THE RAGGED ORPHAN

LINDSEY HUTCHINSON

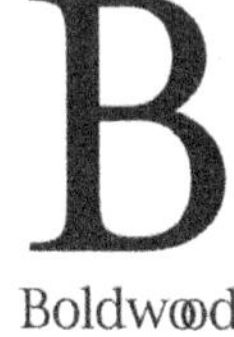

Boldwood

First published in Great Britain in 2023 by Boldwood Books Ltd.

Cover Design by Head Design Ltd

Cover Photography: Shutterstock

A CIP catalogue record for this book is available from the British Library.

Paperback ISBN: 978-1-80162-681-1

Large Print ISBN: 978-1-80162-682-8

Hardback ISBN: 978-1-80162-680-4

Ebook ISBN: 978-1-80162-684-2

Kindle ISBN: 978-1-80162-683-5

Audio CD ISBN: 978-1-80162-675-0

MP3 CD ISBN: 978-1-80162-676-7

Digital audio download ISBN: 978-1-80162-677-4

Boldwood Books Ltd
23 Bowerdean Street
London SW6 3TN
www.boldwoodbooks.com

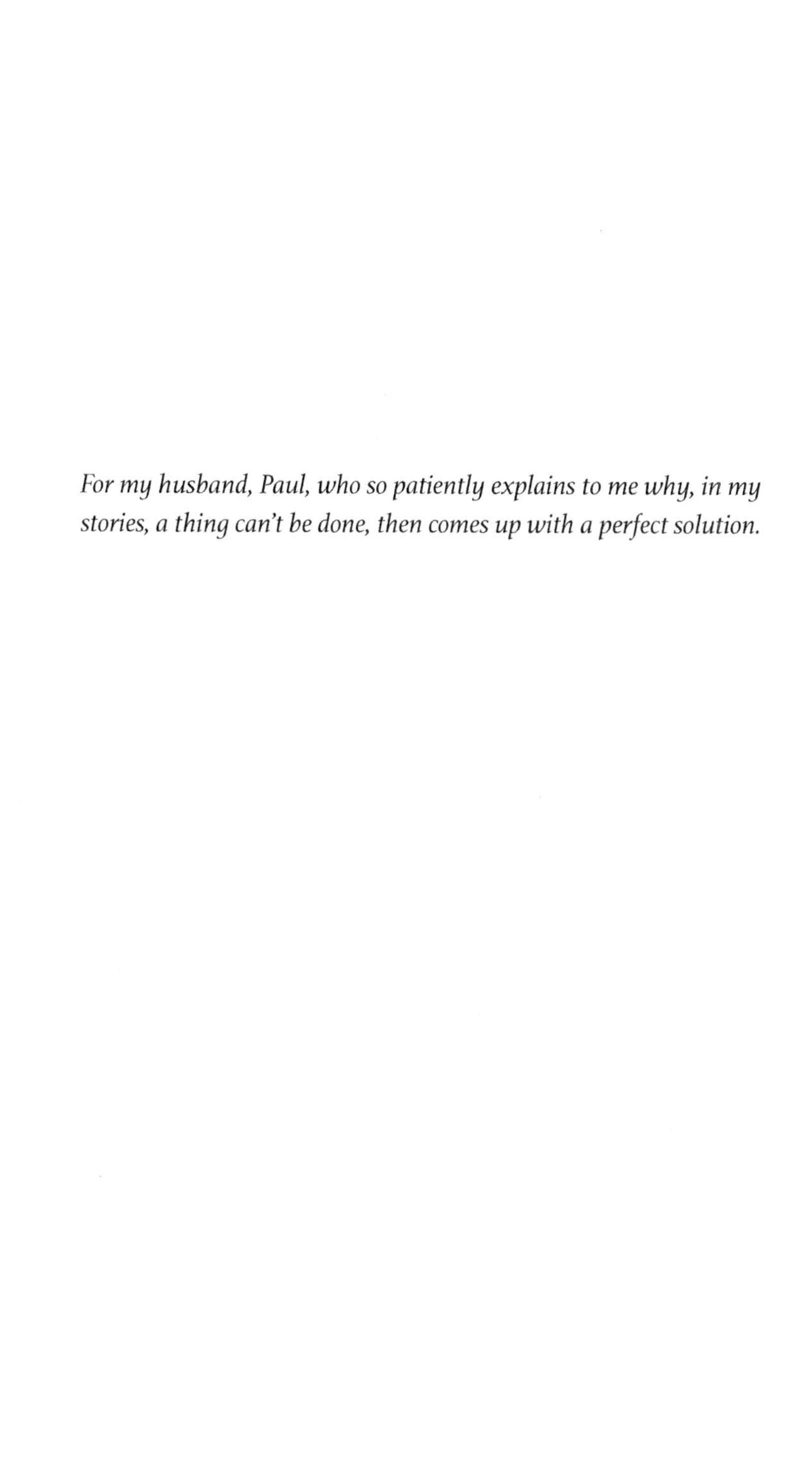

For my husband, Paul, who so patiently explains to me why, in my stories, a thing can't be done, then comes up with a perfect solution.

AUTHOR'S NOTE

It is well known that the women of the Black Country used to swear like troopers. They drank gin mostly, as it was cheaper than Porter, and a lot smoked clay pipes.

I have endeavoured to keep the expletives to a minimum, but for the reader to have a flavour of the character, there have to be some. It is not my intention to offend anyone.

Also, for readers not familiar with the Black Country use of the English language, I will explain a little by giving a short example:

'Is Doris in?'

'No, her's gone down the market.'

This is not my lack of education but is simply how people of the region speak, and I hope it does not detract from the reader's enjoyment of the book.

Mo-shíorghra! (pronounced heer graw) is Irish for my eternal love or my soulmate.

Sláinte (pronounced slaan-sha) means health, as in your good health.

Mavourneen means my darling.
Cailín or *colleen* means girl.

1

Jared Johnson sat on the floor next to the small truckle bed, holding the hand of his younger sister. Maisy's fever had raged for days and she had coughed so hard he thought she might bring up a lung. His legs had gone numb from being in the same position all night, but he didn't move even now.

Maisy's eyes fluttered open and Jared smiled in the grey light of dawn. 'I'm here, kiddo,' he whispered. He watched the little girl as her eyes closed again and he could no longer hold back his tears. Instinct told him the end was near and he gently squeezed her hand.

An hour later, Jared saw his sister take her last rasping breath. He watched her chest, waiting for it to rise again, but it didn't. 'Maisy!' he called. 'Maisy, please don't you leave me as well!' Knowing she wouldn't answer, that she would never speak to him again, Jared laid his head on the edge of the bed and cried until he could barely breathe.

Eventually, he let go of her hand and leaned forward to kiss her cooling brow. 'Sleep well, kiddo, until I see you again.' Dragging himself to his feet, he waited while he felt the pins and needles in his legs and feet. When his circulation was working again, he stamped his feet on the bare floorboards, seeing the dust motes fly up before floating lazily down again.

Steeling himself, Jared lifted Maisy with the utmost care and carried her to his parents' room. He laid her next to his lifeless mother and covered them both with the dirty sheet. It was the best he could do, for he had no money to see them buried.

Making his way downstairs, silent tears rolling down his face, the sound of his boots loud on the bare wooden steps, Jared sat on a kitchen chair and stared out of the window. Now what? Even at twelve years old, Jared knew he wouldn't be able to afford to stay in the house, so where could he go? He raised his brown eyes to the ceiling, his dark hair falling away from his forehead, as he relived the last few weeks. His mother had stopped eating to ensure her children would be fed. Starvation had robbed him of his mum and fever had taken his sister, and Jared felt the anger build inside him. He had begged his mum to share what little food they had equally, but she had refused. He knew she was behind with the rent, and she had warned him they could be evicted at any time.

'You need to take care of Maisy now, Jared,' his mother had croaked.

'*I will*,' he had promised, and he had tried. He had bathed Maisy's forehead and tried to feed her the potato soup he had made, but it was all in vain – he could not save her.

Suddenly it all became too much for him and Jared cried like his heart was finally breaking. A myriad of emotions flowed through him; bitterness at his father for leaving when Maisy was four and he was six; anger at the world that no one had lifted a finger to help. Sadness sliced through his heart at losing his family so cruelly, while guilt gnawed at him for being unable to prevent their deaths, as well as survivor guilt for being the one left alive. Fear settled on him about where he would go and how he would try to stay alive. He could always continue to scavenge, but finding somewhere safe to sleep could prove a problem.

Pulling his emotions under control with great difficulty, Jared thought about the city he lived in. Birmingham was in the heart of the Black Country and was known as the city of a thousand trades, and yet there was no work to be had anywhere. On the days he had walked the miles to the market hall to scavenge, he had seen the men standing in the bread line. Little groups of the out of work idling about on street corners in the vain hope someone might offer them a job, but each time Jared passed, he noticed the line lengthening. How could this be? In the third largest city in Great Britain, why were so many unemployed?

Jared brought his thoughts back to his own plight, the immediate one being where he should go. He realised then that he should let his neighbour know his family had passed away. She could then inform the parish, who would organise paupers' funerals so at least his mother and sister would be laid to rest. However, if he remained here, then he would almost certainly be forced into the workhouse. An involuntary shiver took him as he considered that prospect. No matter what happened, he would not go into that place. He'd heard the stories of folk accepting the ticket from the Relieving Officer and, having entered, they had never been heard of again.

With a sigh, Jared knew he had to make a move. Grabbing an old jacket from the nail hammered into the back door, he slipped it on. He had outgrown his own and even though this one was big on him, he buttoned it up. He'd grow into it. With a last look around, Jared said a silent goodbye to his family and his home before stepping out into the cold morning. He pulled the flat cap from his pocket and slapped it onto his head. Striding across the communal back yard, he walked to the house next to his and banged on the door.

Looking up at the woman who answered, he said sadly, 'They've gone.'

'Oh, lad, I'm so sorry,' the thin woman replied sympathetically. 'Leave it with me, I'll sort it out. But what will you do now?'

'I don't know, but I'll manage,' Jared answered. 'Thanks, Mrs Spittle.'

The woman nodded and watched the boy walk through the ginnel and out onto Watery Lane. Jared looked right then left, trying to decide which route to take. It didn't really matter, for he had no destination in mind. It was his rumbling stomach which decided it for him. He would head for the market hall to see if he could scavenge something to break his fast.

Jared, his hands in his trouser pockets, fell into a steady rhythm as he traversed the streets. There was a low-lying mist and a chill bit the end of his nose. With a sniff, he increased his pace in order to beat off the cold.

Smoke spiralled and puffed from domestic chimneys, mingling with the mist, making it look like a dirty grey blanket had been hung across the street. Cart wheels clattered and a horse's hooves rang hollowly over the cobblestones before the cart disappeared from view.

Listening carefully for traffic, Jared sprinted across the road into yet another thoroughfare. Birmingham's streets were like a rabbit warren and anyone not familiar with them would soon find themselves very lost. Jared, however, knew exactly where he was going.

He stopped short as a front door opened and a yelping dog

flew across his path, followed by a woman's foot. 'Bloody animal!' the woman yelled. 'I'll teach you to piddle on my clean floor!' Jared couldn't help a tiny smile coming to his lips as the door slammed shut, before he continued on his way.

The weak sun struggled to lance through the mist, giving it an eerie yellow tinge as Jared trudged on. Coming to the Bullring, he wondered what it must have been like in years gone by when bulls were tied to an iron ring on Corn Cheaping green. It was there they were baited before being led away to be slaughtered. He was glad the barbaric practice was no longer allowed, but it was this very thing that had given the place its name.

Passing the fish market, Jared wrinkled his nose at the smell, which saturated the air around him. Stepping into the huge building of the market hall which held 600 stalls, Jared breathed easier. The place never failed to amaze him, no matter how many times he visited. The noise was deafening, with vendors calling out their prices. Barrow boys yelled for folk to shift their arses to allow them through.

Wandering down the first aisle, Jared took his time, there was nowhere he had to be. The loss of his family stung again and he felt tears prick the back of his eyes. Struggling to be brave, Jared knew the hardest thing he would ever do would be to live without his mum and sister.

Giving himself a mental shake, he pushed through the throngs of people, each one searching for a bargain. Jared's eyes flitted between the stalls and the floor. He needed to know what was on offer but also whether there was anything worth scavenging on the ground. Maybe he'd be lucky and find a coin which could buy him some food.

The aroma of pies floated on the air and Jared's mouth watered. That's where he'd go if he found a penny. The hunger pain in his belly snatched his breath away but he tried his best to ignore it and plough on. The rattle of tin pots echoed as women sorted through them on the market stall, hoping to find just the right size for their cooking needs, and further along, an argument broke out over a broken cup.

'Look, missus, you knocked it onto the floor!' the vendor yelled.

'I d'aint! It wasn't me!' the woman tried to defend herself.

'You break it, you buy it!' the salesman shouted into her face.

'And you can sod off! It wasn't my fault! You should stack them better!'

Jared shook his head as he walked on. Life was too short to be falling out over smashed crockery.

As he moved on, he came to a bread stall. Pushing his way to the front, ignoring the grumbles from the women he shoved aside, he called out, 'You got anything you're throwing away, please?'

The baker threw a small loaf to Jared, which he caught deftly. 'Thanks, missus,' he yelled and received a smile in reply. The bread was hard but it was food and Jared bit into it eagerly. Dry and difficult to swallow, Jared did his best, his stomach growling loudly in its insistence that he fill it.

Putting the rest of the bread into his pocket, he carried on until he reached a vegetable stall. He scanned the ground and dived for a discarded carrot which was slipped into another pocket. Jared did not consider this to be stealing, the food had been thrown out, so it was fair game as far as he was concerned.

Stepping along to another stall which was piled with fruit, Jared's eyes searched the ground. Nothing. Up one aisle and down the next, he looked longingly at the produce for sale. He *had* to find more food, and so he called out to each stall holder in the hope they had something they couldn't sell and might give to him.

Jared knew it was going to be a long day if he was to wait for the market to wind down, when sellers were more likely to give perishables away, so he sauntered along, every now and then taking a bite of his bread. By lunchtime, however, Jared had found nothing more.

2

Jared walked from the market hall to try his hand at the fish market, but the smell had him gagging so he ran along the street to the meat market instead. His throat constricted at the sight of the blood and pieces of meat laid out on trays. He wondered why he was here, these sellers were unlikely to toss him a joint of beef now, were they? Indeed, but one of them might chuck him a sausage or two, at least that was his hope.

Again, Jared elbowed his way along the stalls until he came to one that was selling bacon, sausages and offal as well as joints of beef and pork. Dead chickens hung from hooks attached to the stall. Jared stood and listened to the seller's patter.

'Come on, wenches, don't be shy, get yer purse out now 'cos you won't get cheaper anywhere else.'

Watching the butcher place a piece of paper onto the flat of his hand, Jared waited. Onto the paper a string of half a dozen sausages landed with a splat, then a thick chunk of bacon was placed on top. The vendor called out his price and women scrambled to be the first to buy. Fists holding money waved in the air as the butcher's assistant took it, giving over the meaty parcels the vendor was rushing to put together.

Wiping the drool from his chin with his coat sleeve, Jared watched the happy customers walk away. As he turned to leave, he heard the meat seller call out.

'Here, lad, you got a penny?'

Turning back, Jared realised it was he who was being hailed and he shook his head. The vendor wrapped two sausages and threw them to the boy.

'Thanks, mister!' Jared shouted.

The salesman gave a little salute before he yelled to the scrabbling women, 'All right, all right, you lot, calm down. Now who's up for a chicken?'

Delighted with his luck, Jared clutched his package tightly. He would enjoy them later when he found a place to cook them. Leaving the building, he went back to the massive market hall where he hoped he might find more food.

Picking up a box, he placed his bread, carrot and sausages inside. Now to search for fruit or more vegetables. An old tin pot would be useful too, that way he could make a good soup, but he didn't hold out much hope that he would come across one. If it came to the put to, or in other words if he had no other choice, he might have to steal a small one which he could carry with him. He hated the thought of having to resort to thieving, but needs must when the devil drives. He berated himself for not thinking to take one from the house before he left. Again, tears threatened as he realised he would never return to the place he had grown up in.

A short time later, he spied a browning cabbage and into his box it went. A lady gave him an apple and another gave him a small cauliflower. Jared returned to the tin pot stall. How could he swipe one without being seen? Then Lady Luck smiled on him again. Two women began to fight over a cheap frying pan and as they struggled, a few pots were knocked to the floor. In an instant, Jared shot forward, grabbed a little pot and shoved it into the bottom of his box, quickly covering it with his food. Then he made his escape whilst the vendor was busy with the arguing women.

Leaving the market, Jared now had to find somewhere to prepare a meal. Making his way to St Bartholomew's church, he slipped into the gardens and hid amongst the trees surrounding the building and graveyard. He could hide here and when darkness fell, he could cook his food. He would need water for a broth so he stashed his box amongst the bushes where it would not be seen. Taking his pot, he crossed the road and knocked on a door.

'What do you want?' a harassed-looking woman asked.

'Would you be kind enough to give me some water, please?'

Looking at the pot held out to her, the woman nodded. 'Wait there.' She closed the door and a moment later came back with the pot full to the brim, along with a pannikin.

'Thank you very much,' Jared said as he took back the pot.

'Here, have this an' all.' The women hooked the handle of the tin cup over his little finger. It was clear the boy had nothing other than what he stood up in, but he had good manners.

'Thanks. You're very kind.' Jared smiled and began to walk away.

The woman shook her head as she watched him go, then she called him back. 'Lad, have you got a spoon? 'Cos I'm betting you'll be eating summat afore long.'

Jared shook his head.

The woman tilted her head for him to return to her door. 'What happened to you?'

'My family just died, I'm an orphan now,' Jared explained, close to tears once more.

'Oh, lad, I'm sorry to hear it. Wait just a minute.' Going back into the house, the kind-hearted woman reappeared with a knife, fork and spoon, which she pushed into his top pocket.

'I can't thank you enough,' Jared muttered, his eyes glistening at her generosity.

'Go on with you,' the woman said with a smile, feeling pleased with her good deed for the day.

Jared hurried back to his box. Placing the pot on the floor, he dipped the pannikin into the water and took a much-needed drink. Then, putting the cutlery and cup back into the box, he set off, looking for bits of wood with which to build a fire later when it was dark.

His wood gathered, he realised he had no matches. Bugger! He had food, water and firewood but nothing to light a fire. Making sure his things were hidden well, Jared wandered out onto the street once more.

There was a public house on the corner of Fox Street, so he made his way there. Outside, a few men were talking and smoking, so Jared approached them. 'Have you a few matches to spare, please?'

The men stopped their chat and turned to the ragamuffin who had spoken to them. 'I s'pose you'll want a fag an' all,' one said with a grin.

'No, thanks, I don't smoke,' Jared answered politely.

'What you want matches for then? You gonna burn summat down?' another asked.

'No, sir! I need to light a fire to cook my dinner.'

The man who had spoken first drew a small box of Swan Vestas from his pocket and gave them to Jared. 'Be careful,' he warned.

'Thanks, I will.' Jared turned and left the men, who had begun their discussion again.

The day had been good where scavenging and luck was

concerned, but as Jared sat beneath the trees cutting up his vegetables for the pot, his thoughts returned to his family. Their loss cracked his heart again and his tears flowed as the daylight faded and darkness fell.

Building a small fire, Jared hoped the smoke would not draw unwanted attention but looking around, he relaxed a little, a fog had dropped to cover the land. Dipping the tin cup, he set it aside for later, then he set the pot onto the fire to boil the water. He stabbed the sausages onto a stick and held them against the flames. He dropped some cabbage and cauliflower along with the carrot into the pot while the sausages began to crackle and sizzle. His mouth watered as the aroma of cooking reached his nose and he constantly glanced around in fear of being discovered. Once he had eaten, he would settle down to sleep, leaving the fire to burn itself out.

Jared ate hungrily and counted his blessings. When he'd finished, he emptied the pot and drank half of his water. Watching the flames dancing, he lay down near the fire.

'God bless Mum, God bless Maisy,' he whispered. Jared Johnson fell asleep with tears on his cheeks.

3

Jared awoke early, his body aching from sleeping on the damp ground. He stretched out his muscles with a groan, then hid behind a tree to relieve himself.

Draining the water left in the pannikin, he placed it into the box and pushed it beneath the low-hanging branches. He hoped it would be safe whilst he went scavenging again. The fog still lay low, so that would help hide his things in the time he was gone.

Cap firmly on his head to ward off the worst of the cold, Jared scouted for more firewood before he went in search of food. As he walked, he knew he would be hungry again before too long, so he sped up. He wanted to be among the first in the market hall. Scavenging was all very well but Jared knew he couldn't go on like this. He had to find work, but he had no idea how. If men on the bread line couldn't get a job, then how was he to do so? He was young and fairly strong but that could count against him. Employers might want fully grown men rather than a boy. Then again, it could aid him in that the wages would be lower for a youngster.

Making a quick decision, Jared decided to forgo breakfast and instead joined a bread line on the corner of Masshouse Lane, which ran along the side of the graveyard. He leaned against the wall of a house, listening to the men complaining about the lack of work.

'You after a job an' all, kid?' a man asked.

Jared nodded.

'Don't bank your hopes up, lad, 'cos we've been here for weeks. There's nothing doing.'

Jared sighed and nodded again.

The men went back to their grumbling, ignoring the boy dressed in rags.

Looking around, Jared couldn't see far due to the fog, but he held out hope for someone to come along who would offer him a few pennies for a day's work.

All morning they waited and eventually Jared thought he would have been better off going straight to the market after all. He sloped off, disheartened, the men's laughter ringing in his ears, their calls of his having no patience disappearing into the fog as he went.

The market was packed and as he had the previous day, he scoured the ground for food. Knowing he couldn't remain in the churchyard for another night, Jared needed to find shelter – somewhere safe where he could reside without being bothered by anyone else. Then a thought struck, why hadn't he considered this before? Behind the brick works near where he used to live was an expanse of heath. There was an old cottage there, abandoned for many years, where he and Maisy used to play. The pain stabbed his heart again as he thought of his sister and how much he missed her and his mother.

Once he had finished scavenging, he would retrieve his box and head over to the cottage. He prayed it would still be empty. As he wandered between the stalls, Jared cast his mind back to the ramshackle building. He recalled the windows were broken, the doors would need some work in order for them to close properly and it would need a good sweep out. But at least there was a fireplace in the living room and an old range in the kitchen. There was also a privy out the back. Jared was certain he could make it habitable over time and he began to feel a spark of hope.

The afternoon wore on and in another box, he collected some stale bread, a chunk of cheese given by a kind lady, an onion and a carrot found on the floor and a threepenny bit which had bought him some sausages and a thin slice of bacon.

The fog had not lifted all day and when he returned to the churchyard, Jared was pleased his things were still where he'd left them. With everything in one box, he folded the other, which could be used to light a fire. With this under his arm, he set out for the heath.

It was as he reached the brick works that he wondered if his family had been moved. Did he have the courage to check? Just as he was debating whether to brave it, he saw a young couple enter his old home. They must be the new tenants. Well, that answered his question. A wave of relief washed over him and he silently thanked the neighbour for keeping to her word to see his mum and sister laid to rest. Jared moved on, knowing he could not dwell on such things. He had to think about his own future and what would become of him.

The old cottage was thankfully still empty but was in an even more dilapidated state than he remembered. Jared stepped in through the door, which hung unevenly on its rusty hinges. There was a battered table in the dusty room onto which he placed his box. It was dark inside the cottage and he felt around in the cupboard on the wall, hoping he might get lucky. He found the nub of a candle which was stuck onto a cracked saucer and pulling out his matches, he lit the wick. A small pool of light was a welcome sight and Jared checked the range.

Leaving the candle on the table, he went out the back to look for more kindling. The light was fading fast so he ran around gathering sticks to add to the ones he'd collected earlier in the churchyard. Arms full, Jared returned to the cottage and using the crushed box and wood, he lit the range, leaving the door open for heat and light. Finding a frying pan with a broken handle, he put the sausages and bacon in and placed the pan on the hotplate. He inspected the chimney in the living room and seeing dim daylight above, he built himself a fire before running back to the kitchen to see to his sizzling food. Pulling a chunk from the loaf, he dipped it into the bacon liquor and munched, his eyes closed in appreciation of the tasty morsel.

After his meal, he built up the fire in the living room once more. Giving the old sofa the once over, ensuring it was free of rodents, Jared lay down, enjoying the warmth from the fire. Tomorrow he'd see about fixing the doors and sorting out the windows. He'd look upstairs too in the light of day to see what was left up there. For now, however, he was content to sleep on an old settee in front of the dancing flames.

The morning saw Jared rifling through the kitchen cupboards, looking for anything useful. He couldn't believe his luck when he found a hammer and a linen bag of nails. Now he could mend the doors, which would help keep out the worst of the cold. An assortment of chipped crockery covered in mouse droppings would need a good wash. An old besom was propped against the wall next to the brownstone sink. Slipping through the back door, he walked to the standpipe. The handle was hard to move at first but with persistence Jared soon had it pumping cool water.

There was nothing to be done about the dreadful smell from

the privy, which was a thunderbox, a board with a hole in the centre laid over a deep hole dug in the ground. Jared gagged and ran back outside. The privy door would have to be kept shut, that was for sure. At some stage, he'd need to find the energy and time to dig out a new latrine – further away from the house.

After spending an hour or so collecting more firewood from the heath, he went back indoors. Dropping the kindling in the grate, he looked around the living room. The windows were cracked, not broken. Clearly this place wasn't quite as dilapidated as he thought, and he wondered why it had been abandoned for so long. He hoped desperately it had been forgotten.

Jared tested the stairs carefully as he made his way to the upper floor, and breathed his relief when they were all good. A filthy mattress lay on the bare floorboards in one room and Jared would lay a bet it housed a family of mice. He would have to drag it outside, well away from the cottage; burning it would draw attention so he would leave it under a hedge where hopefully it wouldn't be seen.

The other bedroom held two rickety kitchen chairs and an iron bedstead. Again, the window was cracked and the plaster was crumbling away from the walls. Spiders' webs criss-crossed from the ragged curtains to the windowsill and bounced gently in the draught from the split glass.

Back downstairs, Jared ate his cheese with stale bread washed down with a cup of water. He wanted to clean out the cottage but with no food in the larder, he knew scavenging would have to take precedence. Securing the property as best he could, Jared set off yet again for the market. As he walked, he thought, *it's not like being at home with family, but it will do me for now.* Tears pricked his eyes and Jared gave himself a shake. He could shed them later in the privacy of his new home.

A good morning's scavenging provided enough vegetables for

his evening meal, and as Jared collected yet more kindling, he moved further afield to explore the heath. It was then he saw a battered, abandoned perambulator and he smiled as a thought struck like lightning.

4

The old pram was shabby and broken, a huge hole in its belly, but the wheels were good. Jared wheeled it back to the cottage and began dismantling it. Having stored the wheels and axles in the kitchen, he dragged the body of the baby carriage and dumped it amongst some bushes near the hedge. Now all he needed was some wood so he could make himself a wheelbarrow.

Striding out, he headed for the timber yard in Lawley Street where he hoped he could beg some offcuts. If not, he might be able to offer to work for them.

Jared shuddered as he crossed beneath the railway bridge, the steam train thundering past overhead. As always, he wondered how the bridge remained standing under the weight of the great iron beast.

Passing a school, he heard the children laughing and shouting as they played in the yard, and not for the first time, he yearned to be there with them. Shaking off the feeling, he marched on.

Turning into the timber yard, he looked around for someone to speak to. Spotting a worker whose clothes were covered in sawdust, Jared walked over to him.

'What can I do for you, lad?' the man asked.

'I wondered if you had any bits of wood I could beg off you. I want to make a wheelbarrow so I can use it to work,' Jared answered.

The man lifted his flat cap and scratched his scalp before slapping it back in place. He blew out his cheeks as he thought, then said, 'Come with me.'

Jared followed where the man led, hope rising in his chest that he would be lucky.

Pointing to a pile of wood of all sizes and thicknesses, the man said, 'Help yourself, you'd be doing me a favour by shifting it.'

'Thanks!' Jared said as he scanned the pile, then he realised he should have left the pram in one piece in order to transport the wood. Then again, the hole in the carriage would have made that tricky.

Seeing Jared's dilemma, the man sighed and nodded to a stack of hessian sacks. 'Use a couple of those and you can drag them.'

Jared smiled his thanks and set to filling the sacks.

'How far are you going?' the man asked as he lent a hand.

'Watery Lane.'

'Bloody hell! You'll never manage, these sacks are heavy when they're full,' the man said, straightening up and rubbing the small of his back. 'Ain't you got anybody to help you?'

'No, sir, my family have all passed away so I'll have to find a way if I want to make a cart. It's really kind of you to give me this; I do appreciate it,' Jared responded.

The two of them worked quietly together, the boss of the timber yard thinking on what the lad had told him about losing his family. Eventually four large sacks were filled.

Jared stood to stretch out and, gazing at their handiwork, he wondered how on earth he was going to get this lot home.

'If I take one now, would it be all right to come back later? I could drag them one at a time if you wouldn't mind storing them for me. I'll move them as fast as I can,' Jared said.

The man shook his head with a smile then whistled loudly, making Jared jump, and a head appeared around an open door.

'Do me a favour, Jed, and help this young 'un shift these sacks, would you?'

'Will do, Gaffer,' the young man answered.

'You'll need the little wagon,' the boss said.

Jared spent a few moments thanking the man again before a horse and cart appeared from around a building.

Jared and the young worker hauled the sacks onto the cart between them as the boss swept up the sawdust.

'Come on, jump up,' Jed said, and Jared joined him on the driving seat.

'Thanks ever so much,' Jared called enthusiastically as the cart lurched forward.

The boss waved and watched them leave his wood yard. 'Good luck, lad,' he whispered before returning to his sweeping.

'Where are we headed then?' Jed asked.

'A cottage on the heath behind Watery Lane,' Jared replied.

'Righto.'

'Your gaffer is a good man,' Jared said as they traversed the streets.

'He is that. He'll help anybody if he can,' Jed answered. 'There ain't many like him left.'

Finally coming to the cottage, the boys unloaded the cart and stacked the sacks against the wall. 'Thanks, Jed, you're a diamond,' Jared said.

'Here.' Jed passed an old saw to Jared. 'You'll need this.'

'You didn't...?'

'No, I d'aint steal it. It's one of mine, I don't use it any more.'

'Thanks and... sorry.' Jared felt wretched at suspecting the boy of thievery.

'That's okay, I would have thought the same in your place. Right, I'll get back to the yard. Good luck, lad. Hope things turn out well for you.'

Once again, Jared called out his thanks as the horse and cart moved off. Jed's hand lifted in a wave, but his eyes remained on the road ahead.

Looking at the bags of wood, Jared couldn't believe his luck. The boss of the timber yard had been so kind, as had Jed, and Jared counted his blessings.

Going into the cottage, he grabbed his grocery box and strode out towards the market, his mood lifted. Building his barrow would have to wait, he had to eat first.

Later that day, on his way home, Jared glanced again into his box. A turnip, a swede, an apple, a couple of potatoes, and a stale loaf. Not bad for a few hours' work. By the time he reached home, he was ravenous. Lighting the range, he filled his pot at the stand-pipe and set it to boil. Chopping the vegetables, he dropped them into the pan. He could have fried his vegetables, but a broth would stretch further, and it would do for tomorrow too. Not having to scavenge the next day would mean he could work on his wheelbarrow. The sooner it was up and running the better, because then he could start earning a wage. Once he had some money in his pocket, he could buy some decent food, and also improve his living standards.

After his meal, Jared lay on the sofa and by the light of a candle nub he drew up a sketch in his mind of a barrow. Feeling his eyelids droop, Jared said his prayers, making sure to include the timber yard boss and Jed. A tear rolled from the corner of his eye as he thought how proud his mum would have been of him.

Another tear followed the path of the first, and as loneliness wrapped itself around him, Jared gave in to his sorrow and cried until he was exhausted. Wiping his eyes and nose on his jacket sleeve, he then blew out the candle flame, before surrendering himself to the blessed darkness of sleep.

5

Eating his breakfast of bacon and eggs, fourteen-year-old Jared looked around the small kitchen and reflected on the past two years.

He had finished his barrow and with a few pennies found on the floor of the market, he had started work. He had pushed his cart around the streets close to his home and called out, 'Any old rags?' day in, day out. A penny had been exchanged for a bundle of old clothes which he had then sorted at home. The better ones he had washed and sold on to a second-hand vendor on the market for a profit. The clothes well past their best were sold to the paper mill to be shredded and used in paper making.

In the evenings, Jared had managed to refit new windows one by one when he had enough money. Next, he had bought and fitted locks on the doors and he had saved hard for a mattress. The cottage was now clean and cosy, although he was yet to tackle the crumbling plaster.

Day by day, Jared had trudged the streets and returned tired but pleased with his efforts. Now he could afford candles and his larder was kept stocked. One extra special day, he had also been a little extravagant and bought a bunch of flowers. These he had taken to the woman who had been so kind in giving him the tin cup and cutlery, and she had been thrilled with the gift.

There was coal in the bunker and bags of kindling stored alongside it. The days of wearing rags were over, as Jared had kitted himself out with clothes from his bundles.

Drinking his tea, Jared nodded. He had done well for himself but for all that he was lonely and still missed his family. With a sigh, he washed his crockery and locked the back door, setting out on another day of work.

Jared walked along the street, pushing his knocked-together wheelbarrow, which he vowed to replace as soon as he could afford to. Inside were the clothes he had washed, dried and folded ready to be sold on. As he was lost in thought, a sharp shout stopped him in his tracks.

'Oi!'

Jared turned to face a young man on the driving seat of a cart.

'Are you addressing me?' he asked.

'You wouldn't be the one tatting on our patch, would you?'

Looking around him, Jared then returned his eyes to the carter. 'I see you are speaking to me.'

'There ain't nobody else near you, is there?' The answer was accompanied by a sneer.

'Indeed.'

'Well?'

'Not that it's any of your business, but I'm on my way to the market,' Jared informed him.

The young man jumped down and Jared instinctively tensed in readiness for a confrontation. At about eighteen years old, the youth had a shock of dark hair and bright blue eyes. His clothes were old but clean, although his boots had seen better days. He strode towards the wheelbarrow and peered in. Seeing the neatly folded garments, he nodded. 'I had to check. It seems somebody has been tatting on our patch and the gaffer asked me to find out who it is.'

Jared said nothing. What could he say in response to that, for it was indeed he who had been collecting old clothes in this area?

'So are these yours?' the youth asked, tilting his head towards the barrow.

Jared nodded. He was not lying, for they did belong to him now. But he knew what the other boy meant – were they his own things he was toting?

'Right, I'll let the boss know what I've learned.'

When the fellow was once more in the driving seat, Jared called out, 'Who is your boss?'

'Toby McGuire.'

'The big Irishman?' Jared asked.

'Yeah, you know him?'

With a shake of his head, Jared answered, 'No, but I know of him.'

'Mr McGuire is not a man to cross,' the older boy said as he picked up the reins and slapped them together. The horse walked on and he waved as the cart rolled away.

Jared watched him go with a sigh. So this was McGuire's patch and Jared had been poaching his business. They must have been looking for the culprit for a while because Jared had already managed to set himself up with a nice little earner. Now he would have to watch his back.

McGuire was king of the tatters, with many young men earning a lot of money for him. His reputation preceded him as being a hard man with no concern for anyone who fell victim to him. Tales abounded regarding people he dealt with going missing, although nothing could ever be proved. It might be that those unfortunates had simply upped and moved away, hoping they would not be discovered by McGuire's men.

These thoughts whirled in Jared's brain as he continued on to the market. Sooner or later, McGuire would find out who was working his patch and then his lackeys would come looking for Jared. He realised he had a choice, either he could go into hiding and find another profession, or he could front up to the man now.

The idea of facing Toby McGuire sent a shiver down Jared's spine, but despite his young age, Jared had never walked away from a problem; his mother had always taught him to tackle difficulties head on and find a solution.

Having sold his goods, Jared pushed his empty cart home, his mind again on the last few years. During his time of becoming a fairly successful tatter, he had managed to avoid coming to the attention of the competition, least of all Toby McGuire. Now it seemed the tatter king had heard of him, albeit not by name, and Jared feared Toby was gunning for him.

Jared knew he could not hide forever and so had made up his mind by the time he reached home. He was going to pay Toby McGuire a visit.

Having stored his barrow, Jared washed and changed into the best clothes he possessed. Combing his hair, he slapped his flat cap on and set out. As he walked, he tried to convince himself that at fourteen he was a man. He was certainly wily enough to talk his way out of a linen bag.

There were two ways this meeting could go: McGuire could have him killed and disposed of or, he might take to Jared and let him live. Either way, the meeting could not be put off any longer, and however much he tried to reassure himself, he was finding it hard to stop his fear taking hold.

Jared walked to the tatters' yard, which was way out on the heath and consisted of an office building and a row of six stables.

The huge yard had a concrete floor surrounded by three brick walls with double gates in the other wall. A slate roof topped the whole site off.

Seeing a group of men working sorting rags, Jared called out, 'Could you point me towards Mr McGuire, please?'

One of the men did exactly that by throwing out his arm and Jared's eyes followed the direction to land on the office. 'Thank you.' Striding over, Jared climbed the steps, knocked on the door and waited, puffing out his chest to try to appear confident.

'Come!' the yell came from inside.

Jared opened the door and stepped into the office. Seeing the huge man sitting behind his desk, Jared felt his bladder shrivel.

'What do you want, boy?' McGuire snapped.

'I'm sorry to bother you, Mr McGuire, but I thought it was time we met. It appears I've been accidentally working your patch.'

'So you're the cheeky young bugger who's been taking away my business?' McGuire's deep brown eyes stared at Jared as he waited for an answer. His grey hair was long and unkempt, his clothes were old despite him being a very wealthy man. Striking a Swan Vesta, he held it to the end of a fat cigar. Blowing out the match, he dropped it into an almighty ashtray on his desk.

'I have been working this area – yes,' Jared admitted, holding out his hands in supplication.

'I suppose you'll say you didn't know it belonged to me, eh?' McGuire asked with a raise of his eyebrows.

'I swear I didn't, at least not until today when one of your lads stopped me to enquire about my business. But we all have to earn a penny where we can, Mr McGuire, as I'm sure you'll agree.'

McGuire's eyes opened wide in surprise at the boy's forthright answer. 'I can't argue with that, lad.' The tatter king was impressed that this young rapscallion had such good manners and afforded him the respect he felt he deserved. McGuire's Irish accent was thick as he asked, 'Where are your folks, boy?'

'Jared, Mr McGuire, my name is Jared Johnson and my family have all passed on.'

Toby nodded curtly. 'So where do you live?'

Jared saw no reason not to tell the big man the truth. He could easily have found out anyway. 'In an old house over the back of Watery Lane.'

'How much did you earn tatting then?'

The past tense of the question was not lost on Jared. 'I make enough so I can buy my food rather than have to scavenge.'

Again, Toby was impressed. He liked this young man, who put him in mind of himself many years ago.

Jared felt the tension in the office as he stood tall and straight. He tried to push his fear away, for he felt now was the time McGuire would make his decision about what was to happen to the kid who had stolen business from him.

The older man studied the boy in front of him before saying, 'I have a proposition for you, young Jared.'

Smiling inwardly at the courtesy afforded him by McGuire calling him by name, Jared waited for him to continue.

'How would you like to come and work for me?'

Quick as a flash and somewhat foolhardily, Jared replied, 'That would depend on how much you're willing to pay me.'

Toby laughed heartily at the boy's brass neck, before tilting his head to the two men standing just inside the office door. 'He's got a big pair on him, to be sure.' The two men nodded but said nothing. Turning back to Jared, Toby went on, 'A crown a week, but you cross me, boy, and you'll wish you'd never been born. There would be nowhere you could hide that I wouldn't find you.'

Five shillings was more than Jared had ever seen in his life, and the thought of this every week was extremely enticing. 'Mr

McGuire, anyone who thought of crossing you would be out of their mind.'

'So, are you out of your mind because if I'm not mistaken, you've crossed me by working my patch,' Toby said, his eyes narrowing dangerously.

Jared shrugged his shoulders and grinned. In for a penny, in for a pound.

Again, Toby laughed loudly at the lad's cheek then, nodding at the two standing by the door, said, 'Show Jared the ropes. Here, take this.' McGuire handed over a slip of paper and a leather money bag. 'Can you read?'

Jared nodded. 'Yes, sir, my mum taught me.'

Again, McGuire was impressed.

As Jared reached the door, he turned and said, 'Thank you, Mr McGuire. Firstly, for not breaking my legs and secondly for giving me a job. I won't let you down.'

McGuire's great belly laugh could be heard all over the yard as his new employee left the office. He was pleased with this new kid and hoped he'd made the right decision. He was fairly sure he had, but it would pay to keep an eye on him nevertheless.

Jared breathed a sigh of relief once he was out of the office. The meeting had gone better than he could have ever expected. At its worst, he could have been breathing his last by now.

The two big men introduced themselves as Dicky and Bobby Cavenor.

'How long have you worked for Mr McGuire?' Jared asked.

'Erm... a long time,' Dicky said.

'What's your job?'

'We... erm, I don't rightly know what you call it, but we looks after the boss.'

'Bodyguards?'

'Yeah, that would be it,' Dicky confirmed.

Jared could tell they'd had very little education, but he didn't pay that any mind. He liked the big brothers instinctively, and hoped they'd become friends.

'You'm lucky, you know,' Bobby said as he led the way to the yard where the carts were kept.

'Yeah, lucky,' Dicky repeated.

Jared smiled confidently. He had stood face to face with the tatter king ready for a confrontation and instead had come away with a job.

'That'll be your cart there,' Bobby pointed out.

'And your 'oss will be Bess,' Dicky added, then both men grinned.

Jared looked at the old mare and felt his pulse quicken. He was surprised to be given a round straight away, as he had expected he'd be put on the sorting. The tatters, or rag and bone men, usually trawled the streets, their familiar call causing children to come running with glee. A battered trumpet or horn would announce their arrival in a street. They plied their trade in rags but occasionally women would bring out the leftover bones after making pots of broth. The tatters would buy these to be sold on to the workhouse, where the inmates would crush them before they were sold on to farmers for fertiliser.

When the carts were loaded or there was nothing more to be had, the tatters would return to the yard for their stock to be unloaded by the sorters, ready for a fresh start the following day. The sorters would pile the bones at one end of the yard to be heaped into sacks for transportation to the workhouse while the clothes were thrown into piles according to their materials: cotton, tweed, wool.

Jared walked slowly towards the aged black mare and rubbed her forehead. He breathed into her nostrils so she could get to know him by his scent. He'd seen farmers do this in the past and had noticed that the horse would then trust them. Jared patted Bess's neck gently as he spoke quietly in her ear and she nuzzled him. The bargain was struck, they would be a team, each looking after the other.

The two huge brothers watched as Jared slipped Bess into the traces with confidence, all the time whispering encouragement and praise to the mare as he worked. His time watching farmers and carters was about to pay off, as he recalled how to hitch the horse to the cart. Breathing a sigh of relief that he had remembered correctly, Jared nodded with satisfaction.

Turning to the brothers, he asked, 'Which one is my round then?'

Bobby nodded at the piece of paper with a list of names on it that had been handed over by McGuire. These were the streets he was to trawl from morn until night. His leather money bag was filled with pennies by Dicky.

Climbing into the driving seat, Jared glanced at the bugle beside him, before picking up the reins and calling, 'Walk on, Bess, my beauty.'

With a flick of her tail, the horse moved forward and headed out of the open double gates of the yard. As the cart rolled along, Jared couldn't stop counting his blessings. Having the courage to visit the tatter king had stood him in good stead; it had landed him a well-paid job.

He noticed then that Bess had no bag to catch her droppings. Stopping the cart, he tied a bone sack beneath her tail with string used to seal the bags. Any manure collected could be sold on to the allotment owners. This would generate more revenue and in turn would please Toby McGuire.

Clucking to Bess again, the cart rolled on. Their route took them this side of the railway line and past the cattle market where the smells hung heavy in the air, down Glover Street which ran alongside the vinegar brewery and back up next to the paper works.

At the end of the day, Jared steered the cart into the yard and was surprised to see Toby McGuire waiting. The cart was unloaded by the sorters and Jared untied the manure bag.

'What's all that about then?' McGuire asked.

'Why allow folks to collect it when we can? This way, we can sell it,' Jared replied.

'That's good thinking, to be sure,' McGuire said with a grin. Turning to the Cavenor brothers, who were only ever two steps behind him, he told them, 'Make sure the others do the same.'

The men nodded and moved off, leaving their boss and Jared to talk.

'I thought the allotment owners would be interested in this,' Jared said, tying the top of the sack.

'Bejesus but you're a smart one.' Toby had known this boy for one day and at every turn he was impressed.

Jared stored the bag by the door, then said, 'If you'll excuse me, Mr McGuire, I'll feed Bess then rub her down before I go home.'

'We have stable boys to do that for you,' McGuire informed him.

'If it's all the same to you, sir, I'd like to do it myself, it will help me get to know Bess a little more.'

'Please yourself.' McGuire nodded as he puffed on his cigar and watched the youngster go. He was thoroughly impressed at the respect Jared had shown him. His other boys didn't bother so much, and they always left seeing to the horses to someone else. They could learn a lot from Jared and no mistake, but even as he thought it, he realised it would not make the boy popular amongst his peers to pick him out as an example. In time, they could grow to resent Jared and call him McGuire's favourite. It was a situation

Toby would have to watch out for and act on it immediately. He felt sure, though, even after this short time, that Jared would go a long way – he just needed a guiding hand.

Further down the yard, Bess snickered and Jared kissed her face.

McGuire watched the interaction between boy and beast and he shook his head in disbelief as the horse followed meekly behind Jared to the stables. That mare never behaved for anyone and yet here she was, eating out of Jared's hand.

Once Bess was fed, brushed and stabled, Jared turned to leave the yard to return home. He was hungry and tired. Not expecting to be working, he had not packed a snap tin to have for his lunch.

A shout he'd heard once before came again. 'Oi!' It was the young man who had stopped him in the street that very morning and the voice was unmistakable.

'Don't I know you?' the youth asked, striding forward.

'I don't know, do you?'

Neither were aware that McGuire was watching them, interested to see the outcome.

'Yeah, you'm the one! The fella who I asked about tatting my gaffer's patch!'

'Our gaffer, you mean,' Jared corrected him.

'What, you working here now?'

'I am indeed. You need to see to your horse, she's sweating.' Jared turned to walk away.

'We don't do that, there's a lackey for that.'

'You want to be careful you don't end up as one of those *lackeys*,' Jared said over his shoulder.

Toby McGuire smiled at the new boy's audacity. Yes, Jared Johnson would go a long way.

6

With a carrot in his pocket for Bess, Jared arrived at the yard bright and early the next day.

Toby McGuire was watching from his office doorway as Bess enjoyed her treat, before being harnessed to the cart. He grinned as a bag was tethered to her hind quarters.

Seth Watkins, the youth who had accosted Jared yesterday, strode over. 'I'm Seth, what's your name then?'

'Jared,' came the reply.

'Was it your idea to put a bag on the 'osses to collect the shit?' Seth asked, clearly annoyed at having to do it himself.

Jared nodded. He could see a confrontation coming and if he wasn't mistaken, it would be quite soon. Hoping to avoid an argument, Jared climbed onto the driving seat and was about to leave when Seth spoke again.

'The lads ain't happy about it. It's another thing to do which we ain't paid for.'

'Take it up with Mr McGuire then,' Jared answered.

'I'm taking it up with you!'

'And I'm telling you – if you are unhappy, speak to Mr McGuire. Now move aside because I have work to do.'

Seth grabbed Bess's bridle to prevent her from moving and she snickered and tried to pull away.

Jared sighed loudly. 'Take your hands off Bess.'

'Or what?' Seth countered, obviously of the opinion should it come to a fight, he would win.

'I won't say it again, Seth. If you boys have a beef, then take it to the boss or we can sort it after work. Now – shift it!'

Seth's anger was evident as his cheeks reddened.

Jared waited a moment longer, staring down at the boy who was shaking with rage, then clucked to Bess. With a snort and a shake of her head, she walked on as Seth let go of her bridle.

McGuire grinned. With each passing hour, he liked Jared more and more. He would, however, have to keep a keen eye on his other boys. The last thing he wanted was for them to jump Jared and knock him senseless.

Once Jared had left, McGuire whistled loudly. The Cavenor brothers came trundling over to the office. 'Gather the boys in here before they go out this morning.'

'Yes, Boss.' The reply came in unison.

Within minutes, the five other young barrow boys, including Seth, stood in the office, wondering why they had been summoned.

'It has come to my attention that yous boys ain't happy about the shit sacks.' McGuire waited, but he knew no one would dare contradict him. 'Well?'

'It ain't that, Boss,' Seth began.

'No? So I'm hearing it wrong then, am I?'

'No – it's just that...' Seth let the sentence hang in mid-air.

'It's just that it's summat else you have to do for no payment. And, I suspect, it's because the idea came from the new lad, eh?'

'He's only been here two minutes and he's taking over already!' Seth's temper was up again.

'Taking over from whom, you?' McGuire waited patiently. When there was no reply, he asked, 'Would you have thought the idea up?'

'I... in time, maybe.' Seth squirmed beneath McGuire's stare.

'Well, see, Jared came up with it right away – on his first day!'

The other four lads took a step backwards, happy to leave Seth in the firing line. Glancing behind him, Seth knew he'd been hung out to dry and he bridled.

'Let's put it this way, if you ain't happy in your work, you can always bugger off! I can fill your jobs tomorrow, remember that. Another thing, I want no harm coming to Jared by your hands. Should that happen and it comes to my attention, you'll all be out on your ear.' McGuire paused to allow his words to sink in. When he was content his message had been received loud and clear, he flicked his fingers, dismissing his workforce. Before they left, he added, 'See to the horses before you go home as well. Now get out of my sight!'

He heard the grumbles as the others berated Seth for being the cause of their dressing down and added workload. Toby McGuire smiled. He had let them get away with far too much and for too long. Now he had cracked the whip and only time would tell whether things would improve. He hadn't been making idle threats when he'd said he could fill their jobs easily if he had to sack them. He knew how scarce work was, so he was certain they would not quit of their own accord.

Striding across to the stables, Toby now addressed his stable boys. 'From now on, those lazy buggers,' he began as he tilted his head towards the tatters getting ready to go, 'will be rubbing down their own horses.'

'So what do we do please, gaffer?' one boy asked.

'Clean out the stables, then you can help out on the sorting. I'll put yer wages up by tuppence a week.'

'Ooh, ta,' came the reply, and the boys' grins split their faces.

One by one, the carts rolled out, Seth being the last to leave. As he went, he made up his mind. Jared Johnson would pay for getting him in trouble with the boss.

Across town, Jared walked Bess slowly down the street, occasionally blowing his bugle. He was wondering whether Seth would be waiting for him after work and if so, how any confrontation would pan out. Seth was a lot bigger than Jared, but it was as his mum taught him, the bigger they are, the harder they fall. For now, he had work to do and worrying about another argument served no purpose.

The street was dusty and dotted with cigarette ends which had been smoked down to where the pin had been pushed in to enable the smoker to enjoy the tobacco to the last bit. The houses were grimy with curtains that had seen better days. The paint on the front doors was cracked and peeling and the whole area reeked of poverty.

A woman dressed in an old frock, patched and worn, called out to him, shouting, 'Hey, cocka!' and Jared pulled gently on the reins. Bess stopped and stood patiently whilst Jared dealt with the woman.

'How much, chick?' the woman asked, revealing her stumpy black teeth.

Jared inwardly winced at the sight, but smiled pleasantly as he weighed her bundle of rags in his hands then said, 'A penny a bundle.'

'Ar, go on then,' the woman said, delighted at the prospect of another copper coin.

Each of McGuire's workers were issued with a pound's worth of pennies first thing every morning. At the end of the day, any left were handed back. Yesterday, Jared had used all of his and today, he hoped, would be much the same. His cart was quickly filling with old clothes and rags. The better-quality items he placed on one side; he knew from experience that if these were washed, they would fetch a decent price on the market. This was something he decided to broach with Mr McGuire when he returned to the yard. As it was, everything went for shredding before being sold on, but McGuire would see a decent profit if he followed Jared's advice.

The question was how to mention it without it seeming that Jared was trying to teach his grandmother to suck eggs. McGuire would surely be quick to point out that he was the gaffer and Jared the employee, so he had to be subtle in his approach. He could offer to take the items to market for McGuire once they were clean and presentable. Maybe that was the way to do it. Of course, the other boys wouldn't like it, they would say he was arse-licking, but Jared was looking out for himself. He wanted to earn some decent money; he was intent on moving up in the world. He had no intentions of being a tatter all his life – unless he was the governor, that is.

By lunchtime, all of his coins were spent and his cart was full, so he turned Bess to head back to the yard.

As he was slowly making his way, another woman yelled out to him from her window and Jared stopped Bess again. 'I'm out of money, I'm afraid,' he confessed as she held out her bundle.

'How about you swap me for that jacket then,' she said, pointing to the item as she peered into the cart.

'Gladly,' Jared agreed and the exchange was made. As he

moved on, he wondered if this was another idea he could share with Mr McGuire. Losing one old jacket but gaining a bundle was good business as far as he was concerned, and he hoped his boss would agree with him.

A little while later, he and Bess pulled into the yard, and as the sorters began to unload, Jared walked across to the office. Cap in hand, he knocked and waited to be called in.

'What's occurring, Jared?' McGuire enquired, a little perplexed at the boy being back so early.

'I'm out of money, Mr McGuire.'

'What, already?'

Jared nodded. 'There was more to collect but I had no pennies left so I swapped an old jacket for a big bundle. I hope that meets with your approval.'

'It certainly does, my boy! Good thinking on your part. To be sure, you're a bright lad and no mistake.' McGuire eyed the youngster shuffling his feet. 'Is there summat else?'

'Mr McGuire, would you mind if I made a suggestion?' Jared asked tentatively.

McGuire nodded. Out of all of them, Jared was the only one to call him Mr McGuire and Toby liked the boy's manners.

'Well, sir, if the better clothes were washed, I could take them down to the market for you and sell them on. The rest could still be ragged, but this way you'd have another income.'

McGuire studied the boy standing in front of his desk wringing his cap in his hands and wondered why he hadn't thought of this himself. 'Ah, lad, may you be at the gates of heaven before the devil knows you're dead!' Jared frowned then smiled when Toby went on, 'To be sure, that's a clever idea of yours.'

McGuire jumped up from his seat and, crooking a finger for Jared to follow him into the yard, he whistled loudly to bring the sorters to a halt. Once they were all gathered around, Toby explained what he wanted doing. From now on, the good clothes were to be put in a separate pile.

Jared smiled inwardly when he realised that although McGuire hadn't actually said this new way of doing things was his own idea, he had certainly allowed the workforce to believe it was.

'Mr McGuire,' Jared said quietly, 'you'll need washer-women now as well.'

Calling to the sorters again, McGuire asked if any of the men had wives who might consider taking on the washing for a small wage. Without hesitation, the men agreed on behalf of their spouses, who evidently had no say in the matter.

McGuire rubbed his hands together, his cigar clutched between his teeth.

'Sir, if you'll spare some more pennies, I'll get Bess back on the road.'

Reaching into his pocket, Toby counted out a pile of coins. 'Good on yer, Jared.'

With a nod, Jared climbed onto his cart as the last of his load was lifted out.

McGuire returned to his office a decidedly happier man. This new kid was turning out to be an absolute diamond.

7

It was gone five in the afternoon by the time Jared arrived back at the yard, again with a full cart. He helped the sorters to throw the bundles from his cart onto the floor then released Bess from the traces after removing her manure sack. He walked to the stables and gave a little smile when Bess followed along behind him without being prompted. The other workers stood with open mouths at the spectacle; Bess was known to be fickle, she could be as stubborn as a mule when the mood took her. Yet here she was, trailing after this tall slim young man adoringly.

Jared then began to rub her down as she drank from a bucket of cool clean water.

'Good girl, you've worked hard today.'

'It don't look like it to me.' Seth's voice sounded behind him and Jared turned.

'Evening, Seth, have you been back long?'

'I got back an hour ago with all my pennies spent,' came the answer.

Jared nodded, aware that the other tatters were watching

closely. Bess flicked her tail and snorted, and he wondered if it was her way of saying she didn't like the young man who was disrupting her grooming time. Jared soothed her with quiet words.

'How much have you got left?' Seth asked, his dark hair greasy and lank around his face.

'None.' Jared tried to keep his patience, despite knowing Seth was pushing for a fight. Clearly, he wanted Jared to throw the first punch, and with the others as witnesses, Seth could plead all innocence. It would be Jared who would be sacked and then things could go back to the way they were.

Neither of the young men were aware that Toby McGuire was watching them from the yard.

'You d'aint get much for your money; the boss won't be happy about you giving his coins away.'

'Seth, haven't you got anything better to do than to needle me? I can see what you're up to but I'm not going to bite. When I'm finished with Bess, I'm going home.' Jared turned away and, in his peripheral vision, caught sight of McGuire but ignored him.

Seth backed down, clearly frustrated that Jared was refusing to take the bait. As he strode over to the other boys, he clenched his hands into fists as he went.

Jared heard them talking quietly but couldn't make out what was being said. Then, as he walked slowly back to the yard from the stables, he saw them glance over to the ever-growing new pile of reasonably good clothes. Now Jared understood.

Seth went to question a sorter, who explained the new system and pointed to Jared. They had guessed it was his idea and not McGuire's.

McGuire's interest was piqued even further as Seth stamped back to the little group to pass on what he'd learned. Over at the gates, Jared shouted, 'Goodnight, Mr McGuire, I'll see you in the morning.'

'For sure, Jared,' Toby yelled back with a wave of his cigar.

Jared heard the others call out, 'Night, Boss,' as he walked briskly away from the yard, and he smiled. Another day gone and Jared Johnson had made himself just that little bit more indispensable.

Later that evening, as he ate his meal of meat and potato pie warmed through in the range, Jared thought about the day's events. Seth was becoming somewhat of a nuisance, constantly goading Jared. He guessed McGuire might be watching out for him, but that was only while he was at work. Jared had a sneaky feeling Seth could push for a fight away from the yard, and if questioned would deny everything. How would Jared deal with that if it came to pass? It was evident to everyone that Seth felt he had been usurped in the pecking order, and he had not taken it well.

Jared could, of course, try to bring Seth onside by kowtowing to him, but that was not going to happen. There was no way Jared would play second fiddle to the arrogant young man. He was determined to become McGuire's right-hand man and he would not let Seth stand in the way of that.

Packing bread and cheese ready for his lunch the following day, he dropped an apple into his snap tin for Bess. Sitting by the range's open doors, he drank his tea and allowed his thoughts to wander once more.

McGuire's business had made the big Irishman a lot of money over the years, and as far as Jared knew, the man had no family to leave it to when he passed on. In his wildest dreams, Jared dared to imagine taking over the business. He saw in his mind's eye the layout of the yard and wondered if it could be put to better use somehow. At present, everything was dumped on the concrete floor in heaps, then as it was sorted, it was thrown onto separate carts for transportation to various destinations. But surely this meant twice the work for the sorters. What if it was sorted as it came off the tatters' carts and tossed directly onto the wagons destined for the market or paper mill? That would mean the boys would be hanging around for a while, but they could be put to doing other jobs. They could paint the office for McGuire, or help load up the bones ready for crushing at the workhouse. Some could take a laden wagon to where it was needed. Jared believed it was all about using the workforce in the most efficient and economical way.

With a yawn, Jared decided his bed was calling. Making sure the range was closed up safely, he used the candle to light his way up the stairs. He would think more on the yard tomorrow on his rounds, but for now he needed sleep.

* * *

At first light, Jared was greeted by his boss's booming voice, carried across to where Jared was feeding Bess her breakfast oats.

'Early again, young Jared?'

'Morning, Mr McGuire, it's going to be another fine day so I thought I'd get on the road as soon as possible.'

'Ah, but you're a hard worker, to be sure. I wish the others were as conscientious.'

Jared shrugged and Toby instantly understood its meaning. Jared did not wish to comment on his colleagues.

'Mr McGuire, would it be possible to have more pennies today? It would save me having to come back then go out again, and it would be easier on Bess.' Jared had asked his question just as Seth and the others strolled into the yard. He saw the scowl on

Seth's face, and he sighed. He had hoped to be gone before anyone else arrived.

'I don't see why not. In fact, all of you lot can take more coin today and see how you get on,' McGuire said, beckoning his boys to follow him to the office.

'You're a bloody menace,' Seth whispered as he strode to catch up with Jared.

'Why's that then?' Jared asked, knowing full well what Seth meant.

'Because we'll have to work twice as hard now,' Seth growled under his breath.

'I'm not afraid of hard work, Seth; I'm just glad of having a good job.' Jared had raised his voice slightly in order for it to reach the gaffer's ears.

Dropping into his chair behind the massive desk, McGuire pulled out a heavy linen bag from a deep drawer. Tipping some of the contents out, he began to make six small piles with the coins. Then he did the same again and then yet again.

McGuire heard Seth shuffle his feet and he looked up at the boy. Seth had the good grace to turn away from the glare of his boss. The clink of coins continued until at last McGuire said, 'Two pounds each.' He leaned back in his seat, eyeing the boys' astonished faces.

No one moved, then Seth said, 'Boss, we can't shift that much in a day.'

Toby raised his eyebrows before replying with, 'Why not? Jared did yesterday.' The boys glanced in Jared's direction. 'He came back for more money at lunchtime and he got rid of the lot. Now, my little leprechauns, if he can do it then so can you.'

Seth was the only one to groan.

Jared stepped forward and scooped the pile of coins into his leather money bag which was then attached to his belt at the front. 'I'll be away then, Mr McGuire, I'll see you later.' With that, Jared turned and walked from the office, a satisfied smile plastered all over his countenance.

As he crossed the yard to the stables, Jared heard Toby yelling from behind him, 'Well, get on, boys! Bejesus, it will be dark before you shift your arses!'

Jared grinned again. 'Come on, Bess, we have work to do.' The horse had been put in the traces by one of the stable lads and Jared called out his thanks, something no one else did. He saw the others dash from the office as he pulled out of the gateway, the grin still wide on his face. There might come a time when those boys worked for him and should that come to pass, he wanted them to be hard workers. It was important he set an example and was setting the standard high. Whether he eventually took over from McGuire or had his own business, Jared Johnson wanted no shirkers working for him.

Seth Watkins watched Jared leave while the stable boy saw to his horse. Although he'd been told he should do this himself, Seth had no intentions of complying with the order. His dark greasy hair fell about his eyes as he climbed aboard his cart. He recalled McGuire's words about no harm coming to the new boy, but the lad was really pushing his luck. Already in the space of a few days their workload had increased, and it was all Jared's fault.

Seth knew he was lazy, but his edict was – why keep a dog and bark yourself? When women came out to him with their bundles, he would tell them to toss them into the cart before handing out a penny. He wouldn't bother to gauge the weight first. Happy to ride the cart around the streets all day, Seth would return at the allotted time whether his coins were spent or not. Sometimes he would pocket the last few pennies and arrive back early.

Jared, however, was not cut from the same cloth. He even went back for more money! Seth had spent a long time training the others to think as he did – do as little as possible over the longest time – and now it had all been turned upside down in the blink of an eye.

Slapping the reins sharply on the horse's back, Seth felt the cart lurch forward. Rolling from the yard, Seth made a decision; it was time to call a meeting. He and the other tatters had to do something about Jared Johnson.

8

At sixteen years old, Sam Jenkins had worked for Toby McGuire for twelve months and he loved his job. A shy, retiring boy, Sam lived with his widowed mother in Bromley Street. As an only child, his mother had constantly tried to keep him as close to her as she could, but he had fought the apron strings that had held him back in order to acquire a job.

Sam's father had worked at the bank and had saved hard to buy the house Sam and his mother lived in. When William Jenkins had died of a heart attack, Sam and his mum had been devastated. And when their money had started to run out, Sam had stepped up to the plate, insisting he go out to work.

Now he was the breadwinner and was happy to take care of his mum. A blue-eyed blond, Sam was a handsome young man and readily drew the glances of young girls. Courting, however, was out of the question for Sam, as his mother would never allow it. He knew his fate was to stay a son before becoming an orphan, then maybe he could become a husband and, with God's help, a father. Although this had occupied his mind many times, his thoughts were being distracted at present by the situation with Jared and Seth.

It was fast becoming clear that there would eventually be trouble between those two and Sam had already decided he wanted none of it. His timid nature usually kept him in the background, but he had debated stepping forward and speaking his mind to the others, to those he could trust anyway. He was fairly sure Dan, Paul and Johnny would agree with him that the best course of action was to leave the rivals to sort things out between themselves. That would hopefully be done well away from McGuire's eyes and ears. Their jobs depended on it.

Unbeknown to him, the other tatters were thinking very much the same thing as they traversed the streets on their rounds. None of them wanted to be drawn into a war between the two adversaries. They knew McGuire would be true to his word and sack them all in an instant if he got wind of any dissention in the ranks.

With Seth being the oldest, the boys had given way and allowed him to become their leader, beneath McGuire, of course. This new turn of events, however, was bound to cause all kinds of upset.

Sam and the lads liked routine, and they liked a quiet life. They just wanted to earn their money and go home happy. Now Seth's jealousy was threatening their livelihood, and it could so easily get out of hand. Sam knew he'd have to say something eventually but for now he concentrated on his work; there would be time enough later to see how McGuire dealt with the problem.

The following day, Jared stopped his cart as an old woman shouted to him. He jumped down and went to where she stood at her gate.

'Do you take bones, lad?'

'I do, Mother,' Jared answered.

The old lady smiled at his use of the endearment. 'How much?'

'Depends on the weight.'

The woman nodded to the enamel bowl at her feet, full to the brim with animal bones which had been used to make broth and were then boiled clean.

'I'll fetch a sack,' Jared said and he did so. Tipping the bones into it, he weighed it in his hands.

'The other fella offered me a penny,' the woman said. Jared frowned. 'Arrogant little bleeder he was an' all. A wash wouldn't have gone amiss either.'

'Other fella? What did he look like, Mother?'

'Greasy dark hair, a look on his face like he was chewing a wasp! He didn't even get off his seat, he expected me to carry this lot and tip them into a sack meself!'

Instantly Jared knew who it was, but what was Seth doing on Jared's patch? The answer was obvious, Seth was out to clear Jared's round before doing his own.

'Well?' the woman asked, bringing Jared's attention back to her.

'Thruppence, Mother.'

'Ooh, ta! That'll do nicely.'

Jared dug in his satchel and brought out a threepenny bit, placing the twelve-sided coin in her hand.

'Thanks for your custom, Mother,' he said, throwing the sack into the cart. On the move again, Jared considered his options. He could call Seth out on his actions or he could tell McGuire he'd had a lousy day. Immediately he dismissed the latter, McGuire wouldn't believe him anyway.

The other decision he needed to make was whether to have it out with Seth quietly after work or shame him in front of the others. He chose the former, it wasn't fair to involve everyone in

Seth's underhand dealings. He would tackle the problem as they left the yard, but first he needed to fill his cart. He just hoped that Seth had not cleared the streets and there was some business left for him.

Having raced around Jared's area, Seth was now in his own and was taking his time. He chuckled, Jared would be lucky to find anything today and he wouldn't be McGuire's blue-eyed boy any more. It would be Seth who would be showered with praise and Jared would be the one left looking like a fool.

As the day wore on, Seth was glad of Jared's takings, for his own round was sadly lacking. Deciding to call it a day, he headed slowly back to the yard.

In the meantime, Jared had made the decision to extend his route, hoping he was not stepping on any of the other tatters' toes. His luck was in when he was informed a tatter had not been around the area for an age.

Children squealed their delight when he sounded his bugle and women poured from their homes with bundles of rags. The pennies he gave out in exchange would help feed their families.

Making a mental note to add Little Ann Street, Rea Terrace and Milk Street to his normal round, Jared turned Bess for home. His cart was full but that was no thanks to Seth. Jared was a naturally patient person and it took a lot to rile him, but the closer he got to the yard, the more his temper rose.

McGuire was waiting when everyone pulled into the yard, a broad smile on his face. The stable boys took the manure sacks and piled them outside, ready for collection by the allotment owners.

Seth had indeed received praise from the gaffer and was now enjoying gloating that Dan, Sam, Paul and Johnny's carts were only half-full. When he spied Jared, a grin split his face, but his smile soon disappeared at the sight of Jared's overladen wagon.

Jared jumped down and, ignoring everyone else, strode to McGuire. 'Mr McGuire, I wonder if I might have a word with you after I've seen to Bess.'

'To be sure, come to the office when you're ready.'

Seth watched the interaction with interest. There was no way Jared could have found out what Seth had done in this short time, surely, so what did he want with the boss?

In the stables whilst rubbing down his horse, Seth kept an eye on the newest member of the team. He would give anything to be a fly on the wall of that office. There was no way of knowing what would be said unless he asked Jared outright and he knew there was no point in doing that.

Once Bess was groomed and fed, Jared walked to the office and knocked on the open door.

'Come away in and shut the door,' Toby said, waving his cigar in the air. 'Sit you down and tell me what this is about.'

'Thank you, sir. I thought I should tell you I varied my round today.'

With a frown, Toby gave a curt nod, indicating Jared should explain his actions.

'The reason I did that, Mr McGuire, was because someone had been on my patch. I didn't want to come back to the yard with a lesser load, so I went down Little Ann Street, Rea Terrace and Milk Street as well. The folk said they were glad to see me so if it's all right with you, I'd like to extend my route regularly.'

McGuire eyed the boy. 'Who'd been there before you, Jared, do you know?'

'I'm not sure, sir, but I have my suspicions, although it's not my intention to make a big thing out of it.'

Toby nodded. 'I'm thinking it might be your man out there 'cos he was early today, which he never is usually. I'm sure he would deny it if questioned. I also think you need to watch your back, Jared, as someone seems set on causing you trouble. But I'll take no further action on it if that's what you want?'

'It is, sir. I didn't come to you to whine but to let you know where I've been today.'

'Good lad. A wise move on your part. Now, if you need my intervention, then you let me know.'

'Thanks, Mr McGuire. Goodnight.' Jared stood to leave.

'Goodnight to you, lad, and well done.'

Jared left the office ready to confront Seth, but there was no sign of him. No matter, there was always tomorrow.

Trudging home, Jared was tired out, and decided he would grab some bread and cheese and a cup of tea and then head straight to bed. In the end, the day had been a success and McGuire was yet again impressed by his business acumen, but he'd need to be ready to go again tomorrow. Walking across the heath, lost in his own thoughts, Jared didn't see Seth watching him from a distance, silently plotting his revenge.

Later that evening, as he lay in bed, Jared thought about his brief meeting with Toby McGuire. He had not intended to tell the boss about one of the other boys poaching his business, but had he not, then Jared would have had to explain why he had made a detour. McGuire was a canny man and would have found out for himself eventually and then Jared would have been in trouble, most likely. McGuire had eyes in the back of his head; he missed nothing. The boss knew about Seth's discontent at having a new boy on the team and about Jared's suggestions to improve the system which McGuire had accepted and implemented.

Smiling into the darkness, Jared settled to sleep. If Seth Watkins was unhappy, that was his lookout, Jared refused to let it worry him.

9

Dan Freeman was fifteen years old and had started out as a sorter. A hard worker, he had proved to be good with the horses and had recently been promoted to the rounds. He was the peacemaker of the group and along with Johnny Baker, who was a real comedian, they could defuse any awkward situation in minutes. Good looking, with dark hair and blue eyes, Dan was always ready with a warm smile.

Like Jared, Dan lived alone after his parents had died when a wave of influenza had swept the town. Although an orphan, he was happy enough with his lot and enjoyed working for McGuire. Dan rarely took a dislike to anyone, but Seth Watkins could never be described as being one of his friends. Other than stepping in to calm a dispute, Dan kept himself to himself, but he had liked Jared immediately and hoped they would become close as time passed. He knew the other tatters felt the same; the only fly in the ointment was Seth. It was Dan's firm belief that the argumentative young man would push his luck too far one day and find himself out of a job. The sooner the better, as far as Dan was concerned.

Every evening, Dan walked home with Paul, Sam and Johnny,

and during their many journeys to and from the yard, they had learned a lot about each other. Dan knew, for instance, that Paul Clancy was the eldest of five kids and lived in Warwick Street. Paul's father used to work the coal pits but now sat at home with a disease of the lungs. His mother took in washing to help subsidise the family income. Sam Jenkins was an only child who lived with his overbearing mother. Johnny Baker, with his titian hair and blue eyes, was a real joker and always laughing. He was twinned with a sister, both of whom drove their mother up the wall with their antics.

Dan knew very little about Seth other than he lived with his bully of a father, so it was no wonder the son had turned out the same. He couldn't help but smile as he saw a woman, who was chatting with her neighbour, bat her child across the head for something he had said to her; the boy then ran into the house crying and the woman continued her canting.

At the end of the street stood a crowd of men hanging around talking and bemoaning the fact that there were no jobs to be had. Despite shiny uppers, Dan guessed the men's boots had holes in the soles. Shirt sleeves were rolled above the elbow and tattered waistcoats were buttoned up, their trousers patched with anything that could be found that would do the job.

Blowing his old bugle, Dan shouted his question. 'Any old rags?' The cart rolled on, pulled by a dependable old mare. All of McGuire's horses were female; less likely to be skittish.

Passing the police station at Digbeth, he turned the cart into Smithfield Street and on past Smithfield market. The streets were quiet today, with little business forthcoming. He had travelled this way every day for a while now, so it was hardly surprising. Dan wondered, if he asked, whether McGuire would give him a new patch. He would gather his courage and enquire when he returned to the yard, but for now, he plodded on, enjoying the sunshine.

Across town, Jared's mind was on Seth and how to tackle the dirty trick the boy had played on him the previous day. The situation needed sorting and soon, otherwise Seth would believe he'd got away with it. McGuire would deal with it if Jared asked him to, but Jared felt it was his responsibility. There would have to be a face-to-face confrontation, something Jared didn't relish, but knew it had to be done.

At the end of the day and with yet another full cart, Jared returned to the yard a little earlier than normal. He wanted to settle Bess so he could wait for Seth outside the yard.

Shouting their farewells, all the boys poured out of the gates, happy that their work had finished for another day. Seth was the last to leave and Jared was waiting for him.

'Might I have a word?' he asked, feeling the other boys stop to see what was occurring.

'You talking to me?' Seth asked.

'I am indeed.'

'What do you want?'

'I want to let you know that I am aware you poached my patch the other day before moving to your own,' Jared said, keeping his voice low. The others gasped and looked at each other in disbelief at this revelation.

Seth laughed but the sound was false even to his own ears. 'When would I have the time?'

'You would have had plenty because, Seth, you are lazy on your own round, and I know you came into work early in the morning yesterday too.' Jared stood in a fighting stance with one leg in front of the other, ready for any eventuality. He saw Seth clench his fists and he was ready if his foe should attack.

The other boys stood back but not so far that they couldn't hear the conversation.

'I'd like to see you prove it,' Seth sneered.

'I can do that if you really want me to,' Jared answered evenly. He saw the colour drain from Seth's face and was sure Seth knew he'd been rumbled.

'I ain't got time for this,' Seth said as he turned away.

'It's not my aim to keep you, I just wanted you to know I'm on to you. I know you don't like me and you know what? I don't like you either. However, I'm warning you now, if you try to get me in bother with Mr McGuire again...' Jared left the sentence hanging in mid-air.

'What? What do you think you can do to me?' Seth puffed out his chest in fake bravado.

The other boys were muttering, but even Johnny and Dan knew to stay out of this one.

'Look, Seth, I don't want to fight you, but I will if I have to.' Jared saw the boy turn deathly pale.

'You wouldn't win even if you tried,' Seth mumbled.

'Maybe not but I wouldn't back down either.'

'I'm not listening to any more of this. I've gotta get home now, so I'll be seein' yer.' Seth strode away and Jared watched him go.

'Bloody hell! I thought he was going to punch your lights out for a minute there!' Sam said as they crowded around Jared.

'So did I, Sam,' Jared said quietly.

'What a cheek, poaching from one of his own colleagues,' Dan said.

'Well, if we all gang together, we could beat him!' Johnny said, his fists raised in a bare-knuckle fighting stance as he bobbed and weaved lightly on the balls of his feet.

Suddenly they all burst out laughing; the tension was broken.

No one spotted Toby McGuire, who was standing watching as the group ambled away in a jovial mood once more.

McGuire had witnessed the confrontation silently and his estimation of Jared grew in leaps and bounds. That boy was destined for great things – provided he didn't get himself killed first!

Jared could look after himself, it would seem, so instead McGuire considered what to do about Seth as he chewed on his cigar. He had known Seth's father for many years. Ned Watkins drank until he couldn't stand up and worse – he was a nasty drunk. Once in his cups, he would pick a fight with a doorpost if he thought it would fight back. He also bullied his only son, Seth. Many times, the lad had come to work with a black eye, but still he went home to hand over his wages. Seth's mother had fled for her life some years ago after Ned had given her a particularly bad beating. The hiding had come after she had told Ned she was leaving and taking Seth with her. She had been informed in no uncertain terms that she would not be taking his son anywhere, so Molly Watkins had slipped away quietly in the night, never to be heard of again.

McGuire walked back to his office and sat behind his desk, shaking his head. He had tried to help the family by hiring Seth, but the boy was lazy and was his own worst enemy. Toby knew this but kept him on anyway, reluctant to make the lad's life any worse. Now Seth was causing problems in the workforce and if it continued, McGuire would have to step in. He didn't want to fire Seth, but he might not have a choice. Then Ned Watkins would be on the doorstep shouting the odds.

The big Irishman was not afraid of Watkins senior, but he could do without the aggravation, if truth be told. With a sigh, McGuire decided to go home and think more on the matter.

10

The boys laughed and joked as they walked home together, then Dan decided to share his thoughts about asking for a new round with Jared.

'The trouble is, well, I don't fancy asking the boss.'

'I could do it on your behalf if you want me to,' Jared replied.

'Would you really? That would be great 'cos my patch is all worked out and it's getting harder to fill my cart every day.'

'Would you ask for us as well?' Sam asked.

'Of course. I'll suggest it when I get the chance.' Jared was delighted that the other boys were growing to trust and respect him.

Just before they parted company, Paul Clancy spoke up suddenly, clearly itching to get something off his chest. 'Jared, I think Seth is stealing money from McGuire.'

Hearing the sharp intake of breath from the other boys, Paul felt their gaze on him and he flushed.

'How? What makes you say that?' Jared asked.

'I've been counting his bundles for a while now and they don't tally with the money. Seth never returns his unused pennies to the boss, but his bundles are short.'

'Bloody hell!' Johnny gasped.

'If McGuire finds out, he'll go wild!' Sam put in.

'We could all be sacked,' Dan said, 'and if we are because of him, I swear Seth Watkins won't be walking for a long time!'

'All right, let's all calm down,' Jared said. 'We can't accuse him without proof.'

'So how do we get that?' Sam asked.

'I don't know – yet. Look, leave it with me and I'll have a think about it.' Jared gave the others a reassuring smile then added, 'I'll ponder it tonight and see you all tomorrow.'

Relieved that Jared was going to come up with a plan, they said their farewells, and each of the boys made their separate ways home.

That evening, over his meal of broth and bread, Jared was true to his word and thought long and hard about what he'd been told. He knew he couldn't take the problem to McGuire until he had evidence of Seth's thievery. The decision he made before he went to bed was that he would do as Paul had done and count Seth's bundles. He would make a note of the tallies each day, and only then if he found repeated inconsistencies would he feel he could inform his employer that Jared suspected he was being robbed.

* * *

Several days later, Jared requested a meeting with McGuire.

'Sir, the boys are worried their patches are dry and you might get angry if you think they're not pulling their weight,' Jared said.

'I've been meaning to draw up another route plan but I ain't got round to it,' McGuire answered; he was annoyed with himself for being so remiss. Pulling out a map of the town from a drawer in his desk, McGuire slapped it down and unfolded it. 'Now then,' he said with the obligatory cigar clenched between his teeth. He rubbed his forehead as he studied the paper. Then, looking up at Jared, he said, 'Have a look and tell me what you think.'

Jared frowned, then stepped forward. With a whisper, he said, 'Mr McGuire, forgive me but – can you see the map?'

McGuire growled. 'Of course I can, I just wanted to see what you'd come up with.' Then, with a loud sigh, McGuire dropped into his chair, rubbing the bridge of his nose between his finger and thumb. Looking at Jared once more, he pointed at the boy, saying, 'Not a word, do you hear me?'

'I swear, but you should see about getting some spectacles,' Jared suggested.

'I will, but for now, I'll rely on you to work out new areas for the boys. Remember, not a bloody word to anyone or else!'

'Yes, sir.' Jared's eyes swept over the map and his pencil raced over six scraps of paper. Before long, he had it all worked out and explained to McGuire what he'd come up with. 'I've worked it like a grid pattern then, after a while, maybe a week or two, we can draw up another round further away. Eventually, when we've spread out quite a distance, we can start all over again from the beginning.'

'Excellent! We should be able to cover the whole town this way,' McGuire said, clapping his hands together.

'Shall I pass these out then, Mr McGuire?' Jared asked, holding out the scraps of paper.

'By all means do, and thanks for your help, Jared.'

'Sir, please go and get some spectacles. Your eyes are very precious and as my mum used to say, once they've gone...' Jared shrugged his shoulders as his words hung in the air.

'That's the truth of it, boy. Very well, I'll see to it today.'

Jared could barely contain his grin but when McGuire realised what he'd said, Jared burst out laughing.

'See to it,' McGuire repeated, then his belly laugh resounded around the office.

Jared left to distribute the papers for the new rounds and as he handed Seth his, the sulky boy asked, 'What's this?'

'Your new round, Seth. Mr McGuire thought it was time to have a change,' Jared replied, aware the boss was listening.

Seth looked at the list of streets. 'I can't manage this lot!'

'Why not? We all have the same number,' Jared said.

'But mine's way out, the other side of the railway!' Seth complained loudly.

'And your point is?'

'It'll take me forever!'

'You have a week or two to cover it, then Mr McGuire will issue you a new round.' Jared turned to walk away, but Seth grabbed Jared's arm roughly and swung him around. 'This is your doing, ain't it?' he growled.

'I have no idea what you mean,' Jared called over his shoulder as he snatched his arm back and walked away.

Once the horses were ready and the barrows were hitched, each cart rolled out of the yard and the boys in turn waved to Jared – all except Seth.

Jared was pleased the boys were happy with their new allocations and he smiled as he set off on his own round.

Bess pulled the cart along the streets to their new patch, which was down Cheapside past the carriage works and the horse repository. Up into Dean Street, Moat Row and down the tramway into Bradford Street.

Glad to see a tatter at last, women and children came out of their houses with bowls of bones and bundles of rags.

Jared was courteous and polite to each of his customers and

his cart filled quickly. Heading back to the yard earlier than he'd hoped, he realised bigger carts might well be needed if business continued to be this good. Yet another good suggestion he could put forward to Mr McGuire, but he would see how things went first. It could be that because a tatter had not covered this area for a while, that was why he had done so well. By the end of the week, he would know for sure.

Jared had fed and groomed Bess by the time a grumpy Seth arrived back, his cart only half-full. Standing with the others in the yard, Jared listened with half an ear as they enthused about their new patches. He wasn't paying full attention as he was too busy counting the bundles as they came off Seth's wagon, then waiting to see if any coins were given back. There were none. Two pounds in pennies had been doled out that morning by the Cavenor brothers; nobody had any left. But it was clear to Jared that Seth's bundles only amounted to having spent a pound at best. Jared was horrified. Even if Seth had paid out two or more pennies, which Jared doubted, then he had still pocketed a good amount.

Pulling out his slip of paper and the nub of a pencil, Jared made a note, then shoved both back into his pocket. Then he and the others left for home; he knew they had seen him scribbling on the slip so decided to share his thoughts when they were further away from the yard lest they be heard.

As the boys made their way towards the heath, Jared explained what he planned to do to keep track of the discrepancy with Seth's takings. 'At the end of the week, I'll total up how much I think Seth has stolen then I'll take it to McGuire,' Jared said.

'There'll be ructions, I'm telling you,' Sam said.

'McGuire will murder him!' Johnny added, pushing his titian hair out of his eyes.

'Well, whatever he does, Seth can't be allowed to get away with it,' Jared said.

'I wish I'd never said anything now. If Seth finds out we're on to him, he'll lather all of us,' Paul said wearily.

'I'm glad you did, Paul, just imagine how McGuire would react if he discovered we knew but did nothing about it,' Jared countered.

Paul nodded but he didn't feel any better about it.

'What made you check on Seth in the first place?' Jared asked.

'We all, including Seth, only had half-full carts a few times recently, and we all handed in our unspent coins, but Seth didn't and I grew suspicious.'

'Wouldn't the Cavenor brothers have questioned that?'

'No disrespect, Jared, but they're not very bright. I'm not sure they can count. They just follow McGuire's orders blindly,' Sam said.

'Right.' Jared nodded, knowing what he said was true. 'Let's see what the end of the week brings.'

They waved to each other as they went their separate ways, and as Jared headed home, a dread settled over him. It would be up to him to enlighten their boss about the pilfering, and although he couldn't actually prove the coins were going into Seth's pocket, he had to report it. It would then be up to McGuire what he did with the information. Jared just hoped the Cavenors didn't find themselves in trouble too; he liked the big men and would, if needs be, help fight their corner if blame should be placed at their feet. One thing was for sure. All hell would break loose on Saturday evening.

11

The rest of the week passed without incident and Jared continued to note down the discrepancies between coins and bundles on Seth's cart.

On Saturday evening, the boys were given their wages after seeing to their horses. Sunday was their day of rest, with only the stable boys coming in to feed and water the mares. McGuire, however, would, as usual, be in his office.

Pleased he had taken Jared's advice and got himself some spectacles, McGuire was in a good mood.

'Jared, my boy, spare me a minute before you go home,' McGuire called out.

'Will do, Mr McGuire,' Jared replied.

'What's going on?' Seth demanded to know.

'You know as much as me,' Jared said with a shrug.

'What does the gaffer want with you?' Seth pushed.

'Seth, I didn't know a minute ago and I don't know now. In fact, I won't know until I get in there now, will I?' Jared tilted his head towards the office.

The other boys watched and waited with bated breath to see if this conversation would blow up into a confrontation. Seth seemed to be bruising for a fight, but Jared kept his cool and winked at his pals as he strode to see the boss. His friends hung around outside the office, chatting quietly amongst themselves. Whatever was occurring, they didn't want to miss it.

Knocking on the door, Jared entered when McGuire yelled for him to, 'Come in, lad.'

'You wanted to see me, Mr McGuire?'

'I did that. Shut the door.'

Doing as he was bid, Jared stood before the desk.

McGuire removed his new spectacles and said, 'Good idea of yours, Jared, to be sure.' He waved his glasses before placing them gently on the mahogany surface.

'They suit you, sir, make you look distinguished.'

McGuire chuckled and nodded, before saying, 'The change of rounds went well, don't you think?'

'Yes, sir,' Jared replied, wondering what this was all leading to.

'I've drawn up some new routes for next week; cast an eye over them, would you?'

Jared relaxed and checked the lists against the map. Happy with what he saw, he nodded. 'These look good, Mr McGuire.'

'Right, I'll get the Cavenors to pass them out to the boys on Monday morning.'

Jared shuffled his feet, his eyes on his boots.

'What's up, lad? You look like you have something on your mind.'

'Mr McGuire, I'm not sure how to put this so I'll just come out and say it. I think you're being ripped off.'

'What?' McGuire frowned, the anger evident on his face as he jumped to his feet.

Jared handed over the slip of paper on which he'd made his calculations and McGuire stared at the figures incredulously. 'I don't believe this! Who is it?' he said at last as he dropped despondently into his chair.

'Mr McGuire, before I tell you, I ask that you don't lay any blame on the Cavenors. They carry out your orders to the letter but, as I'm sure you know, they are not very well educated. I'm not sure they always understand the numbers, sir.'

'I do know that, Jared, and I won't hold them responsible for any of this.' McGuire stabbed a finger on the paper lying on the desk. 'Now, tell me everything.'

Jared spent the next ten minutes explaining what he knew and how he had come by the information he had passed on.

'Do the others know all this?' McGuire asked when Jared had finished speaking.

Jared nodded. 'We thought it best you should be told as soon as possible, sir.'

McGuire rubbed his chin as he considered what he had heard.

'I have to be totally up front, though. I can't prove any of it, Mr McGuire. It's only what I've worked out for myself and I could be quite wrong, in which case I apologise. But I hope you understand why I had to let you know.'

'Quite right, boy. I think I need to keep a watch for myself, lad, that way if it turns out to be true, then no one else need be involved.'

'Thank you, sir, I'll let the boys know what you've decided.'

'Thanks, Jared, for bringing this to my attention. I'll sort it from here on in.'

Jared left the office and joined his mates. Quietly he related what McGuire had said and as they walked towards the gates, Seth called out, 'Well?'

'Oh, Mr McGuire said we all have a new patch as of Monday,' Jared replied.

Seth nodded and strode away, annoyed that it was Jared who had been summoned to the office and not him.

'Phew!' Sam muttered. 'I thought he was going to call you out again.'

'I told him the truth, we are getting new rounds next week.'

'Now he's gone, tell us again what McGuire said,' Johnny demanded, excited to hear the inside scoop.

By the time Jared reached home, he was tired to the bone. The stress of keeping the tally and having to tell McGuire about his suspicions had drained him. He sat down at the kitchen table with a great sigh.

In the short time he had worked for McGuire, he knew he had helped to improve the business. He also felt sure that he had won the boss's trust, which is what he wanted. But he hadn't wanted to rock the boat and now he felt he'd betrayed a colleague. And more to the point, his accusations were based only on speculation.

Jared didn't like Seth one bit, that was true, but he didn't relish seeing him sacked, which he undoubtedly would be if it was proved the lad had been stealing. Jared would feel responsible for that, no matter what anyone said, and he already felt wretched about it.

He realised that if he wanted to be a gaffer himself, he would have to grow a thicker skin. He wouldn't be able to feel sorry for people, for all he might want to. McGuire had earned himself the reputation of being a hard man, ruthless in his dealings with others, and Jared knew he would have to be the same.

Pulling his wages from his pocket, he laid the coins on the table. The money was all his and he couldn't help but smile. He had earned this with hard work, politeness and quick thinking. Scooping up the money, he added it to the little he had managed to save in a small box under a floorboard.

Then, giving himself a mental shake, Jared made himself a

meal of faggots and grey peas, chunks of bread and butter and a pot of tea. After he had eaten, Jared decided he would start to tackle the crumbling plaster on the walls before he retired for the night. Tomorrow was Sunday, his day off, and he thought he would stroll down to watch the boats in the basin of the Warwick and Birmingham Canal. With luck, it would lift his spirits ready for work the following day.

After a good night's sleep, Jared packed bread and cheese and a bottle of cold tea. He strode out into the sunshine of a Sunday morning and headed towards the basin. As he strolled along, he admired the brightly painted narrowboats, adorned with colourful traditional flowers and castles, and listened to the laughter and chatter of the owners. Someone whistled a ditty and before long women joined in to sing along as they worked unloading their cargo. A couple of young children on one boat chased a puppy around the deck, squealing with delight as the little hound turned on them and returned the chase. Jared smiled at their antics and ambled onwards.

Sitting just off the towpath, Jared ate his lunch, waving occasionally to the boats leaving the basin on another journey to earn a living. He read the names as they chugged away: *Not So Fast*, *Aboat Time*, *Nauti-Bouy*, and he smiled at the ingenuity. He watched women painting pots and kettles with animals and birds in bright colours as they sat in the sunshine on deck. Children raced around playing 'tag', a dog yapping at their heels. For all it was hard work on the canals, the people appeared to be happy with their lot. Having finished his food, he stood to retrace his steps homeward. He was about to pass a public house when two men strode outside, taking off their jackets as they did so and handing them to their friends. Jared stood to watch. He knew what was coming.

The two men took the stance of bare-knuckle fighters, their

left legs forward and their fists raised. Other drinkers poured out of the pub to watch the spectacle as the two danced around each other, occasionally making a jab for the other. Each time, the crowd roared their approval at the effort and yelled their support of one or the other of the fighters. Suddenly one of the men shot forward and landed a punch, knocking the other to the ground, and the onlookers cheered. The fallen man got to his feet, rubbing his chin in disbelief the blow had landed. Then he raised his hands once more, determined to carry on. The crowd applauded his bravery as the fellow planted his feet in a solid stance. Again, he was punched to the floor and as he scrambled to his feet, he held up his hands, palms towards his opponent. The man had conceded and the fight was over. The onlookers clapped loudly as they discussed the merits of each opponent.

Jared smiled as the two men flung an arm around the other's shoulder and everyone pushed their way back into the pub. If only everything could be sorted out so easily.

12

Monday morning saw the sun shining and a buzz of excitement in the yard about the new rounds. Jared's patch took him in a loop around New Street Railway Station and he was eager to get started. He collected his money satchel and went to feed Bess. Giving his thanks to the groom who had fed the horse already, Jared helped fit his mare into the traces. But before he could get going, he heard shouting.

He exchanged a frown with the groom before walking back to the yard from the stable.

Johnny nodded towards the office. 'Seth.'

'What?' Jared asked.

'He's complaining again,' Johnny replied quietly.

The boys stood to listen to the argument raging in the office.

'I'll remind you, in case you've forgotten, I am the boss here!' McGuire's voice boomed out.

'I know that, but this round is...'

There was a pause before McGuire asked, 'Is what?'

'Boss, it's at the other end of the town!' Seth whined.

'Correct, but it ain't as though you have to walk now, is it?'

'No...'

'Then get to it! The quicker you're out, the sooner you're back.'

'I won't be able to get here by closing time unless I...' Seth was about to say he would have to cut short his time on the road, but obviously thought better of it.

'Seth, just get on, or do you want to find yourself out of work?'

'No, Boss, my dad would kill me if I lost this job.'

'Right, so move out and let's have no more whingeing.'

The boys in the yard immediately began to walk towards the stables as Seth left the office. They didn't want to be caught earwigging by the boss.

'Bloody hell, he's pushing his luck,' Paul whispered.

Jared just nodded. He was still feeling bad about sharing his suspicions about Seth with McGuire, but the boy wasn't helping himself.

'See you later,' he called to his friends as he climbed onto his cart.

As he led Bess down Smallbrook Street, Jared blew his bugle and wondered how well he would do today. He hoped his new route would be a good one and he would return with a loaded cart. However, after one circuit, he had done very little business, so he decided to extend the loop to take in the next few blocks of streets.

Holloway Head proved better pickings and Jared smiled happily as women came out to call to him. Bundles containing patched dresses, children's clothes which were now far too small and men's shirts which would not stand another mending were brought out. Children gathered around Bess and stroked her neck, the horse snickering with pleasure at the unexpected grooming. One brave boy even gave her his apple core and the others laughed as she munched away happily. Having finished his business with the women, Jared clucked to Bess to move on, the children running behind happily shouting a goodbye. The morning passed quickly and by lunchtime, Jared was ready to eat.

'Whoa, Bess,' he said, pulling gently on the reins. He was halfway down Irving Street and once he was parked up, he jumped down from his seat. Pulling the sack of oats from the cart, he hung it over Bess's neck before returning to his seat. Taking his bread and cheese and bottle of water from the tin by his feet, Jared began to eat.

As he chewed, he looked around him. The houses, the bricks covered in grime, were crammed one against the next, allowing no light to filter between them. The once white net curtains were a dirty grey as they hung at dusty windows. Despite the weather being bright and warm, chimneys puffed out spirals of smoke as fires were lit in an effort to beat off the damp and cold inside the dark rooms. A small flock of birds swooped and soared before flying high and out of sight. Jared heard the church bell chime and a dog barked in the distance. He smiled at Bess as she nuzzled to reach the bottom of her nose bag.

Man and beast finished their lunches and Jared clucked to Bess to move on, having taken off her food bag and tossed it into the back of the cart.

Cutting down Speaking Stile Walk brought him out onto Holloway Head once more, so he crossed into Washington Street, passing St Thomas's Church. Before he knew it, Jared had a queue of women waiting patiently in line. They gossiped loudly as they moved forward, their bundles clutched in their arms.

Jared worked quickly and soon he was ready to move on, but the women remained on the street, their conversations continuing. The arrival of the tatters was always a good excuse to catch up with friends and neighbours.

The rest of the day was busy and by home time, Jared's cart

was full. His money satchel was empty, so he turned Bess and walked her back to the yard.

Pulling in through the gates, Jared was surprised to see he was the last to arrive.

'Blimey, Jared, we thought you'd got lost,' Bobby Cavenor said as Jared handed him the money bag. He peeped inside and, seeing it was empty, he went on, 'Another good day, I see.'

'It was indeed, Mr Bobby,' Jared said respectfully.

Bobby grinned at the boy's politeness, then passed the bag to his brother.

'No pennies left again, Jared?' Dicky asked.

'All spent, Mr Dicky,' Jared replied.

'Good lad.'

Jared turned back to release Bess from the cart, a frown forming. This was new. Normally the Cavenors just collected the leather bags without looking inside them. Clearly Toby McGuire had instructed them to check who had money left and how much it was. This way, Toby could keep a close eye on Seth to see whether he was indeed stealing from his employer.

Jared laughed as Dan shouted, 'How come you always get the best round?'

''Cos he's the favourite,' Seth muttered under his breath, just loudly enough for Jared and the others to hear it.

'I guess I'm lucky, Dan,' Jared returned.

'Lucky my arse!' Seth spat nastily.

Jared ignored the remark and walked away to the stables, Bess meekly following behind. He was busy rubbing her down as Seth entered the stables.

'So, spent out again?' Seth asked.

'Yes,' Jared replied shortly. He really didn't want to get into this right now, he was tired and hungry and just wanted to go home.

'You sure you ain't giving the boss's money away?' Seth pushed.

'I am – in exchange for bundles.'

'Funny man,' Seth sneered.

'Look, Seth,' Jared began as he fed Bess, 'I'm shattered and I'm off home, so don't start.'

The stable boys looked on, wondering if a fight might ensue, ready to run for the gaffer if it did.

'I'm just asking how come you always manage to use up all your coins,' Seth said as he followed Jared out of the stables.

'I buy bones and rags, Seth, what else do you think I do with it?' Jared replied.

One of the grooms called out to Seth, 'Ain't you gonna feed your 'oss?'

'You do it, that's what you're paid for!' Seth shouted back.

In the yard now, Jared walked to join his friends who were waiting for him and they all left together after waving to McGuire, who stood watching them.

'Hey, I asked you a question!' Seth yelled.

'Leave it,' Sam said quietly as Jared made to turn, 'don't get into bother with McGuire over that toerag.'

'Sam's right,' Paul concurred, 'he's not worth it.'

Jared nodded and the group walked on, discussing the events of their days.

Behind them, Seth threw down his leather satchel on the floor in frustration and marched away.

Bobby Cavenor picked up the bag and peeked inside. Turning to Toby McGuire, he shook his head, grimly confirming there were no coins left.

Toby nodded and returned to his office chair to chew on his cigar.

13

A little while later, one of the sorters knocked on the door and entered Toby's office. 'Four hundred bundles on that particular cart,' he said.

McGuire nodded, and the sorter took his cue to disappear.

Seth, in common with all the others, had been given two pounds' worth of pennies that morning and had only collected 400 bundles at a penny a go. That left a discrepancy of eighty pennies, so where was the money? Either Seth was overpaying or he was pocketing the remainder. Either way, with 240 pennies to the pound, McGuire was losing out big time.

Toby shook his head as he wondered how long the theft, if it was proved, had been going on. With a sigh, he knew that by the end of the week, Seth could find himself out of a job. He also knew that Ned Watkins would beat the boy mercilessly if that should happen and he felt bad about that, but he could not condone what the lad was doing, no matter the reason for it.

Hearing everyone leaving outside, Toby got to his feet. Locking the office, he went down the stairs and walked across the yard. Dragging the gates shut, he locked those too. Then he walked home with a heavy heart.

Meanwhile, Jared and his pals had discussed his altercation with Seth, and how the Cavenors were checking the money bags.

'McGuire will be keeping an eye on all of us, but more so on Seth,' Jared explained.

'If Seth is pilfering, he's a fool,' Sam said.

'I dread to think what McGuire will do if it turns out to be true,' Johnny added.

'How will he know for sure?' Paul asked.

'I don't know, but that's McGuire's problem now,' Jared answered.

'Seth's dad will murder him if he's sacked,' Paul said, 'because Seth provides Ned's beer money.'

'Likes a drink, does he?' Jared asked.

'Phew!' Paul went on. 'Ned Watkins is a drunkard and nasty with it. When he's had a skinful he will fall out with his own fingernails!'

'I heard the rozzers often throw him in the cells overnight, then, when he sobers up, they let him go,' Dan added.

'Not much of a life for Seth,' Jared said.

They had reached the point where the boys parted ways, and after saying their goodbyes, each walked home with Seth on their minds.

That evening, whilst Alice his housekeeper was busy working away in the kitchen, Toby McGuire sat by his fireside, cigar in one hand and a whisky in the other. He studied the yellow flames dancing around the coal nuggets, which burned scarlet.

He knew he would have to challenge Seth at the end of the

week by asking the boy to turn out his pockets. Any money produced would almost certainly be left over from the round. He wondered if Seth was giving the pelf to his father each night or whether he was hanging on to it for himself. Perhaps he would find out on Saturday when Seth had finished work for the week.

McGuire wondered how Seth would react when faced with having to explain himself. He was sure the lad would deny everything, at least at first.

With a hefty sigh, McGuire emptied his glass with one swallow. For sure it was a dirty business leaving a nasty taste in his mouth, but it had to be sorted out as soon as possible. It would do no good if the other boys thought they could get away with skimming money off the takings.

'Yer tea's on the table, Toby. I'm off now; see you tomorrer,' Alice called.

'You will if you keep your eyes open. Thanks, Alice,' Toby replied with a grin.

Walking to the dining room, Toby sat alone at the huge table. A plate of lamb, potatoes and vegetables smothered in thick rich gravy awaited him. Breathing in the aroma, he nodded contentedly. As he ate, he thought about the lady who came in every day to 'do' for him. Alice Crawford was a woman he'd known since their school days, and she had worked for him for years. She was short with a little meat on her bones and could out-swear the best of navvies. Her twin boys were grown and married with little ones of their own. Her husband, Stanley, was tall and thin, and McGuire smiled as he thought that, when standing together, they resembled the number ten. Alice stood no nonsense, even from him, and would often call a spade a bloody great shovel.

Their relationship consisted of trading insults in a playful manner and he liked that about her immensely. She cooked and cleaned for him and she was not afraid of hard work.

Taking his empty plate to the kitchen and laying it in the sink, Toby retired to his chair in the living room. Pouring another whisky, he sat and poked the fire before settling back to ponder again the matter of Seth Watkins and the missing money. He would have to wait and see what the following days brought forth.

The rest of the week played out as usual but added to that was the Cavenors checking the satchels, which had not gone unnoticed by the boys. Unknown to anyone else, the sorters were inconspicuously counting Seth's bundles, informing the boss quietly of the number each night.

On Saturday evening, the boys lined up for their wages, then one by one they left the office, leaving only Seth waiting to be paid. Watching the others go, Seth turned back to McGuire and began fidgeting impatiently.

'Seth, turn out your pockets,' McGuire said, eyeing the boy standing in front of his desk.

'What for?' Seth asked, feeling the Cavenor brothers' eyes burning into his back.

'Just do as you're asked, boy,' McGuire replied.

'Why me? You d'aint ask the others,' Seth said indignantly.

'Seth, your loads haven't been tallying with the money spent.'

Seth frowned as the colour drained from his face. 'I don't know what you mean.'

McGuire sighed and nodded at the Cavenors. In a flash, Bobby pinned Seth's arms behind his back and Dicky searched the boy's pockets. The four pennies pulled out were laid on the desk and Toby counted them before nodding again. Seth was released and gave the men a scathing glance.

'Open your snap tin,' McGuire ordered.

'What?'

'Snap tin – now!'

Seth's face was pale with fear, but he did as he was told.

McGuire looked inside the tin and there, wrapped neatly in a tea towel, was the rest of the missing money. Tipping it out to join the other four pennies, he eyed the boy standing before him.

'How do you explain this?' McGuire asked, pointing to the coins with his cigar.

'It's my savings,' Seth said rather too quickly.

'So you carry it around with you all the time, do you?'

Seth nodded. 'You know my old man, Boss, he'd drink it up the wall if he got the chance.'

'I've no doubt on that score, lad, but look at this.' McGuire pushed a paper across the desk on which he'd made a note of each day's takings from Seth's round.

Seth shuffled his feet as he glanced at the paper and sweat formed on his brow.

'Where's the rest of the money, Seth?' McGuire asked, his voice low and even.

'I... spent it – buying bundles.'

'I don't believe you.' McGuire's voice took on a menacing tone now. He was done with being patient.

Seth glanced up at Bobby and Dicky standing either side of him then lowered his eyes to his boots.

'Well, what have you to say for yourself?' McGuire demanded.

'Boss, you don't understand. It's my dad, I have to get out from under him!' Seth's words came out rapidly.

McGuire waited for the boy to continue.

'I thought if I could save enough, I could move out and live somewhere else, away from my father!'

'And the only way you could do that was by stealing my money.'

'I'm sorry, Boss, I really am.' Seth twisted his flat cap in a tight strangle-hold.

'An apology won't cut it, Seth. You've been pilfering from me for god knows how long and treating me like a fool. Probably laughing up your sleeve at getting one over on Toby McGuire.'

'It wasn't like that, Boss, I swear!'

'Well, that's how I see it. Now, on Monday morning, I want everything you've stolen from me right here on this desk. Do we understand each other on that point?' Seth nodded. McGuire cupped his ear.

'Yes, Boss.'

'Good. I will consider what's to be done with you and let you know when my money is returned. Now, get out of my sight!'

Seth turned and fled.

'What you gonna do to him, Guv?' Bobby asked.

'I'm not sure yet; let's see if he gives back what he's pinched first.'

'He could do a runner,' Dicky said.

'Sure, that would be a mistake, but if he tried, I would request you gentlemen hunt him down and bring him to me.'

'Yes, Boss,' the brothers said in unison.

'Right, boys – your wages, and have a good day off.' McGuire pushed the envelopes towards the men.

'Thanks, Guv'nor,' Bobby said.

'Ta muchly,' Dicky added.

McGuire watched them go then gathered up the wages to take to the sorters and grooms. Once all the staff had been paid, McGuire locked up and walked home, wondering as he walked if Seth might actually do a moonlight flit.

14

On Sunday morning, Jared woke to a banging on his front door. Climbing from his bed and opening up, he was surprised to see Dan standing there.

'Hello, sleepyhead, I thought I'd pay you a friendly visit,' Dan said cheerily.

'So I see. Come in and put the kettle on while I get dressed,' Jared answered with a yawn.

Dan had rekindled the coals in the range and made tea by the time Jared had washed and changed. Staring at Jared's clothes, Dan shook his head. His friend was dressed in trousers with holes in the legs, an old pair of bedroom slippers which were torn and tatty and a vest which was battleship grey. He was about to ask the reason for this when Jared asked, 'To what do I owe the pleasure?'

'To be honest, I get fed up on Sundays, and I thought you might as well seeing as you live alone like me.'

'Actually, I'm in the process of re-plastering the walls in the living room so that stops me having the time to feel lonely...' Jared began.

'Ah, that would explain the clothes. I can help with that, if you like,' Dan put in quickly.

'Fair enough. Have you eaten?' Dan shook his head. 'Right, bacon and eggs for two it is then.'

The boys chatted happily as Jared cooked breakfast, then Dan washed the dishes as his friend mixed the plaster in an old bucket. They both worked hard and had fun slapping the plaster onto the walls and trying to smooth it flat. By lunchtime, they were tired from their exertions and leaving the doors open to help dry the walls, they sat outside with a cup of tea.

'That's a job well done, thanks, Dan.'

'Pleased to have helped. I've been thinking about Seth and McGuire and what happened after we left last night.'

'I'm sure we'll find out soon enough,' Jared answered.

'McGuire is bound to tell you.'

'Why do you say that?' Jared asked.

''Cos he relies on you and trusts you,' Dan answered simply, before adding, 'I wonder if Seth will get the sack.'

'I hope not, I wouldn't want that to happen to anyone, even Seth.'

'But he stole McGuire's money, Jared!'

'I know, Dan, but how would he live without a job? And sounds like his dad would come down hard on him too.'

'I suppose, but I wouldn't want to be in McGuire's shoes, having that decision to make.'

'Neither would I,' Jared concurred.

After a bite to eat, the boys strolled down to the basin, enjoying the sunshine.

'We should do this every Sunday,' Dan proffered, 'we could ask the others to come too and bring a picnic while the weather is still good.'

'I like that idea. We could all contribute something for our lunch and make a day of it.'

'That's if Sam's mother will let him come, you know how possessive she is,' Dan said.

Jared nodded and waved to a little girl sitting on a narrowboat. 'We can suggest it and see what they say.'

As they walked back the way they had come, Dan said, 'Would you like to come to my house for tea?'

'That would be nice,' Jared answered and both boys picked up their pace.

Arriving in Miles Street, Dan led his friend into the terraced house. It was an old building, but Jared saw that Dan kept it clean and tidy. In the kitchen, Dan fed the range and Jared filled the kettle from the standpipe in the communal back yard. A ready-made meat pie was pushed into the oven to warm through and Dan peeled potatoes while Jared made tea. They worked well together, stepping around each other in the small space.

'How come you still live here after you lost your parents?' Jared asked, hoping Dan would not take offence at his question.

'My dad bought the house from the landlord. He had a good job as manager of the brick works so he made an offer on the place and the landlord agreed to it. I'm glad he did, otherwise I'd be on the streets.'

Over their evening meal, Jared told Dan about losing his mum and sister and how he'd lived rough for a short while before finding the empty cottage.

'What about your dad?' Dan asked.

'He left us when I was six years old.'

'Why?'

'I don't know. All I can remember is Mum and Dad arguing, then the next day he was gone,' Jared answered.

'It's hard being on your own, ain't it?'

'Yes, but at least we're not beholden to anyone. I'd rather live alone than with someone like Seth's father.'

'Me an' all,' Dan agreed.

'Right, then, I'd best get home and pack my lunch for tomorrow,' Jared said at last. 'Thanks for the meal, help and company.'

'I enjoyed meself today, ta, Jared.'

Jared walked the short distance home, also thinking how much he'd enjoyed the day. It was nice to have friends, and he and Dan had a lot in common.

The sun was setting and it cast an orange glow over the land. The birds chattered and squabbled in the treetops, each vying for the best roosting spot. Jared realised that autumn was almost upon them, when the brown leaves would fall into a golden carpet at the feet of the tree trunks. Squirrels would be scampering to hide the nuts they had gathered ready for winter, and Jared thought he would have to be sure to fill the larder and coal bunker in readiness for the cold winter weather too.

He reached home just as the sun slipped beneath the horizon, although it would be a while yet before the light faded completely. Time enough to sit outside and enjoy the fresh air before bedtime.

* * *

McGuire was woken on Monday morning by Alice screeching up the stairs. 'Get yer arse out of bed, you lazy bugger, yer breakfast is ready!'

'I'm glad I ain't married to you,' McGuire yelled back as he got up to wash and dress.

'I wouldn't have you! My Stanley is the one for me.'

'Your Stanley is a long streak of liquor, no further through than a slat!' McGuire said as he walked into the kitchen.

'Maybe, but he won me over, d'aint he?'

'He was a fool to himself, for sure. He should have run while he had the chance.'

Alice laughed. 'Yer only jealous, you big Irish bugger.'

McGuire wiggled his eyebrows and tucked into his food.

'Yer snap tin is there,' Alice said, pointing to his lunch bag. 'Bread, cheese, pickles, cake and fruit.'

'Same as always then. When am I to get something different?'

'When you make it your bloody self!' With that, Alice left via the back door, leaving McGuire grinning like a fool.

Arriving at the yard first, as always, McGuire opened up the gates and office. He watched as the sorters and grooms filed in, then he saw the boys come in one by one. The Cavenors followed and came straight to the office to collect the money satchels. McGuire had already counted out the coins for each and when he pushed the full bags across the desk, the brothers left to stand in the yard to give out the satchels.

McGuire stood in the office doorway, waiting for the last boy to arrive. He watched the carts roll away but still there was no sign of Seth Watkins.

Going to sit in his chair once more, McGuire began to wonder if the boy had taken his chance and run away.

15

All day, McGuire waited, but Seth still didn't show up for work. The dilemma facing him now was whether to see if the boy came in tomorrow, or go to his home to enquire if Seth was ill. Toby knew that Seth's father would be there, most likely inebriated up to his eyeballs, and that if Ned wasn't aware his son had not been to work, then it would cause trouble for the boy.

A passing thought gave him cause for concern that maybe Seth had taken another beating and was in no fit state to work, or he had indeed absconded.

'Bobby, ask Jared if he will spare me a minute before he goes home,' McGuire said quietly.

The big man nodded and, followed by his brother, went out to the stables to do as he was bid.

Moments later, there was a knock and Jared popped his head round the door. 'You wanted to see me, Mr McGuire?'

'Yes, lad, come in.' McGuire dismissed the Cavenors to watch over the sorters and Dicky closed the door as they left. Grimly, McGuire set out his concerns about Seth, and his fears for the boy when he hadn't returned the stolen funds.

'If you tell me where he lives, I can go in your stead and see if Seth's okay,' Jared offered.

'What about Ned? He's aggressive when drunk.'

Jared pondered a moment, before replying, 'I can say Seth and I work together and I forgot to ask him to come to tea with me and the others.'

'All right, but take someone with you 'cos I don't trust Ned Watkins. He's a mean drunk and can be unpredictable. Thanks for doing this, Jared, I appreciate it.'

'Leave it with me, Mr McGuire, I'll take Dan and let you know the outcome in the morning.'

Toby nodded and Jared went on his way, a slip of paper with Seth's address in his hand. Once he was back with the other tatters, Jared explained to his friends what was going on.

'I'm coming as well,' Paul said.

'And me,' Johnny put in.

Dan had already agreed and all eyes turned to Sam. 'My mother will have a blue fit if I'm late home,' he mumbled.

'That's okay, don't worry, there's enough of us,' Jared said sympathetically.

Suddenly Sam piped up, 'Oh, bugger my mother – I'll come!'

Spontaneous applause rang out and Sam beamed. It was about time he crawled out from beneath his mother's apron anyway.

Making their way through the town, they eventually came to High Street Deritend.

'Wouldn't you just know it, Seth lives right next door to the pub,' Paul commented.

They all looked up at the building to see the sign, the Old Leather Bottle, hanging above the door. The premises was in a sorry state, but raucous laughter could be heard within.

Jared banged on the door of the Watkins house and waited. No one answered so he hammered louder.

'Maybe he's in there with his father,' Johnny muttered as he tilted his head to the pub.

'Unlikely,' Jared said.

'Why not?' Sam asked.

'I suppose he could be, but I'd be surprised. I don't believe Seth is a drinker. I would have thought with his dad being a drunk that Seth would steer clear of alcohol,' Jared answered.

'Well, wherever he is, he ain't in there,' Johnny said, pointing at the front door of the house.

'Unless he's hiding,' Sam put in. 'He might be scared, thinking it's the Cavenors come to batter him.'

'That's a possibility, but there's nothing more we can do now. At least we tried. Let's go home,' Jared said as he turned to walk away.

'Seth, you in there?' Johnny yelled, causing Jared to turn back.

'Shut up! You'll have the street up and nosing, then we'll have Ned on our backs!' Jared reprimanded.

The boys passed four more public houses before they reached the tramway, each one a possible drinking hole for Ned Watkins. Staying close to the edge of the street, they sauntered along, still chatting about the whereabouts of Seth.

Stopping to peer at the boat in the lock for a while, they saw one set of gates close behind it, stopping the water from passing through. Further along, a hefty woman dug her heels into the ground and pushed her back against a sturdy wooden beam which opened the gates there, allowing the water to rush forth.

'That looks like hard work,' Paul said, pointing to the woman.

'It's clever, though, ain't it?' Johnny said as they watched the water pour in, slowly raising the narrowboat.

They walked on, their discussions moving from the canal

boats and the genius of the lock back to Seth and where he might be. Eventually they reached Watery Lane, where they said their farewells, Jared assuring them he would inform McGuire in the morning of their fruitless visit to Seth's house.

* * *

The following morning saw Jared reporting to McGuire.

'It looks like he's legged it, then,' McGuire said thoughtfully.

'I'm sorry, Mr McGuire.'

'That's all right, lad, you did your best and I appreciate that for sure.'

'Can I get off, then?'

'Aye, Jared, and thanks.'

McGuire puffed on his cigar, sending plumes of smoke up towards the ceiling as he considered his options. He could let the whole thing go and write it off as a bad debt and just put processes in place to make sure it never happened again. Or he could visit the Watkinses himself. If Ned was in the pub, he could go in there and ask about Seth. It was a tricky situation, having to speak with a drunken man about why his son hadn't been to work, but when that man was prone to fighting as well... McGuire thought he could always take Bobby and Dicky with him, maybe then Ned Watkins wouldn't be so quick with his fists. He decided to wait and see how the day panned out then have a word with the Cavenors at close of business.

Jared and the others set out on their rounds, hoping for a fruitful day, but all had their minds on Seth and where he might be. Jared thought about calling round to Seth's house again after work; he had a niggle at the back of his brain telling him that things were not right. He was not of the opinion that Seth had absconded, although he couldn't be sure. Jared was afraid something might have happened to the young man; maybe he was lying hurt somewhere. Whatever the reason, Seth had not come into work again today and Jared wanted to find out why.

The week's new rounds proved successful for all the boys, as Jared realised when he arrived back at the yard that evening.

There was an audible sigh from the sorters as the carts were positioned side by side, piled high with rags before the horses were released and taken to the stables. A few sorters climbed up onto the carts and began to throw the bundles to the floor. There was loose clothing and some shoved into old pillowcases. Other men on the ground bent to begin their task of sorting through, occasionally standing to rub their lower backs.

After seeing to their horses with help from the grooms, the boys gathered together and Jared asked, 'Sam, were you in trouble with your mum for being late last night?'

Sam rolled his eyes as he answered. 'She started with, "You're late, where have you been? Well, your tea's gone cold now. I don't stand cooking all day for you to waste good food..." So I told her I'd been with you lot to help a colleague out. And we would have – had we found him.'

'What did she say to that?' asked Paul.

Sam blew out his cheeks then said, '"Oh, my sweet boy, you're so thoughtful." So I told her I'm sixteen years old now and you have to stop mollycoddling me. It's time I was treated as a man.'

'Blimey, I bet that went down well,' Johnny said with a laugh.

Sam shook his head. 'Nah, she said, "You're just a baby yet, you have plenty of time to grow up." So I said, "I tell you what, any more of that and I'll leave home!"'

The others grinned widely at Sam's imitation of his mother.

'You won't be leaving any time soon 'cos your mum looks after you and you have it pretty easy compared to some,' Dan put in.

'You're probably right, but maybe the threat will be enough for her to see sense and get her to give me a bit more independence,' Sam answered.

All of them looked up at the sound of a whistle and McGuire hooked a finger for the friends to go to the office. Once inside, McGuire said to the assembled boys, 'I wanted to thank you for going with Jared last night and to tell you I'll be visiting Seth myself shortly.'

'Do you want us to come with you, Mr McGuire?' Jared asked.

'No, Jared, I'll be taking the Cavenors with me just in case there's any bother.'

'Good luck, sir, I hope you can get to the bottom of all this,' Jared responded.

'Me too, to be sure. I'll have to be finding somebody else to fill Seth's place if he's not coming back, so if you hear of a lad looking for work, let me know.'

The boys nodded and filed out to go home. As they made their way through the streets, full of the sounds of families getting ready for their evenings, the boys chattered about their days. In a pause in conversation, Dan piped up.

'Oh, by the way, lads, Jared and I thought we could all meet up on Sundays for a picnic when the weather's nice,' Dan said.

'Sounds a good idea,' Johnny replied with a smile.

'Count me in,' Paul said.

'Sam?' Dan asked.

'Yes, I'd like to and, before you ask, Mother will just have to put up with it!'

The boys all laughed as they clapped Sam on the back before they took their separate paths home.

* * *

McGuire, Bobby and Dicky set out after the workers had all left and walked across the town. People moved out of the way at the ominous sight of the big man, followed by two even bigger men. McGuire knew folk were whispering behind their hands about him as he marched past, and they were wondering who was next in line for a pasting.

'Ready?' McGuire asked as they arrived at the Watkinses' house. A nod and a roll of the shoulders told him the brothers were indeed on their guard. McGuire's fist banged loudly on the door and all three men took a step back. No answer came, so McGuire banged again.

'The curtain moved, Boss,' Dicky said.

McGuire gave a curt nod and hammered louder, intending to keep the knocking up until someone responded. After a moment, he heard the key turn in the lock and a pair of eyes peeped through the crack of the open door.

'Seth, let us in, lad,' McGuire said quietly.

'I can't,' the reply came as a whisper.

'Why not?'

'My father...'

'Is he there with you?' McGuire asked.

'No, but...'

'Then open up and let's talk about this. We don't want to be discussing your business on the doorstep for all to hear.'

The gap between door and jamb widened and McGuire gasped at the sight before him.

16

'Dear god in heaven! What's he done to you?' McGuire was shocked at the state of the boy leaning heavily against the door. He saw silent tears roll down Seth's cheeks from his almost-closed eyes, so swollen he could barely see. 'Let us in, Seth,' McGuire coaxed.

'He'll kill me if I do,' Seth said, a catch in his voice.

'He bloody well won't! We'll get to him first, lad,' Dicky rasped.

Slowly, Seth moved aside to allow them entry and closed the door behind them.

McGuire watched the boy limp back towards the living room, then the three followed behind.

Seth lowered himself carefully onto a kitchen chair next to an empty fireplace. Other than Ned's armchair, there was no other furniture in the room. There were no rugs, just bare floorboards and the once pretty wallpaper was hanging off the walls in shreds. Candles on saucers adorned the fireplace, ready to be lit when darkness fell.

'Tell me what happened,' McGuire said gently.

Seth shook his head and winced. His arm lay across his ribs as if fighting off the pain.

'Seth, I can't help if you don't explain.' McGuire kept his voice calm in the hope of Seth divulging what had befallen him.

'My father... he found my savings,' Seth began.

McGuire sighed heavily. 'Go on, lad.'

'He wanted to know where they came from. I was gonna bring them back to you, I swear!' Seth was becoming agitated, glancing at the window regularly, clearly afraid his father would come back and catch them there.

'All right, Seth, I believe you,' McGuire said soothingly.

'He started hitting me and I... I had to tell him how I'd got the money. I'm sorry, Mr McGuire but – he took the lot!'

'The money doesn't matter, Seth, what he's done to you is what concerns me, so it does.'

Seth's tears fell in a torrent and each time he took a breath, he winced.

'Looks like Ned's broken the kid's ribs,' Bobby said quietly.

'That's what I thought,' McGuire agreed. Then to Seth, he said, 'We have to get you out of here for your own safety.'

'No! He'll find me and kill me if I try to leave!'

'He won't find you, don't you worry about that, son,' McGuire said. 'Come on, you can stay with me until we decide what's to be done.'

Seth cried harder at the kindness shown to him by the man he'd stolen from.

'Bobby, go and hail a cab 'cos there ain't no way Seth can walk that far.'

Doing as he was bid, Dicky helped Seth to his feet and then to the front door. Between them, they got him into the cab.

'Drive slowly,' McGuire instructed the cabbie.

'Yes, sir,' the reply came. The cabbie shook his head, seeing the poor boy's injuries. Slowly the cab took them to McGuire's house and again Seth was helped into the house. McGuire paid the cabbie handsomely. 'Not a word about this, all right?'

'I ain't had a fare all evenin',' the cabbie said as his finger tapped the side of his nose. He smiled gratefully as a large tip was handed over to accompany the fare.

As he opened his front door and entered the hallway, McGuire and Seth were met by a screech from the housekeeper. 'You're bloody late again! What the...' her voice trailed off as she saw the Cavenors aiding Seth to walk. 'Oh, you poor boy!'

'Alice, make up the spare room, will you? Seth will be staying here for a while,' McGuire said quietly.

'Right away,' Alice nodded and trundled off.

Seth was led into the living room and eased into a large armchair.

'Thank – you – Mr – McGuire,' he panted once he was settled, 'and – you – too,' he said to the Cavenors.

'No trouble, lad,' Dicky answered.

'You just get better,' Bobby added.

'I'll need you to help him to bed after he's had something to eat,' McGuire said, and the men nodded.

A few moments later, Alice joined them. 'His room is ready. I've laid out a spare nightshirt and there's water in the jug for a wash.'

'Thanks, Alice, the boys will take him up after he's had some dinner...'

'No, they won't. You get yourselves off home, I'll see to Seth.'

At McGuire's nod, the brothers left quietly. 'Thanks,' Toby called out.

'See you tomorrow, Boss,' Dicky answered.

Alice disappeared to the kitchen and came back with a tray on which was a plate of hot food.

'I hope that's not my dinner,' McGuire said with a smile.

'As it happens, it ain't, but it should be 'cos you could do with losing a few pounds!' Alice answered with a grin.

Seth watched the banter between the adults through one eye. The other had now completely closed.

'Sit you down and I'll fetch yours, you can eat in here with Seth tonight,' Alice said as she placed the tray gingerly on Seth's lap.

'Thank you,' the boy muttered as he eyed the food, his mouth watering. Thick onion gravy covered potatoes, vegetables and slices of beef. He didn't know whether he would like the meat because he'd never tasted it before.

Alice brought in McGuire's tray, and then went back to the kitchen to make tea for them all.

Seth began to eat tentatively, his jaw aching from the punches he'd received at his father's hands. Then, as the delicious flavours tickled his taste buds, he tucked in with relish, forgetting all about the pain.

Alice came back with the tea tray and sat down to pour them all tea. She watched the injured young man as he cleared his plate.

'Thanks,' was all Seth could manage, out of breath from the effort of eating.

Alice whipped his tray away and gave him his cup of tea. As she tidied up in the kitchen, she couldn't help but wonder what on earth had happened to the boy, but she knew McGuire would tell her in his own good time. Returning to the living room, she saw Seth had finished his tea. 'Right, my boy, let's get you to bed.'

'I can manage,' Seth said, embarrassment written all over his face.

'Seth, I have a husband and two sons, you ain't got anything I ain't seen before.'

'I wouldn't argue with her, Seth, she's a dragon, so she is,' McGuire said with a laugh.

'You shut up else I'll box yer bloody ears!' Alice snapped back, but her smile belied her temper.

'See what I mean?' McGuire grinned and saw Seth attempt a smile.

Alice helped Seth to his feet, muttering soothing words. 'That's it, good lad. You'll feel better by morning 'cos I've got a medicine that will help with the pain.'

It took a while to get Seth up the stairs, but Alice managed. She led him to a bedroom where the gas lights on the wall were burning low, giving the room a cosy glow.

'Right, let's get you out of those clothes and into your nightshirt.' Seth hung his head as his tears began again. 'I know you're embarrassed, but try not to be. I just want to make you comfortable and get you well again.'

Seth screwed up his mouth in the semblance of a smile and allowed Alice to undress him; he couldn't have stopped her anyway with those injuries of his.

Talking to him all the while to distract him, Alice kept her shock to herself as she saw the bruises, old and new, all over Seth's body. This boy had clearly been beaten badly on many occasions and Alice's heart went out to him. Carefully, she washed and dried him, allowing him to do his own intimate ablutions. Then she slipped the nightshirt over his head. 'There you go, all done. Now, into bed and take some of my medicine and you'll sleep like a babe.'

Seth settled onto the feather mattress and sighed with pleasure and relief. He swallowed his medication and smiled at the woman who had ministered to him.

'I'll leave the lights burning in case you wake in the night and wonder where you are.' Alice bent down and retrieved the chamber pot from beneath the bed. 'I'll put this here so you can reach it.' She placed the pot on the dresser next to the bed.

'Thanks, angel Alice,' Seth muttered as his eyes began to close.

Alice felt tears sting her eyes before she tiptoed from the room, closing the door with a quiet click.

'How is he?' McGuire asked as Alice joined him in the living room.

'Sleeping. His bones and bruises will heal but I doubt his tortured mind ever will.'

McGuire and his housekeeper sat with whisky in hand, discussing the battered boy asleep upstairs.

'Christ, Toby, that lad is a mess. He's bruised yellow and black from top to bottom. God alone knows what might have happened if you hadn't got there when you did,' Alice said quietly.

'I've seen him with a black eye now and then, but I had no idea it had got so bad.'

'If Seth said nothing, then how could you know?'

McGuire sighed long and deep.

'What's gonna happen next is my concern,' Alice said.

'Mine too, Alice, for I feel sure Ned Watkins will be at the yard tomorrow once he finally realises his son is not there.'

'I don't envy you that, Toby, but promise me you won't let him take Seth home.'

'I promise I'll do everything in my power to keep them apart, it's the best I can do.'

Alice's satisfaction at his answer was confirmed with a nod. 'Toby, does Ned rent that house?'

'I've no idea but I suspect he does, and what's more, I wouldn't be surprised if he's in arrears with his payments. He seems to spend all his money in the boozer.'

'So he'll be chucked out then if Seth's not earning for him.' Alice's words were more statement than question.

'I expect so. In fact, it's a miracle it hasn't happened already.'

'He's always been a bad 'un, even at school, do you remember?'

'I do, Alice, he thumped me a couple of times until I fought back. Once he'd measured his length on the floor, he left me alone, so he did.'

Emptying her glass, Alice stood. 'I'm going home before my Stanley thinks I'm canoodling with you.'

'Perish the thought! My mares are prettier than you.'

Alice laughed before adding seriously, 'If Seth cries out in the night, give him a spoonful of the medicine on the dresser. Talk to him gently, reassure him he's safe and he'll go right back to sleep.'

'Thanks, Alice, you're an angel.'

'That's what Seth called me – angel Alice.'

'Sure, then he's right,' McGuire said with a smile.

'I'll see to him in the morning and to your breakfast, you old devil.' With that, Alice left McGuire to his musings, having absolutely no idea he had loved her all of his life.

17

The following morning, McGuire called the boys into his office and explained what had happened to Seth, and that he had taken the lad into his own home. He was struck by the solemnity of the moment as the boys bowed their heads. He was fully aware that Seth was not liked by the others, but he could see they felt sorry in their hearts for him.

'Mr McGuire, what about Seth's dad?' Jared asked at last.

'I'm expecting a visit from him sometime today, Jared,' McGuire answered. 'However, I don't want you to worry about that, if he causes a ruckus I'll send for the police. Now let's all get to work.'

The boys left the office, sharing what they'd been told in mumbled discussions.

Minutes later, Jared clucked to Bess as they rolled through the gates, still feeling wretched for Seth. He somehow had known when he and the boys visited Ned's house that something bad had occurred, and now he fretted that he had been unable to do anything about it. Quite what a fourteen-year-old could have done about Seth's dad beating him up he had no idea, but that didn't make him feel any better. He was also concerned for McGuire's safety. The man had been good to him in the time Jared had worked for him and he didn't want his boss to suffer the same fate as Seth. Despite his fearsome reputation, McGuire had a soft side, and Jared felt strangely protective of him. The saving grace was that McGuire had the Cavenor brothers to guard him. As he traversed the streets, Jared wondered if Watkins senior would be arrested for assault; Jared thought he should be.

Heading up Jamaica Row and then on to the Bull Ring, Jared wrinkled his nose at the smell as he passed the meat market. He turned into Moor Street and was immediately hailed by a woman with half a dozen young children hanging onto her skirts. She held up a single child's dress and asked how much he would give her for it.

'I only buy bundles, missus,' Jared said.

'This is all I have. I shouldn't really sell it, but I need the money to feed the kids.'

Jared stared at the woman and her offspring, and his heart ached. She was stick thin, with eyes which looked too big for her face. Her pallor was pasty, despite the fact that the weather was unseasonably hot and sunny that day. The children's bellies were distended from malnutrition, their little arms and legs like twigs.

Reaching into his satchel, Jared pulled out three pennies and passed them to the woman's outstretched hand. 'Keep the dress and don't say a word or I'll lose my job,' he said quietly.

'God bless you!' the woman gasped as she clutched the coins to her chest.

Jared nodded and clucked to Bess to move on. He had just given away money which did not belong to him, but he would replace it tomorrow from his box beneath the floorboard. It was the woman's dignity which had swayed him in the end; she had not been begging for a handout, but was prepared to sell what

Jared suspected was her daughter's only other garment. She couldn't have had anything left of her own to barter.

You're a soft touch, Jared Johnson, he thought as the cart rolled on, and you'll never have any money if you start giving it away.

However, by lunchtime, his cart was half-full. Jared hung the nosebag over Bess's head then fed himself. He was keen to get on, so he kept his lunch quick and was soon heading down Smallbrook Street and then onto the tramway at Horse Fair. In all these streets, the houses were tightly packed together with a ginnel every few buildings allowing access to the rear of the properties. There was a pub, a church – St Catherine's – and a bank and Jared didn't think he would do any good business in this fairly well-to-do area. He couldn't have been more wrong. Cleaning ladies came out with bundles from almost every house, and Jared knew these good-quality clothes would be sorted to be sold on.

With all his money gone and his cart full, Jared led Bess past the Looking Glass Manufactory and along the smaller streets, which were quieter at this time of day, back to the yard.

The other boys were back already and they greeted Jared heartily as he pulled in. He called out a hello and headed to the stables to bed Bess down for the evening. As the tatters finished in the stables, they all stopped dead as they heard a shout.

'McGuire!'

The boys exchanged a glance and ran back to the yard, where they saw a tall, well-built man, swaying from foot to foot.

'Seth's father?' Sam asked in a whisper.

'I'm guessing so,' Jared answered just as quietly.

'McGuire!' the shout came again.

Toby McGuire walked to the doorway of his first-floor office and looked down to see Ned Watkins. He had known Ned would come but was surprised it had taken him so long to get there; clearly he had been too drunk to manage the journey before now.

'Where is he?' Ned yelled.

McGuire spoke to Bobby, who nodded, and with his brother descended the steps to the yard. 'Mr McGuire asks you to join him in his office,' Bobby Cavenor said.

'Where you two brutes can jump me? I don't think so,' Ned replied.

McGuire sighed heavily and came down to stand facing a very drunk Ned Watkins. All the hatred and anger McGuire was feeling showed in his eyes as they burned into the man opposite him.

'So, McGuire, where's the boy?' Ned asked.

'*The* boy? Don't you mean your son? The one you beat half to death,' McGuire answered coolly.

'That's none of your business! Just hand him over.'

McGuire merely shook his head, puffed on his cigar and stared at Ned. Then he said, 'Seth isn't here.'

'That's true,' whispered Jared as the tatter boys, grooms and sorters all stood together, watching the confrontation.

'Now you listen to me...' Ned said, taking a step forward with fists raised. But he stopped short as the whole workforce walked to stand behind McGuire in a show of solidarity.

McGuire didn't move so much as a muscle. 'I've told you, Seth is not here. Now I suggest you go home, sober up and think on what you've done.'

'You can't keep him from me forever, McGuire!' Ned yelled. 'I'll find him and when I do...'

'You'll what? Finish the job you started the other day? You're a disgrace, Ned Watkins. Look at you, hardly able to stand up. You have no furniture in that tip you call a house, taking every last penny Seth earns to buy your drink. What sort of father treats his son like that?'

'How we live is up to me, so I'll thank you to keep your nose out!' Ned shouted. The effort of raising his voice caused him to wobble and almost fall over.

'This conversation is over. Gentlemen, please see Mr Watkins off my property.' McGuire turned and strode towards his office.

The Cavenors grabbed Ned's arms and frog-marched him out of the gates, where they pushed him away. Ned fell to the ground, screaming obscenities, but the brothers ignored him and returned to the yard, brushing their hands together in order to remove the filth they thought might contaminate them.

Ned's yelling could be heard slowly receding as he got to his feet and staggered away across the heath.

Jared began to clap the Cavenor brothers, and before long, everyone else joined in. With a little bow, Bobby and Dicky climbed the stairs to join their employer.

McGuire smiled as he heard the applause. Now all he had to do was decide what he was going to do with Seth Watkins.

18

Alice Crawford had stayed with Seth all day, ensuring he ate and slept whilst McGuire was at work. Having raised her own children, Alice had dealt with bumps and scrapes kids acquired from everyday play, so tending to Seth was no great hardship for her. However, she did worry the young man's mind could be affected by the abuse he had clearly suffered over the years.

A quiet thank you had been the only words Seth had uttered after she had fed him chicken broth for his lunch. He had sipped homemade lemonade before lying back, exhausted.

Alice had made up a medicine of turmeric and ginger to help reduce inflammation and ease the pain, which she had given to Seth on a teaspoon. Then she made a pot of peppermint tea to help soothe any muscle spasms and aid sleep. Tenderly she applied Arnica to the bruising on his body, explaining it was an anti-inflammatory.

'This lot should see you feeling better in no time, although your ribs are gonna take a bit longer to heal.'

Seth tried to smile, but his split lip prevented it and he winced. 'Need to...' Seth's eyes moved to the chamber pot on the dresser.

'Come on then, I'll help you.'

'No...'

'I've done this before, Seth, so don't fret,' she said, helping him out of bed. 'I tell you what, I'll hold the pot under your nightshirt and close my eyes, all right?'

Seth nodded carefully.

Once the trickling stopped, Alice put the pot on the floor and helped Seth back to bed. 'There you go, that wasn't so bad, was it? Now you can rest a while.'

'Thanks, you're so kind,' Seth muttered.

Alice saw his tears welling and rather than embarrass him further, she grabbed the pot to be emptied and washed. 'It's no bother. You sleep while I cook tea.' With that, she flung open the window and left the room.

Having emptied and washed the pot in the bathroom, she placed it outside Seth's room ready for the next time she went in. Washing her hands, she then went downstairs and set about preparing an evening meal.

As she worked, Alice thought about the boy in her charge. 'Poor bugger, ain't never had a kind word nor been given any love,' she mumbled. 'Well, my lad, you'll get both from me.'

Around four o'clock, she brewed a pot of tea and adding a few biscuits, she took it all upstairs on a tray balanced on one hand, holding her long skirt away from her feet as she ascended with the other. Letting go of her skirt, she managed to grab the pot with her now free hand. Having left the door ajar, she nudged it open with her foot and was pleased to see Seth was awake.

'Did you manage forty winks?'

'Yes, I think the medicine helped,' Seth said, sounding brighter than he had that morning.

'Good. I've brought you this.' Alice placed the tray on the bed beside him then laid the pot back on the dresser.

Seth sipped his tea then took a biscuit.

'Time for some more medicine, oh, and I have liver and onions for later, I hope you like it.'

'I do!'

Alice was gratified to see a light in his eyes at the thought of another delicious hot meal.

'Excellent. So how are you feeling now?'

'Sore but I'll mend, I always do,' Seth answered sadly.

'Well, once you're fit again, there'll be no more mending for you – ever,' Alice said sternly.

'You don't know my dad.'

'Oh, but I do. I went to school with that bleeder and he was vile even then.' For a while, Alice regaled the boy with stories of his father in his younger years, ending with the time that McGuire had laid Ned Watkins out cold after Ned had been the ringleader in a particularly nasty bout of bullying.

'Blimey, I never knew that. My dad don't talk to me much. He just takes my wages and goes to the pub every night.'

'What about food?' Alice asked.

'I always bought some on Saturdays after I got paid and before I got home, otherwise we would have starved.'

'Oh, lad! My heart bleeds for you having to put up with that sod for so many years. No wonder your mother took off.'

'I wish I could have gone with her, but my dad wouldn't allow it,' Seth said with a sniff.

Alice shook her head. Then, seeing he was struggling to stay awake, she said, 'I'll go and check the liver but before I go, do you need to pee?'

Seth's eyes crinkled in a grin. 'No, I'm all right, thanks.'

With a smile, Alice returned to the kitchen.

McGuire arrived home just as Alice was dishing up. 'That smells good. How has Seth been today?'

'He's doing well; a couple of days should see him up, but he'll have to be careful with those ribs.'

McGuire sat at the dining table and Alice placed his food before him. 'I'll take some up to Seth now.'

McGuire was aware they had exchanged no insults as was usual. All their lives, they had hurled scornful abuse at each other but always in a playful manner. Today there had been none and McGuire guessed it was because Alice was worried about Seth.

A few minutes later, she was back and sat down to relate her earlier conversation with Seth.

McGuire listened as he ate, giving a nod every now and then. When she'd finished speaking, he said, 'The lad has had a hard life with Ned, to be sure, but he's safe now and will be well in no time with your ministering to him. Anyway, you'd best get off and see to that skinny fella you call husband.'

Alice grinned and, pointing to his plate, said, 'I bet you wish you'd married me now.'

You'll never know how right you are, McGuire thought, but said instead, 'What, with your foul mouth?'

'I don't know what you bloody mean!' she said with a grin. 'There's apple pie and custard in the kitchen. I'll leave you to take some up to Seth.' Turning on her heel, she called, 'Tarrar,' and was gone.

Once he'd finished his dinner, Toby went into the kitchen to make tea and with a bowl of sweet on the tray, he ascended the stairs. 'Alice said you're feeling a little better today,' he said as he put the tray on the bed and removed the tray that had had Seth's dinner on it. 'She also said you have to eat all of that. And we don't want to go disobeying Alice, do we?'

'I'll do my best,' Seth said with a smile and proceeded to tuck right in to his pudding.

When he had finished, Toby decided he should tell the boy what had happened that afternoon.

'Your father came to the yard today looking for you.' He saw Seth's face fall. 'He was as drunk as a lord, shouting the odds.'

'So what happened?'

'I had him thrown out,' McGuire said with a grin.

'He'll be back, Mr McGuire, and he'll keep coming until I go home.'

'Do you want to go back there?'

'No, but I can't stay here. You've been kindness itself to me, especially after what I did, but once I'm on my feet, I'll leave you in peace.'

'Where will you go, Seth? You have no money.'

'I don't know, but I have to get away from *him*!' Seth felt tears prick his eyes and he tried to swallow them away but they fell anyway.

'Look, let's not worry about any of that yet. We need to get you fit and well first, then we can decide what's to be done,' McGuire said gently.

'Thanks, Boss.'

'Right, I'll have my pudding then I'll come back and we can chat if you want.'

'I'd like that, Mr McGuire.'

Downstairs, Toby ate without tasting a thing. His mind kept turning over and over the problem of how to keep his promise to Alice, and keep the Watkinses away from each other.

19

It was around midnight when McGuire woke with a jolt at the screaming coming from the next room. He jumped out of bed and bolted into the corridor. By the time he'd entered the spare room and turned up the gas lamp, the sound had turned to pitiful crying.

'It's all right, Seth, you're safe, lad,' McGuire soothed as he approached the bed where Seth sat bolt upright with tears streaming from his eyes.

'Sorry,' Seth managed between the heart-wrenching sobs.

'It's okay, son, let it all out,' McGuire said softly as he sat on the side of the bed.

Taking a breath as deep as he could manage, Seth said, 'I was dreaming, I'm sorry I woke you.'

'No matter, I'm here and I won't let anything happen to you whilst you're under my roof.'

Seth's tears continued to fall, and McGuire held out his arms. Seth leaned forward and despite the pain in his ribs, he let McGuire hold him while he cried himself out.

'I was prepared for this, so don't you fret none. Alice warned me it might happen and said for you to have some more medicine.'

Seth could feel the strong arms wrapped around him gently, something he hadn't experienced since his mother had left, and he began to relax a little.

McGuire sensed the small movement but didn't let go until the boy's arms released him.

For a moment, they looked at each other in the glow of lamplight. Seth saw the tenderness in his boss's eyes which belied his reputation as a hard man, and McGuire saw the anguish and fear in the boy's.

McGuire measured out the medicine on a spoon and fed it to Seth, then said, 'Do you fancy a cuppa before you go back to sleep?'

Seth nodded with a sniff.

McGuire got to his feet, saying, 'You know what Alice would say? "Bloody kids getting you up in the middle of the night!"'

Despite the ache in his ribs, Seth chuckled. 'She's a special lady.'

'Sure, but you're right there.'

'Mr McGuire, you should have married her, you know.'

'I do, lad, but someone got there before me, so he did. Now you rest a minute while I make us a nice cup of tea.'

Seth watched him go and shook his head in wonder. He had seen for himself now just how kind McGuire was, and Seth learnt an important lesson about not taking people at face value. McGuire was known to be ruthless in business and not a man to be crossed. He could instil fear in a person with just a word, as Seth had discovered for himself. But beneath that iron carapace was a gentle soul with a heart of gold. Since he had been saved by McGuire just a few days ago, Seth had received more affection than he had had from his own father for many years.

The sound of McGuire's footsteps on the stairs broke Seth's train of thought and moments later, the two were enjoying a hot brew by gas light. A little later, as Seth settled down to rest once more, McGuire returned to his own bed, his thoughts swirling on what he'd like to do to Ned Watkins.

The following morning, McGuire sat with his breakfast and related the events of the previous night to Alice – omitting what Seth had said about them being wed to each other, of course.

'It was bound to happen, Toby, that boy has such a lot of misery in his brain; years of abuse tormenting his mind while he sleeps,' Alice responded sadly.

'He held on to me so tight, Alice, even though his ribs were hurting,' McGuire said.

'He sees you as his saviour and it was his way of thanking you. I'll stay with him again today. Knowing he's not alone might help.'

'Thanks, Alice, you're a diamond.'

'What I wouldn't give for one of those,' she said on a sigh.

I would have given you the biggest I could find, McGuire thought but said instead, 'Ah, now quit your moaning, woman, you had a gold band from that old man of yours.'

'I did,' Alice agreed wistfully, 'but to own a diamond – if only a little one... Still, I'd best get Seth his breakfast.'

McGuire watched her go to the pantry, the aching in his heart as sharp as it ever was, from the very first day he'd seen her in school. It was then he decided – one day, he would buy Alice a diamond.

* * *

At the yard, Jared had collected his money satchel and was ready to set off on his round. He slipped three pennies inside to replace those he had given to the starving woman and his mind felt at ease. He had decided not to mention it to anyone, and now the money was back where it belonged, he felt no reason to speak of it again. The last thing he needed was for McGuire to lose faith in him after all his hard work to gain the boss's trust.

Travelling the list of streets which constituted his round, Jared wondered what would happen to Seth once he was up and around again. He very much doubted Seth would return to his father's house, but would McGuire allow him to stay in his own home indefinitely? Jared shook his head at the very idea. His guess would be that McGuire would ask Seth to leave once he was fit enough, then it would be up to Seth what he would do and where he would go. Jared couldn't see Seth on the rounds again either because he would be too easy to spot by Ned Watkins.

Jared pushed the thoughts away when his stomach rumbled to tell him it was time for lunch. With Bess's nosebag in place, he pulled out his bread and cheese and sat on the driving seat to enjoy his food. As he was munching and minding his own business, out of the corner of his eye he saw a man tumble from the doorway of a nearby pub. Jared felt a ripple of fear as he heard the shout, 'Oi, you!'

Ned Watkins staggered across the road towards the cart. 'You work for McGuire!' he yelled.

Jared put down his food and, feeling around, he located the reins. If the situation turned ugly, he could urge Bess forward despite her having her nose in the oats bag.

Ned stood swaying in the street. 'Well?'

Jared didn't answer, his mind working overtime on how to escape. He was about to pick up the reins when he felt himself yanked from the cart and land heavily on the cobbles.

'Answer me, you little toerag!' Watkins bellowed into Jared's face.

'Yes, I work for Mr McGuire,' Jared said, getting to his feet.

'Where's my boy?' Watkins asked.

Jared turned to walk away back to his cart, but Ned grabbed his arm and swung him around. 'Get your hands off me!' Jared growled.

'Or what?' Ned taunted.

Jared strode around the cart to remove his horse's nosebag, which he tossed onto the driving seat. As he was about to climb up, he was dragged backwards. In an instant, Jared spun round and let fly a hard kick which landed squarely between Ned's legs. The man went down to his knees with both hands clutching his injured parts. Tears welled in his eyes as he rolled onto his side, gasping for breath.

Leaning down, Jared ground from between clenched teeth, 'Stay away from me! Don't you ever touch me again!' Then he climbed aboard the cart and snapped the reins together. Bess set off and was soon picking up speed. As the cart hurtled around the next corner, Jared didn't look back but kept his eyes on the road ahead.

Behind him, Ned Watkins lay on his back, his knees pulled into his chest, rocking from side to side, his lungs desperately seeking air as tears rolled down the sides of his face.

Jared's heartbeat didn't slow until he reached the yard. Pulling in through the gates, he halted Bess and jumped down, racing towards McGuire's office.

'Jared?' McGuire asked as the boy barged in through the open door.

'Mr McGuire,' Jared panted, 'I've just been accosted by Ned Watkins!'

20

McGuire leapt from his seat and rounded the desk in one stride. 'Are you all right, lad?'

Jared nodded, still breathing hard.

'Get your breath back, then tell me what happened,' McGuire said as he looked the boy over for any signs of injury.

The Cavenors entered the office, having seen Jared arrive back early, and stood quietly to listen in.

Eventually, Jared was able to explain what had happened as he described the confrontation between Watkins senior and himself.

Bobby and Dicky exchanged glances before looking at their employer once more.

McGuire sighed audibly. 'That man is a menace, so he is, but I'm glad you are not hurt.'

'I'll have a bruise from where I landed, but otherwise I'm okay,' Jared responded. 'I'm sorry I came back early, Mr McGuire, but I thought you should be aware. I just hope Watkins doesn't come across any of the others.'

'Aye, lad, that is a worry, to be sure. Right, you go and give the sorters a hand till the end of the day and leave this with me.'

When Jared left the office, Bobby said, 'Something needs to be done, Boss, we can't have Ned harassing the lads.'

'I know. Let me think on it.'

The brothers nodded and left McGuire to do just that. As they stood in the yard watching Jared explaining to the sorters why he was back early, Bobby said quietly, 'Ned Watkins needs sorting out.'

Dicky chuckled, 'Sorting out – sorters, get it?'

Bobby sighed with a shake of his head. 'The trouble is we can't do anything without the boss's say-so.'

'I'm more than happy to give him a kicking,' Dicky pushed.

'Me an' all but like I said, McGuire needs to give the word first.'

The two then went to stand guard at the gates in case the man in question decided to put in another appearance.

Up in the office, McGuire thought hard about the debacle between Jared and Ned. He knew it was possible that it could happen again, maybe with one of the other tatters, and if it did, then someone could get hurt. Not about to let that happen, McGuire knew he would have to warn Ned to leave the boys alone or face the consequences. But when would be the best time to visit Watkins? McGuire felt an early-morning call would be the best, after Ned had slept off some of the alcohol he'd drunk the night before. That way, he'd be less inclined to start a fight, but McGuire would be sure to take the Cavenors with him anyway, just in case.

The sound of a cart pulling into the yard prompted McGuire to get to his feet and go to check on the yard from the doorway, but it was an allotment owner come to buy some manure. Jared and one of the sorters carried the bags and placed them on the cart. The man offered the money to Jared, who shook his head and pointed to Bobby, who had followed the cart in. Taking the money, Bobby shook hands with the man who climbed onto the cart and led the horse out of the gates, waving to Dicky as he went. Bobby brought the money up to McGuire, then re-traced his steps to the gates. Work might have been carrying on as normal, but the mood in the yard was jumpy.

* * *

The afternoon passed quietly and soon the tatter boys began to return one by one, each of them surprised to see Jared helping with the sorting.

'Bobby, I need to see the lads before they go home,' McGuire yelled.

'Yes, Boss,' came the reply.

Half an hour later, all five boys lined up in McGuire's office.

'Jared, tell your pals what happened today, if you would,' McGuire said.

Paul and Dan exchanged a worried look, then all eyes turned to Jared.

When Jared had finished explaining what had happened with Seth's dad, McGuire took up the story. 'Now, I've decided to pay Mr Watkins an early-morning visit tomorrow so you've no need to be worrying.'

'Are we coming as well?' Bobby asked.

'It would be appreciated,' McGuire answered.

The brothers grinned, secretly hoping they'd be allowed to give Ned a black eye at the very least.

'However, until this nonsense is dealt with once and for all, I want you boys to go out in pairs. Sam and Johnny, Dan and Paul.'

'What about me, Mr McGuire?' Jared asked with concern he might be relegated to the yard for the foreseeable future.

'I want you to take one of the sorters with you, Jared, so you make your choice. And this way has the benefit of giving the horses a rest too, if you alternate them each day.'

Jared nodded. 'I'll ask Tom Brooks then.'

'Fair enough. Bobby will tell him he's promoted to tatter temporarily and if he proves his worth, he can have the job permanently. Right, that's it, so get off home and stay together.'

The boys filed out and Bobby followed along to have a word with Tom Brooks. When he returned, he said, 'Young Tom is delighted and sends his thanks.'

'Good. Now, about tomorrow…' McGuire laid out his plan on how best to deal with Watkins senior before giving the brothers leave to go home too.

Locking up a little while later, McGuire kept his eyes peeled for any signs of Ned, and continued to be on his guard as he strode purposefully back to his house.

'Hey up, the boss is back,' Alice called out as she heard the front door open and close. Receiving no answer, she walked to the hall to see why. A frown drew her brows together as she asked, 'What's up?'

McGuire nodded towards the living room, and once they'd taken seats, he told her about the events of the day, taking care to keep his voice low lest Seth should hear him.

'Christ, Toby! That bloody man needs a thrashing and I've a good mind to do it myself!'

McGuire then went on to relate his plan for the following day. 'I'm taking the Cavenors with me early in the morning to pay Ned Watkins a visit.'

'What are you going to do when you get there?' Alice asked quietly.

'I think it's time Ned was reminded about how it feels to be punched black and blue.'

'You watch his neighbours don't call the bloody bobbies out and have you arrested!'

'I'll let the boys rough him up a little, just enough that he aches for a few days, and we'll do it quietly.'

'Just be sure you do.'

'I'll be back before you get here, though.'

'Be careful, you know how Ned can be when the mood takes him,' Alice said, smoothing her hands down her apron.

'I will, the brothers will be with me.'

'Good, I don't think even Ned would tackle one of them buggers, let alone two.'

'So how is Seth?' McGuire asked.

'Better still today. He's finally realised he's safe and you're not gonna force him to go back to Ned.'

'I'll nip up and see him and then I'm having a large whisky,' McGuire said, wiggling his eyebrows.

Ten minutes later, Toby was handed his drink by a smiling Alice as he sat in his armchair. 'Ah, may you live long enough to pour me many more,' Toby said gratefully.

'And may you live long enough to say thank you,' Alice retorted.

'Why should I break the habit of a lifetime?' McGuire asked with a grin.

'Ooh, sometimes you rile the life out of me! Come and get your tea while I see to Seth.'

McGuire watched Alice's hips sway as she walked away to the kitchen and he felt his pulse quicken.

'Get your eyes off my arse!' Alice said without turning around.

McGuire took a gulp of whisky and coughed as the liquid burned his throat.

'Serves you right, that does,' Alice called, and McGuire had to agree.

A little while later, Alice brought Seth's tray downstairs and left it in the kitchen. Finding McGuire in the living room with another drink, she tutted loudly. 'Tch, you'll end up a drunkard if you're not careful.'

'There's no chance of that – I'm Irish, woman, and we know how to hold our liquor.'

'Hmm, so they say. Anyway, I'm off now. Remember what I said and watch yourself in the morning.'

'Anybody would think you cared,' McGuire teased.

'I don't give a bugger,' Alice said with a crooked smile.

McGuire's heart melted. 'Away with you, I'll spend some time with Seth.'

'You gonna tell him?' Alice asked.

'About today, yes, but not about tomorrow.'

With a curt nod, Alice left him to it. She had a husband at home waiting for his evening meal.

McGuire stood, walked to the stairs and with a sigh began to climb them. He was not looking forward to relating the day's events to Seth but knew it had to be done.

21

When Jared and the others walked home together, the questions came thick and fast.

'Did you really kick Watkins in the trossocks?' Johnny asked.

'Yes.'

'Was he very drunk again?' This came from Paul.

Jared nodded. 'It happened exactly as I told you in Mr McGuire's office.'

'Weren't you scared? I would have been,' Sam said.

'At first I was, then I was just plain angry,' Jared answered.

'I think it's a good idea to work in pairs for a while,' Dan added.

Everyone mumbled their agreement as they ambled along. They stood for a while to chat before they said farewell and went their separate ways.

The weak sun slipped towards the horizon, its yellow hue bathing the heathland in a glow that held no warmth. Birds chattered loudly in the treetops and Jared caught sight of two huge ears before the hare scampered away. The scrub was dry and it crackled beneath his feet as Jared headed towards the cottage, where he saw the last of the sun glinting on the windows.

Once inside, Jared locked the door. He didn't think Ned Watkins would come looking for him, but it paid to be careful. Checking his larder, he knew he would have to grocery shop on Saturday after being paid, but for now he settled for cold meat pie and a cup of tea. Then he had a good wash and retired to bed early, and he fell asleep almost immediately.

Across town, McGuire was telling Seth about Ned accosting Jared.

'He's never going to give up looking for me, is he, Mr McGuire?'

'Your father is just angry that we got the better of him, Seth. He doesn't have your wages coming in now, so he has no beer money, and I suspect that's what is sticking in his craw.'

'That would be about right, never a thought for me,' Seth agreed sadly. 'Will you tell Jared I'm sorry?'

McGuire nodded. 'I'll go and make us a cuppa. I believe Alice has left us some cake and if we don't eat it, she'll chew my ears off.'

'She's lovely, I wish she was my mum,' Seth muttered.

'I won't be long,' McGuire said and left the room. Down in the kitchen, he thought about what Seth had said, and not for the first time, he wondered where Molly Watkins had gone when she left Ned. Of course, she could be anywhere after all these years, but something told McGuire she wouldn't be too far away from her son. His gut told him she would be watching from afar, her heart breaking at being unable to help him.

Pushing the thoughts aside, he took the tea and cake upstairs but when he entered the bedroom, it was immediately obvious that Seth had been crying again. Toby didn't want to embarrass the boy, so he made no mention of it.

Instead, he tried to cheer Seth up. The two enjoyed their

supper snack and chatted a while before McGuire said goodnight and headed for his own bed.

* * *

Very early the next morning, McGuire and the Cavenors were standing on the street outside Ned Watkins's house.

'Ready?' Toby asked.

The brothers nodded and Bobby rubbed his hands together, relishing the thought that today Ned could get finally his comeuppance if he didn't behave.

McGuire banged on the door continuously and only stopped when a woman yelled from an open upstairs window next door. 'Shut yer row, folk are trying to sleep!' Then, seeing who it was, she called, 'Sorry, Mr McGuire,' before pulling the window closed.

McGuire ignored her and carried on banging until at last the door was opened by a bleary-eyed Ned Watkins.

The Cavenors pushed their way in, forcing Ned backwards into the living room.

'Hey!' Ned's objections fell on deaf ears as McGuire stepped inside and closed the door quietly. When they were all in the sparse and depressing living room, McGuire stared at the man, who was rubbing his eyes and still hardly able to stand up from the after-effects of the alcohol he'd imbibed the night before.

'What do you think you're doing?' Ned snapped as he looked from one to the other of the three men in his living room, at the same time pulling his braces up over a dirty vest. Clearly, he'd slept in the clothes he wore yesterday.

'Ned Watkins, you are sorely testing my patience!' McGuire ground out.

'I ain't done nothing!'

'Is that right? So you call shouting the odds at my yard and accosting one of my workers *nothing*?' McGuire's temper rose as he glared at the drunk trying desperately to keep his balance.

'I d'aint accost anybody! I only asked the lad where my boy was.'

'You laid hands on one of my staff!' McGuire yelled into Ned's face, so loud that Ned fell back and landed in his armchair.

'Don't shout. I've got a headache.' Ned rubbed his temples, trying to dispel the thumping in his brain.

McGuire shook his head as he glanced at Bobby and Dicky. Looking at Ned again, he said, 'If you come near me, my workers, my yard or my house, I swear it will be the last thing you ever do!'

'Look, all I want is Seth back here.'

'Well, that's not going to happen, so you'd better get used to the idea. Seth is somewhere safe and he's going to stay there. He will never return to this doss hole. Now, you push me one more time, Watkins, and you might never see another day.'

'You threatening me?'

'You bet I am and it's also a solemn oath, so think on the next time you get bladdered. In fact, I think Bobby and Dicky should give you something to remind you.'

'What?' Ned asked, clearly not thinking straight.

At McGuire's nod, Bobby said, 'This!' As he spoke, his fist shot out and caught Ned on the chin, snapping his head back. Then Ned was dragged to his feet and held upright by Bobby as Dicky landed a punch in Ned's stomach.

With a hiss like a balloon going down, Ned doubled over in pain and gasped for air. He received a couple more punches for good measure before he was flung into his chair.

'Remember what I said.' McGuire turned and walked out, followed by the Cavenors, who were grinning from ear to ear.

'Right, boys, let's go and see if Alice has some breakfast for us,' McGuire said as they strode away, glad of a good morning's work.

22

‘I’ve just put the bacon on,’ Alice said as McGuire entered the front door. ‘Hello, Bobby, Dicky, how’s your old mum?’

‘Doing well, Alice, thanks for asking,’ Bobby returned.

‘Good. Go on through. Breakfast won’t be long.’ Alice ushered the three men into the dining room and in a few moments brought through a tray of hot tea. ‘Hungry?’ she asked as she poured.

‘Starving,’ Bobby said.

‘Famished,’ Dicky added.

‘I’d rather feed you two for a week than a bloody fortnight,’ Alice said with a laugh. Then, to McGuire, added, ‘Seth is pretty good this morning, so I thought I’d get him out of bed and moving about a bit.’

McGuire nodded, then, when Alice returned to the kitchen, McGuire and the brothers quietly discussed their visit to Ned.

After the men had eaten, Alice made a fresh brew and sat listening to McGuire relating the events at the Watkins house all over again for her benefit.

‘Let’s hope he takes some notice this time,’ she said.

'To be sure.' McGuire gave Bobby the keys to the yard, saying, 'Open up for me while I let Seth know where we've been.'

Thanking Alice for a scrumptious breakfast, the brothers left quietly.

'You're looking tired, *cailín*,' McGuire said.

Alice smiled – even after all these years, he still called her a girl, and she loved it. 'I am. When I'm done here, I have to go home and start again. Cooking, cleaning, washing – it all has to be sodding done.'

'Tell Stanley you're leaving him and come and live here with me,' McGuire said with a cheeky grin.

Alice burned with longing to do just that, but like most women, she knew she couldn't. She had made her bed and now she had to lie in it. Even before the day she had wed Stanley Crawford, she knew her heart would always belong to Toby.

'You don't have to stay here all day, Alice, Seth can look after himself.'

'We'll see how he goes on today, then if he can manage, we can get back to normal,' Alice replied.

With a nod, McGuire went to speak with Seth. The boy needed to know that his employer had threatened his father and McGuire hoped Seth would understand what he and the Cavenors had done.

* * *

Over at the yard, the tatters had arrived and with satchels in hand, they paired up and set off.

Dan and Paul had elected to do Dan's round and Paul's the following day. Sam and Johnny agreed to start with Sam's. Tom Brooks, the temporary tatter who was joining Jared, was eager to be gone, but Jared asked him to wait a moment.

'Mr Bobby,' Jared asked, approaching the big man, 'is Mr McGuire all right? It's not like him not to be here first thing.'

'He's fine, Jared,' Bobby replied.

'He's having a word with Seth 'cos we...' Dicky began but at a dig in the ribs from his brother, he snapped his mouth shut.

'Righto, I'll see you later.' Jared returned to his cart, wondering what was going on. Clearly something had happened, and he would dearly love to know what it was.

'Can I blow the bugle, Jared?' Tom asked excitedly.

'Of course you can, but let's get out of the yard first, shall we?' Jared grinned.

'Yeah, sorry,' Tom said sheepishly.

As the morning wore on, Jared patiently taught Tom how to deal with customers politely as well as weigh the bundles. The two quickly formed a good relationship, despite Tom being something of a chatterbox. Already he had told Jared how he lived with his older sister and her husband, their parents having died years before.

'Eventually I'd like to have a house of my own,' Tom said, 'but that's a ways off yet because it's so expensive.'

Jared was content to listen as Tom prattled on, but always at the back of his mind was the mystery of what Bobby and Dicky had been up to earlier in the day. Whatever it was, it concerned Seth, and Jared was itching to be in the know. Maybe tomorrow he would ask Mr Bobby and Mr Dicky, with luck they would tell him in confidence.

After speaking with Seth, McGuire patrolled his enormous house in Ivy Lane, chin in hand, his thoughts tumbling over each other in his mind. Where three properties once stood, now there was only one, McGuire having bought them and knocked them through to provide a single residence. He meandered around beautiful furniture, and passed expensive drapes which were pulled back from windows looking out onto extensive gardens.

He breathed deeply as his mind went over, yet again, his conversation with Seth. The boy had taken it rather well, but Toby had seen the sadness in his eyes. Naturally Seth would be loyal to his father and despite the beatings probably still loved him in some way, but McGuire wondered for how long. Seth was eighteen years old now and he'd lived alone with his father for ten years. McGuire wondered if it was worth seriously considering whether Seth's mother could be found. On the off-chance that she could, would she want to see Seth after all this time? McGuire had no idea if Molly and Ned had divorced, but if they had, it could be that Molly had a new family now. Should that prove to be the case, then Seth turning up on her doorstep would be a tad uncomfortable to say the least. Whatever the outcome, McGuire felt it was worth trying to find Molly before mentioning it to Seth.

Having made up his mind, McGuire set out for the yard. His hope was that someone there might know where Molly Watkins had disappeared to.

Back at the house, Alice helped Seth out of bed and down the stairs. 'You can sit in the living room and read the paper, or you can come in the kitchen with me.'

'I'll come with you,' Seth said.

Alice smiled, clearly the lad didn't want to be alone and needed some company.

The two chatted over a cup of coffee for a while before Alice brought out the ingredients for baking. Flour, butter and the last of the soft fruits were laid on the table to be made into a pie for afters. As she was bustling around, busy in her work, she was stopped short when Seth said, 'What's going to happen to me now?'

'That's a question you should be asking Toby, sweetheart.'

'He won't put me back on the rounds, though, will he?'

'I don't know, Seth. What I do know is you're safe here,' Alice said kindly.

'I'll always be grateful to Mr McGuire for coming to get me, but I'm sure as soon as I'm fit enough, he'll chuck me out.'

'He wouldn't do that, lad, don't you worry.'

'I wonder why he never got married.'

Alice flushed as she busied herself with making pastry. 'Probably because he was wed to his business.'

'If he had and then had children, he would have been a fantastic dad.'

'I agree with you there, but I suppose he thinks it's too late now.'

'It isn't, though, is it? To be married, I mean,' Seth said as he watched the knobs of butter in the flour turn to crumbs and flow through Alice's fingers.

'I guess not.' The old feelings of fondness and love stirred in Alice's heart as she considered what her life would have been like had she and Toby tied the knot.

Struggling to his feet, Seth muttered, 'I have to...'

'Can you manage on your own?'

'Yes, thanks.'

'This is one time when I wish Toby had kept the old privy out the back,' Alice said, happy at the change of subject.

'It's posh to have an indoor one, though,' Seth said as he slowly and carefully headed for the door.

Listening to him climbing the stairs, Alice whispered, 'Toby, you have to make up your mind about that boy, and soon.'

The boy had touched her heart, and she had been moved to hear how fond he was of Toby. Of course, the boy was right, Toby would have been a fantastic father. Alice felt her heart would break for want of Toby McGuire.

23

'All right, Boss?' Bobby called as McGuire entered the yard.

McGuire nodded, still deep in thought.

'What did Seth say?' Dicky enquired as they followed Toby up to his office.

'Not much. I think he expected his dad to cause trouble, although it made him a little sad it has come to this,' McGuire answered as he dropped into his chair behind the desk. 'Do me a favour, will you, and think back a few years. Can you remember Molly Watkins?'

The men nodded. 'Ar, she run off in the middle of the night,' Dicky said.

'Might you have any idea where she could have gone?'

The brothers exchanged a puzzled glance. 'No, Boss, I can honestly say I have no idea,' Bobby said.

McGuire sighed as he picked up his cigar cutter and snipped the end from the rolled tobacco.

'Can I ask why you'm talking about Molly Watkins all of a sudden?' Bobby asked.

'I was wondering if we could find her. Maybe then Seth could have the chance of a real family,' McGuire said, after lighting his cigar with a Swan Vesta match.

'She could be anywhere,' Dicky said.

'Is there anyone who would have an idea of her whereabouts?'

'We could ask around the town,' Bobby answered.

'You do that, but – be discreet. I don't want it getting back to Ned, understand?'

The men nodded. 'Shall we go now, Boss?'

'Aye and let me know if you hear anything useful.'

McGuire watched the brothers leave his office, but without much hope that their enquiries would get them anywhere. His gut was telling him that Molly Watkins had covered her tracks well.

Late afternoon saw the carts roll in one by one, the tatter boys in good spirits, having enjoyed working in pairs for a change.

Jared noticed immediately the absence of the Cavenors, and took it upon himself to collect the money satchels. Going up the stairs to the office, he knocked on the open door. 'I brought these, Mr McGuire, as I couldn't see Mr Bobby or Mr Dicky.'

'Thanks, Jared. Before you go home, I'd like a word with you and the others.'

'Righto,' Jared responded and left the room to see to Bess.

'What's going on?' Sam asked.

'I'm not sure but Mr McGuire wants to see us when we've finished here.'

'Maybe the Cavenors have jacked it in and got jobs elsewhere,' Johnny said with a little laugh.

'We'll soon find out,' Tom put in.

'How was your day on the cart?' Paul asked.

'I loved it!' Tom replied. 'I learned a lot from Jared.'

Ten minutes later, the boys were crowded in McGuire's office, where their employer explained the events of his early-morning visit to Ned Watkins. 'So, I think you're probably safe to go back to your own carts,' McGuire finished.

'What about me, Mr McGuire, do I have to return to the sorting?' Tom asked.

'I was thinking you could take Seth's place for a while and see how you get on. Would you like that?'

'Yes, please. Excellent! Thanks, Boss.' Tom's grin spread across his face.

'There's another matter I'd like to share with you, but you have to swear to keep it a secret, lads. If you breathe a word of what I tell you, it could put people in danger, do you understand?'

'Yes,' the boys chorused, looking serious.

'Well, then, I thought you should know that Bobby and Dicky are out trying to discover where Seth's mother, Molly, might be.'

The boys exchanged glances at the revelation.

'My hope is that if we find her, she might take Seth in. They would have to move away from the area to keep themselves safe from Ned, of course, but it could solve all of our problems. So now you see why I ask for the secrecy, for if Ned finds out, he could go on the rampage, and we don't want to raise Seth's hopes either.'

'Is there anything we can do to help, Mr McGuire?' Jared asked.

'I don't think there is at present, unless any of you boys have any information? But I reiterate that your silence will keep Seth and his mum safe, wherever she is.'

The boys trailed out of the office and set off home, talking quietly amongst themselves. McGuire watched them go, hoping he'd done the right thing in sharing what he had in mind, and wondering how the Cavenors were getting on with their search.

* * *

As they had walked into the town earlier in the day, Bobby said, 'I don't know where to start.'

'Me neither,' Dicky concurred.

'Molly took off ten years ago, surely she wouldn't have stayed around here.'

Dicky shook his head. 'I wouldn't have thought so.'

'It's my guess she would have put as much distance between herself and Ned as she possibly could,' Bobby said as he glanced at his brother.

'Yeah, I agree. Should we start at Deritend?'

'No, it's too close to Ned, he'd hear about us asking questions in no time. What about the market? Molly would have shopped there. Those traders on the market don't miss a thing.'

'Good idea,' Dicky said.

The brothers strode off purposefully with what they thought were the beginnings of a plan. A little while later, they stopped at a fruit stall and Bobby asked the seller, 'How long have you had this pitch?'

'Ten years, why?'

'We're looking for someone who would have shopped here about ten years ago,' Dicky said quietly.

'Are you having a laugh?' the woman asked.

'No, and I know it's a long shot, but we really need to find this person,' Bobby answered.

'Look around you,' the woman spread her arms to encompass the crowds, 'do you have any idea of how many folk come in here every day?'

The brothers glanced at the hundreds of stalls and sighed. The woman had a point.

'I'm thinking you're looking for the proverbial needle, and it's my guess you ain't gonna find it.'

Thanking the vendor for her time, the men moved on. 'She's right, Dicky, I don't think we'll have much luck here.'

'So where do we go?' Dicky asked.

'To be honest, brother, I ain't got a clue.'

They stood a moment, taking in the hustle and bustle of the busy market place, watching people come and go. The noise was deafening as vendors called out their prices to women who were counting their pennies. The squeal of barrow wheels set their teeth on edge as they were jostled about by the barrow boys. The scent of fruit mingled with the fragrance of fresh-cut flowers was cloying, and as the brothers walked away, the smell that hit them next was of wet fish. This was soon replaced by the aroma of newly baked bread and cakes. At the nearest bakery stall, women queued with their baskets over their arms, their purses clutched tightly in their hands, knowing the pickpockets would be out in force. As the women were served and walked away, the hems of their long skirts brushed the dirty floor, picking up bits of detritus on the way.

Bobby's eyes scanned the crowd, wondering if one of these women with their small bonnets tied beneath their chins could be Molly Watkins.

'This is a waste of time,' Bobby said eventually.

'Back to the yard then?' Dicky asked.

Bobby nodded and they sauntered away out of the market.

24

Alice Crawford, despite having married and had her children at a young age, kept herself trim as best as she could. Her dark hair showed no signs of greying and her blue eyes still sparkled when she laughed. Always the optimist, Alice endeavoured to see the good in everyone, all except Ned Watkins, that is. Ned and the whereabouts of Seth's mother were occupying her thoughts as she busied herself in Toby's kitchen, feeling Seth's eyes watching her.

'When I've finished here, we'll take tea in the garden, on the bench under the oak tree,' she said.

'That's a nice idea. I'll make it, Alice,' Seth volunteered, getting to his feet carefully.

'Thanks, sweet'eart,' Alice said with a smile, happy that Seth's health and confidence were improving with each new day.

Ten minutes later, they sat in the shade of the majestic tree, listening to the birds singing and chattering. Insects buzzed rapidly around them and the sun tried desperately to raise her head to cover the lawns, which had previously been bleached to the colour of straw.

'It's nice here, ain't it? I always wanted to live in a house like this,' Seth muttered.

'Ar, me an' all,' Alice responded.

'Alice...' Seth began, 'I know the other tatters don't like me and I know why but...'

'Are you missing them?' Alice interrupted. Seth nodded sadly. 'Well, maybe you could go into the yard with Toby one of these days.'

'I'd like that except – I don't want my dad to know because he'll bring trouble for Mr McGuire.'

'Seth, Toby ain't afraid of anyone, least of all your dad, so set your mind at rest on that score. He's Irish and they'm known for fighting, as you well know. Besides, Toby's put your father on his arse more than once,' Alice said.

Seth grinned. 'I've caused enough bother...'

'No, lad, you haven't. It's Ned's fault – all of it, and the sooner you realise that, the better off you'll be. Now, when Toby gets home, we'll put the idea to him and see what he says.'

'Thanks, Alice – for everything,' Seth said as his face flushed around the black and yellow bruises.

'I'll go and see how that pie is doing in the oven; you stay and enjoy the fresh air.' With that, Alice took their cups back to the kitchen.

Taking the pie out, she put it to cool and sat for a moment. That poor lad was racked with guilt for something he'd not done. The blame lay squarely at his father's feet but the son was carrying the burden of it. Seth was constantly afraid and would remain so as long as Ned Watkins was alive. Alice shivered, knowing it could be many years before Seth would be free of fear and worry.

A moment later, Seth joined the housekeeper in the kitchen.

'You all right, bab?' Alice asked.

'Yes, can I do anything to help?'

'Ar, you can peel these spuds,' Alice said as she passed over a sharp knife and a few potatoes, 'and I'll string the beans.' Quietly the two of them settled to their jobs.

Across town, Bobby and Dicky had returned to the yard and were explaining to McGuire how their difficult task had borne no fruit so far.

'Sorry, Boss, but it's impossible. We asked at different stalls and no one could remember that far back,' Bobby said.

'We d'aint know what else to do so we came back here,' Dicky added.

'It was a long shot to be sure, but worth a try, I suppose. Thanks anyway, lads.' McGuire dismissed the men, feeling a little disappointed that they had no leads as to Molly Watkins's whereabouts. He hadn't really expected any, if truth be told, but he had hoped someone might have known something.

Lighting another cigar, McGuire wondered if Seth could recall anything more about the night his mother left. McGuire could ask him, but that would give away the fact that a search for Molly was underway. Toby supposed just knowing they were looking in itself was not a problem; but the outcome could be. If Seth was aware they were looking for Molly but she couldn't be found, then his mental health would suffer yet another blow. Even worse was if they found her and she wanted nothing to do with her son. Then again, could McGuire, in all conscience, deprive the boy of a possible meeting with his mum after so many years of being apart?

The only thing for it, McGuire determined, would be to discuss it with Seth once he got home.

In the yard, the sorters were busy forming big piles of rags for shredding or washing to be sold on. Being a man down now Tom was on the rounds meant the work was slower but it was getting done. Over in the stables, the grooms were mucking out the stalls, laying fresh straw and filling water buckets ready for the mares' return. Bobby and Dicky stood by the gate to deter any unwelcome visitors and McGuire counted out the pennies for the following day.

Out on his round, Jared was thinking about what McGuire had told him about Seth's mother when a woman yelled out to him. Pulling Bess to a halt, he jumped down and walked to where the woman stood by her front door.

'I've got a box of junk here, can you take it?' she asked.

'I only usually take rags and bones,' Jared answered.

'I don't want paying, I just want it gone. I need the space.'

Jared peeped into the box and saw it was filled with small statuettes and trinkets. He scratched his chin as he considered what to do. 'All right, I'll shift it for you, I just hope the boss won't mind.'

'Thanks, lovey,' the woman said as she stood aside so Jared could retrieve the box. Carrying it to the cart, he placed it down carefully, not wanting to break anything. With a wave, he climbed aboard and set off once more. McGuire would probably have his hide for this, but then Jared hadn't paid out for it and it might be that someone might like what was in the box. Maybe he could swap a trinket or two for a bundle; the thought eased his conscience. Alas, as the afternoon wore on, nothing was traded other than pennies for rags, and having to return with the junk had Jared a little concerned. Nevertheless, he turned Bess towards home and if it came to the put to, he could always take the box home with him. In fact, the contents might even brighten up his home. With that solution decided, Jared clucked to Bess to get a move on.

25

McGuire was waiting in the yard when the carts came in and cast an eye over each as the bundles were dragged off.

‘How did you get on today, Jared?’ he asked, spying the box.

‘Good, Mr McGuire. A lady asked me to shift this for her but I didn’t pay out. If we can’t do anything with it, I’ll take it home and dispose of it from there.’

McGuire nodded as he sifted through the box. The movement told Jared all he needed to know.

‘Mr McGuire, how is Seth doing?’ Jared asked.

‘Improving every day, Jared. I’ll tell him you were asking after him.’

‘Is he coming back to work?’

‘It’s a bit early to say yet. I think a lot will depend on whether we can find the person we’re looking for.’ McGuire’s eyes slid sideways to where the sorters were busy and who were not privy to the secret.

‘I understand,’ Jared said as he picked up the box. ‘I’ll feed Bess and then head home. See you in the morning, Mr McGuire.’ Placing the box by the gates, Jared then went to the stables.

Once work there was finished, Jared collected his box and after being joined by the other boys, he set off home.

'What's in there?' Dan asked.

Jared told his friends the story about the woman who wanted rid of her junk, and amid taunts of being a soft touch, the little group walked on, laughing happily.

Once he was back at home, Jared sorted through the box, pulling out a plaster statue of a shepherdess, a broken brooch, a pair of woollen gloves with holes in them, a rag doll missing an arm, and at the bottom, a tin box. Intrigued, Jared prised open the rusty lid and lifted out some photographs. Gazing at the pictures, Jared could see they were of the woman who had given him the box, but the photos were from her younger days. The image of the girl looked back at him, the hint of a smile at the corners of her mouth. A small hat adorned her hair, which was piled up in neat curls, and her high-neck blouse had a lace trim.

Jared wondered why the woman was discarding the photographs or even if she realised they were in the box when she handed it over to him. As he stared at the pretty face, he debated returning them to her the next day in case she wanted to keep them after all.

Replacing the pictures in the tin box, Jared set it to one side. The rest of the junk he put outside the back door to be thrown out later.

Making himself a meal of cold meat, tomatoes, cheese and bread with hot tea, Jared's thoughts moved to Seth and what was to become of him. There was part of Jared that hoped Seth would not be returning to the yard, for in his absence things had settled into an easy-going routine and the tension in the group had gone. If he *did* come back, Seth could upset the balance again with his disruptive attitude. But another part of Jared couldn't help but feel sorry for the lad. Seth had been through so much in his young life, and Jared couldn't imagine what it must have been like living with a bullying father.

Jared's life with his sister and mother had been tough but it was happy, and tears stung his eyes as their faces appeared in his mind. He still missed them terribly and probably always would.

With a sad sigh, Jared packed his lunch for the following day, washed the dishes and went to sit on the doorstep in the dying rays of the sun as it sank slowly towards the horizon. Feeling the chill in the air, he pulled up the collar of his jacket then stared out across the empty heath. In the distance, he could just see the houses in Watery Lane where he had lived with his family, now shrouded in a mist.

* * *

Whilst Jared was musing about Seth, over in Ivy Lane, Toby McGuire had just arrived home, happy to see his house guest up and sitting in the kitchen with Alice.

'So this is what you do while I'm out grafting, is it?' McGuire asked with a smile.

'You, graft? That'll be the bloody day,' Alice responded.

'Button your lip, woman, and pour us a cuppa.' Turning to Seth, he asked, 'How are you feeling today, lad?'

'A lot better, Mr McGuire, thanks to you.'

Alice watched Toby take a seat at the table and a small frown etched her face. Toby almost never sat in the kitchen. Something was afoot.

'Seth, I want to ask you a few questions and I'll explain why in a minute. I need you to trust me,' McGuire said gently.

Seth glanced at Alice, a worried look in his eyes. Alice nodded and Seth said, 'All right.'

'Can you remember the night your mother left?'

Seth nodded.

'Good lad. Now, you said before that your parents were arguing, is that correct?'

'Yeah. My mum wanted to leave and take me with her, but Dad was having none of it.'

'Was there any mention of where she was going?' McGuire probed.

Seth shook his head. 'I don't think so, it was a long time ago and I was only a scared little kid.'

'I understand that. All right, let's try another tack then. Can you recall what the row was about?'

Seth screwed up his face as he thought hard, then a dry sob escaped his lips. His eyes were tightly closed as he whispered, 'Dad was hitting her.'

Alice's hand went to her mouth as she glanced at McGuire, who shook his head, telling her to say nothing.

'Mum was crying,' Seth went on, opening his eyes and bowing his head, 'but he didn't let up. It was when he unbuckled his belt that Mum ran out of the back door. She came back when it was very late and I went to the top of the stairs from my bedroom. I listened and Mum said she was leaving for good.'

'Did she say where she was going?' McGuire asked very quietly.

'No. Can I ask what this is all about?'

'We're trying to find your mum, Seth.'

'Why?'

'It might be that you could go and live with her, but you mustn't build up your hopes because there are many reasons why that might not happen. We might not be able to find her, for one thing.'

'I'd give anything just to see and talk to her,' Seth mumbled.

'We need to know as much as possible so we might know where to start looking.'

'I'll keep on thinking and trying to remember.'

'That's all we can ask,' McGuire said. 'Now, I'm starving, so what's for tea?'

'Pie and vegetables. I'll serve, then I'll away to do Stanley's,' Alice replied, 'and you two – make sure you eat the bloody lot!'

'You're a dragon, Alice Crawford,' McGuire said.

'You mind I don't breathe fire and set your arse alight,' Alice called over her shoulder as the men retired to the dining room and she smiled as she heard them chuckling.

26

The following morning, Seth came downstairs to join McGuire for breakfast.

'I'd like to come to the yard with you today, Mr McGuire, it would be nice to see the lads.'

'Good idea, but it's a fair trek so we'll catch a cab. Not sure those legs of yours are up to the walk yet, Seth,' Toby replied.

'Thanks.'

'The boys will be pleased to see you up and about.'

'I hope so,' Seth said, hoping McGuire was correct but suspecting he wasn't.

* * *

Whilst the two broke their fast, across town, Ned Watkins rolled out of bed with a dreadful headache. He had spent the last of his money in the pub the previous night and now didn't have a penny to his name.

Stumbling around the kitchen, he made tea with yesterday's leaves and grumbled at the foul taste.

Ned hadn't worked for years and knew he probably never would again, for jobs were scarce, even for a handyman. At one time, Ned could do anything from mending a broken chair to pointing a chimney. Now he couldn't even make a decent cup of tea.

Gingerly lowering himself into his armchair, Ned held his head in his hands as he rued the day he took up drinking. However, he knew from experience that when the banging in his head ceased, his body would once more cry out for alcohol. The demon drink had him firmly in its clutches and Ned could not break free. With every hangover he suffered, he wished he could quit and even voiced it aloud at times, but he didn't hold out much hope that he would be able to do so.

Ned moaned as he tried to recall his actions of the night before. Slowly it came back to him – he'd been thrown out of the pub for instigating a punch-up. The reason why escaped him, but he knew that it was one more pub he'd been banned from entering again, that much he could remember.

Once his eyes began to focus, he saw that his clothes were dirty. He dragged his hands through his greasy hair then over his chin, which was badly in need of a shave. Holding out his arms, he saw the shake of his hands and dismissed the idea of scraping his face with a cut-throat razor.

Resting his head on the back of the chair, he winced as the movement increased the banging in his skull. Trying to formulate a plan for what to do about his financial situation, Ned realised he just didn't have the strength to think. Closing his eyes, he gave up and slowly drifted off to sleep once more.

It was hours later when Ned woke again. The hammering in his brain had ceased but the shake in his hands remained. He stood up to go looking for food and stumbled into the door jamb. In the kitchen, Ned found only a crust of rock-hard bread and a few old mouse droppings. Even the rodents had deserted him in search of better pickings.

Slamming a cupboard door, Ned jumped back as it fell off its hinges and landed with a clatter on the floor. He kicked out at it with a mumbled expletive. Staring out of the dirty window onto the communal back yard, Ned Watkins knew he was sinking fast. He was out of food and money and the rent arrears were piling up. Soon he would be without a home and would have to resort to begging on the streets. Once that happened, he would be at rock bottom and would most likely die in a doorway somewhere. He would never survive the winter but even as the thought struck, his addiction to alcohol overruled everything else in his mind. Ned desperately needed a drink but how to get one without coins in his pocket eluded him. There was only one answer to his problems. Ned might have no money, but he knew someone who would.

* * *

McGuire and Seth arrived at the yard by cab and stood to greet the tatter boys, sorters and grooms.

'How are you feeling?' Paul asked Seth kindly.

'Better, thanks.'

'You have a couple of cracking shiners there,' Johnny said, pointing to his black eyes. Seth nodded.

'It's nice to see you're on the mend,' Jared put in.

Each of the boys gave Seth a welcome of sorts as McGuire made his way to his office and Toby couldn't help but be proud of them for being so fair.

'Before you all go off on your rounds, lads, I just want to say I'm sorry,' Seth said quietly. 'For everything.'

The tatters shuffled their feet and exchanged glances, each of them feeling a little embarrassed, but not for themselves. They recognised that the apology was a big thing for Seth, but it was way overdue.

Turning to the grooms, Seth went on, 'I was rude to you too, expecting you to do what I should have done with my mare.' To the sorters, he added, 'You lot as well – I should have helped where I could.' Eventually he came back to the tatters. 'You and I should have been mates, but I ruined that right from the start. I thought if I acted tough you would respect me,' Seth shook his head, 'except it backfired on me. I'm so sorry.'

It was Jared who stepped forward first and held out his hand and when Seth took it, they shook. One by one, all of the others did the same, including Bobby and Dicky, who had witnessed Seth's little speech.

McGuire smiled from his place in the office doorway. The boy had come a long way.

Seth watched with longing as everyone went about their business before climbing the steps to McGuire's office.

'I'm proud of you, son,' McGuire said, indicating a chair for Seth to sit.

Seth nodded, too choked up to speak. No one had ever said such kind words to him other than his boss and Alice.

'Now, what are we going to do with you? It ain't a good idea to be sending you out on the rounds again, that's for sure. It would be just our luck for your dad to spot you.'

'I could help sort, Mr McGuire,' Seth suggested hopefully.

'Not with those ribs, you can't, you'd be on your knees in no time,' McGuire answered.

Seth's face fell, knowing McGuire was right.

'How well can you read and write?'

'Pretty good,' Seth replied.

'Right then, this is what I propose,' McGuire said.

27

Jared put the tin box of photographs in a linen bag alongside his lunch, deciding to return them to where they belonged. If the woman *had* put them for throwing out, then it was no great hardship for Jared to discard them with the other items, but he wanted to check first.

He remembered the house because it was such an unusual request and he hoped the lady was in when he got there.

The grey sky overhead told him the weather was on the turn and autumn was upon them. Everywhere there was an eerie calmness as the trees were well into their hibernation in readiness for winter. Pulling up his jacket collar against the chill, Jared clucked encouragement to Bess.

Arriving at the house, he halted the mare and, grabbing the tin box, he jumped down from the cart. Jared ignored the twitching curtains from the neighbour's house and knocked on the door. A moment later, it was opened by the woman he'd spoken to the day before.

'I'm sorry to bother you, but I found this in that box of trinkets I shifted for you and wondered if you might want to keep it.'

The woman frowned as Jared handed her the item.

'It contains photographs, and I thought they might be precious,' he added.

Flipping up the lid, the lady pulled out the pictures and looked through them. 'I haven't seen these for a long time,' she said, a small smile crinkling the corners of her eyes. 'I'd forgotten they were in the box. Thank you. That was very thoughtful of you.'

'You're welcome. My name is Jared and I'll be around this area for the rest of the week, so if you need me, just flag me down, Mrs...?'

'Shipton. Thanks, Jared. Much obliged to you.'

Tipping his cap, Jared went back to the cart and with a wave he called for Bess to walk on, his good deed for the day completed. A warm feeling of satisfaction settled over him, knowing he had made Mrs Shipton happy by returning her property. The photographs were worthless to him but to that lady they clearly had great sentimental value.

Picking up his bugle, he blew it with gusto, sending out a sound like a cow in labour. 'Any old rags?' Jared bellowed as Bess plodded along. 'Rags and bones,' he called out before blowing into the instrument again.

Front doors opened and women spilled out onto the street, all rushing forward with their bundles, each eager to be the first to claim their penny.

'All right, ladies, I've coin enough for all,' Jared said as the throng closed in on him.

'Oh, hark at him, the millionaire tatter!' shouted one, much to the amusement of the others.

'I ain't yet, missus, but I will be one day,' Jared replied as he weighed her bundle and handed her the penny.

'Well, when you are, I hope you'll remember all of us who helped you get there,' yelled another.

'I will indeed, I'll think of you every time I eat steak and sip champagne,' Jared said with a laugh.

'What I wouldn't give to afford a bit of steak,' he heard another woman mutter.

'Give over, you're making me feel hungry and I only have bread and cheese for my dinner!'

'Think yourself lucky you have that, some ain't even got a pot to piss in!' came the reply.

'Ain't that the truth! Thank you, ladies,' Jared said as he retook his seat and gently snapped the reins together.

'Tarrar, cocka,' the lady who had called him a millionaire tatter said, before turning away to gossip with her neighbours.

Jared moved on, happy with his haul.

Meanwhile, McGuire had cleared a small table in his office and placed a chair next to it. 'These are the books for the bones for the workhouse and the manure bags,' he said, placing two huge ledgers on the table. 'I need you to tally what goes out with the money that comes in and mark it down in there.' He tapped the books with a finger before fetching a tin money box.

'You're going to trust me with your money?' Seth asked incredulously.

'I am, lad,' was all McGuire said in response. 'Now, can you manage the steps when the deals need doing?'

'Yes, Mr McGuire, thanks.'

'Alright then, let's get to work because here comes your first customer.' McGuire nodded to the wagon pulling into the yard.

Grabbing a pencil and a notebook, Seth headed for the door,

still being careful with his sore ribs. 'How much do I ask?' he asked as an afterthought.

'It's all in the ledgers,' McGuire answered. 'You're a bright boy, I know you can work it out.'

Seth took a quick look in the books and nodded, then made his way down to the yard to begin his new job. He enjoyed his day at the yard feeling useful again, but by five o'clock he was tired and weary, and his ribs ached like the devil.

McGuire sent Bobby to hail a cab to take Seth and himself home and once everyone had left and the yard was secure, they climbed into the cab.

'You did well today,' McGuire said.

'Thanks, it was nice doing something different,' Seth replied, 'and the takings were good for the bones and the manure.'

'Aye, lad, you know what Alice would say – "Where there's muck, there's money."'

Seth grinned. 'Can I come again tomorrow?'

'I don't see why not.'

'I'll walk so you don't have to pay a cabbie.'

'We'll see how you feel in the morning,' McGuire replied, amazed at how different the boy was now he was away from his father.

McGuire paid the fare and as they entered the house, they heard Alice yell, 'I hope you haven't tired that boy out today, Toby McGuire!'

McGuire rolled his eyes and Seth smiled. 'No, Alice. He went on his round, helped the sorters and then mucked out the stables,' McGuire yelled back as they hung up their jackets in the hall.

Alice came flying through, full of thunder, to see both men chuckling. 'You're a...! Get in here, the pair of you, your tea is ready.'

Following meekly behind Alice, Seth and McGuire took their seats in the dining room, still grinning widely.

'For that little prank, you can wash the dishes,' Alice said as she placed their meals on the table.

McGuire's grin slipped from his face and Alice burst out laughing.

'Two can play at that game. See yer tomorrer, boys,' Alice said cheerily as she left them to enjoy stew and dumplings.

28

Jared was also sitting down to eat, but rather than Alice's delicious home cooking, he had a bowl of broth with fresh bread he'd bought on the way home. 'Happy birthday to me,' he said aloud.

He'd celebrated another birthday as he had the previous two years, quietly and alone. He hadn't mentioned to anyone that today he'd turned fifteen years old, he didn't see the point. To him, it was just another day.

As he ate, he mulled over the day's events. He'd learnt about Seth's new job on his return to the yard and was glad that the boy was being offered a new start. He also thought about Seth's apology that morning and the discussion he'd had with the others on the way home. He wanted to believe Seth meant what he'd said, but somewhere in the back of his brain, a little warning bell rang.

Jared wasn't sure a person could change so drastically in so short a time. Agreed, a beating like Seth had taken might have been a deciding factor, but Jared had told the others to remain on their guard. It might well be that once Seth was fully recovered, he could revert to his old ways. None of them wanted that to happen, so they had promised to keep a sharp lookout.

After cleaning up the kitchen, Jared went to the front room and lit a fire. The cottage held a chill now the weather was turning and being at work, he couldn't keep a fire in all day. Sitting on the old settee, he watched the yellow flames lick around the coal nuggets as the kindling burned through. Before long, the room had a cosy glow and he felt the heat coming from the hearth. Slowly, his eyelids began to close, and he surrendered himself to the sleep which was claiming him.

* * *

Across town, it was in the early hours that McGuire woke with a start. Something had disturbed his sleep and a moment later, he realised what it was. Someone was hammering on the front door. Jumping out of bed, McGuire grabbed a dressing gown and ran down the stairs, muttering to himself as he went. 'If this is Ned Watkins, I'll lay him out, so I will!'

Opening the door, all set to throw a punch, McGuire stared at the person in front of him. Standing in the gloom of the first light of day was Alice, tears streaming down her face.

'Alice, what's happened? Come in, *colleen*.'

'Toby...' Alice stumbled inside and McGuire closed the door. Lighting the gas lamp in the hall, he turned to his housekeeper.

'Oh, Toby!' Alice fell into his arms and sobbed her heart out.

'Come on, *mavourneen*, I'll make some tea and you can tell me what this is all about.'

In her distress, Alice didn't realise he had called her *my darling*. She allowed him to take her to the kitchen and sit her in a chair. He lit the lamps and it was then she finally managed to sob out the words, 'Stanley's dead!'

'What? But how, Alice? I don't understand.' McGuire was shocked.

'He passed in the night, whatever shall I do?' Alice wailed.

'You'll have tea while I dress, then we'll go and see him,' McGuire said gently.

Feeding the range, he banged the kettle onto the hotplate. As he turned, he saw Seth standing in the doorway.

'I heard banging. Alice? Whatever is the matter?'

'Seth, make tea, lad, while I get dressed,' McGuire urged.

'What's going on?'

'I'll explain later, but I have to take Alice home and see to some things.' McGuire hurried from the room, leaving Seth baffled and Alice crying.

'Alice, how can I help?' Seth asked.

Between sobs, Alice answered, 'You can't, lad, nobody can. I've just become a widow.'

'Oh, no, I'm so sorry,' Seth said, then, unable to find anything more to say, he began to make the tea.

A short while later, Toby and Alice left and Seth returned to bed but was unable to go back to sleep. The lady who had cared for him so tenderly was breaking her heart and he couldn't do anything to help.

Arriving at her house, Alice led McGuire inside. 'He's upstairs,' she whispered.

'You sit there and I'll go up,' McGuire said, helping her to a chair in the warm kitchen. He made his way to the bedroom with the open door and peeped inside. He could see the outline of Stanley lying on his back but could hear no sounds of breathing. Crossing the room, he opened the curtains, allowing the light in so he could get a better view of what he was dealing with. Going to the bed, he sighed, and moving to the still figure of Stanley, he closed the dead man's eyes. 'Rest well, my friend,' he said, then quietly left the room.

In the kitchen once more, he held Alice's hands and said, 'We'll need the doctor. I'll see if I can find a cabbie to fetch him.'

Alice nodded, unable to answer.

McGuire ran out into the street and looked both ways before it dawned on him it was too early for the cabbies to be abroad. 'Bugger!' he muttered as he rubbed the stubble on his chin. Then he saw an urchin sitting in a doorway across the road. Giving a whistle, he beckoned the boy.

'What you want? I was sleeping!' the boy said angrily.

'I need the doctor bringing here and if you fetch him, there's a florin in it for you.'

'Two bob! I'll be back in a minute.' With that, the boy took to his heels.

McGuire went back indoors to try to comfort Alice, but he was at a loss as to how to do so. Her tears and sobbing were breaking his heart and he wanted nothing more than to hold her in his arms and kiss the hurt away.

Half an hour later, there was a knock on the door and McGuire let the doctor in. He paid the urchin the promised two shillings, then led the doctor upstairs.

The doctor took his time, but his examination confirmed that Stanley had indeed died and there was nothing to be done to help him. 'What's his name?' the doctor asked.

'Stanley Crawford.'

'Because Mr Crawford passed unexpectedly, the coroner will need to determine the cause of death, although I think it was his heart. I will inform the office and get Mr Crawford moved as soon as possible.'

'Thank you, I'll explain what's happening to his wife. She's my housekeeper and she came to get me,' McGuire said.

'Will you be staying with her?'

'Yes, until Stanley... then I'll take her home with me.'

'Very well.'

McGuire paid the doctor's fee and saw him out before going back to the kitchen, where Alice was sitting staring into space. He told her what the doctor had said but he wasn't sure she had taken it in.

'Tea, I'll make us a cuppa,' he said and saw Alice nod. 'Later you can come home with me. I don't want you on your own just now.' McGuire made the brew as he talked and placed the steaming beverage on the table in front of Alice. She didn't bat an eyelid, she just kept staring at nothing.

McGuire was worried, he knew she was in shock and needed time to process everything before she could begin to come to terms with her loss. He sat quietly, watching the lady he had loved since he was a boy, feeling wretched that he couldn't make things better for her.

After a while, McGuire answered the door to the men from the coroner's office and pointed to the stairs. 'When will we be able to bury him?' he asked in a whisper.

'As soon as the boss says so. You'll be notified by letter and you can then arrange for the funeral parlour to collect him. I'm sorry for your loss.'

'Thanks,' McGuire responded. He told them where the letter should be sent as Alice would be staying with him. He watched the two men carry a stretcher with a cover upstairs. He listened to them shuffling about, then saw them appear on the landing. Carefully they manoeuvred the stretcher down the stairs and out through the front door and into the wagon outside. A third man stood holding open the door in the back of the black vehicle. With a nod, the man closed the door and all three climbed onto the driving seat. Two black horses walked on, pulling the cart down the street.

McGuire shut the door and, taking a deep breath, he turned to go back into the kitchen but was surprised by Alice standing in the doorway.

'He's gone, then?' she asked.

'Yes, love,' McGuire answered softly.

Alice ran to him and he wrapped his arms around her as the sobs racked her body once more. He kissed her hair tenderly and felt her arms tighten around him.

All his life, he'd longed for this – just not under such circumstances.

29

Seth was up and dressed when McGuire and Alice arrived home and he immediately set to making them tea and breakfast.

'Seth, I want you to take care of Alice for an hour or two. I have to open up the yard but then I'll be back.'

'I'd be happy to,' Seth replied, looking at the distraught woman who had been so kind to him.

'Alice, love, I won't be long,' Toby said, resting his hand on hers.

'Toby, I have to let my boys know...' she began.

'I'll see to it, don't you worry about a thing.' McGuire left Alice in the care of Seth and hurried over to the yard, where everyone was waiting by the locked gates. Opening up, he said, 'Jared, I need a word right away.'

The other boys frowned, wondering what was going on, as Jared followed McGuire to his office.

'Shut the door,' McGuire said quietly. 'Last night, my housekeeper and friend, Alice, lost her husband, so I'll be staying at home with her for a while. The coroner is involved as the death was unexpected, so god knows how long it will be before Stanley can be laid to rest.'

'I'm sorry to hear it, Mr McGuire,' Jared said. Although he didn't know Alice personally, he felt sorry for her and his boss. Thoughts of his own family dying rose in his mind and he knew how badly grief could affect a person.

'I'm going to give you the keys and leave you in charge while I see to Alice and help her with Stanley's affairs.'

Taken aback by the trust his boss was putting in him, and the weight of the sudden responsibility, Jared merely nodded.

'There's nobody else I can trust, Jared, to take care of my business while I'm gone. Bobby and Dicky will help, but they've got no head for business.'

'Thanks, Mr McGuire, I won't let you down.'

'I know, lad, that's why I chose you. Now, I'll be home if you need me for any reason.'

'Yes, sir.'

'The Cavenors usually collect the cash from the bank on a Monday morning, so you don't need to worry about that. It's kept in the safe there,' McGuire pointed to the iron box behind his desk, 'and this ledger is for the wages, so you know who earns what.'

'I'll manage, Mr McGuire,' Jared said confidently.

'Seth will come in and do his bit with the manure sacks and bone collections, will that be a problem?'

'Not for me, Mr McGuire,' Jared answered truthfully.

'Good. I'm sending Bobby and Dicky to let Alice's sons know the news of their father's passing, so they won't be around much today.'

Again, Jared nodded.

'I don't think we'll see Ned Watkins again, but you never know, so be careful. Send for the police if there's any trouble.'

'I will.'

McGuire handed over the keys then said, 'Ask the Cavenors to come up, please, and – thanks, Jared.'

A few minutes later, the Cavenor brothers were seen leaving the yard in a hurry.

'What's amiss?' Dan asked as Jared joined him in the stables.

'I'll explain everything later, but for now, I'm in charge.' Jared's voice carried to the grooms and tatters as well as the sorters in the yard.

There were a few grumbles from the older men who separated the rags as to why a boy had been chosen over them.

Jared called out as he stood between the yard and the stables. 'Mr McGuire has urgent business to attend to, so he asked me to step up in his absence. It will only be for a short while, but let me say this only once. If you don't like it, there's the door.' Jared threw out his arm towards the huge wooden gates. 'As I see it, the only thing that's different is that I'll be in the office rather than on the rounds. Now that's settled, I suggest we all get on with our work. Mr McGuire needs our support and I know we'll all want to give it to him.'

The tatters and grooms exchanged glances before settling to their jobs. Jared marched away, feeling the sorters' eyes burning into his back.

In the office once more, McGuire said, 'Well done, lad, I can see I made the right choice.' Then, as McGuire left, Jared sat in the oversized chair behind the desk, a determined look on his face. This was his big chance to prove himself and he wasn't going to let anyone down.

* * *

Penniless and desperate for a drink, Ned Watkins set out to find his son. He walked along High Street Deritend, passing three public houses in close proximity to each other, all of which he had been banned from entering. It was as he stepped onto the tramway that he saw a piece of paper fluttering in the gutter. Unsure at first what it was he was looking at, he stepped closer. With a quick glance around to ensure he wasn't being watched, Ned quickly bent down and picked up the paper. Moving on, he inspected the paper back and front, then, shoving it into his pocket, he grinned widely. Turning at the corner, he walked into Adderly Street, passing beneath the two viaducts. Presently he reached his destination – the pub. The five-pound note in his pocket would see him in ale for quite a while. Still hardly able to believe his luck, Ned threw open the double doors and strode inside, happy he wouldn't have to seek out his son for a few days yet.

Bobby and Dicky chatted quietly in the cab which was taking them to Wednesbury. They had been given the unenviable task of informing Marcus and Luke Crawford that their father had passed away.

'Poor Alice,' Bobby said.

'She's such a nice lady,' Dicky replied.

'She is, but she has a mouth on her when it suits.'

Dicky grinned. 'How do you think the twins will react when we tell them about Stanley?'

'I don't know, bruv, but I'm guessing their greedy wives will be wanting to know if Stanley had a will and whether he left them anything,' Bobby said.

'I feel sorry for Alice. I don't just mean about losing Stanley but 'cos she ain't seen her sons for years.' Dicky shook his head.

'It ain't up to the twins, though, is it? It's those sisters they married. Gold diggers, the pair of them.'

'It's wicked if you ask me,' Dicky put in. 'Alice ain't seen her grandkids since they was born.'

'*Were* born,' Bobby corrected his brother. 'I agree with you; they'll grow up never knowing their grandma, and now it's too late for Stanley.'

The thought was sobering and the men lapsed into silence as the cab rattled over the cobblestone streets.

At last, the cab drew to a halt and the brothers stepped out onto Bridge Street. The cabbie nodded when they asked him to wait. The brothers knew this wouldn't take long.

Standing in front of the White Horse Hotel, Bobby sniffed. 'It's a doss house,' he said.

'It used to be a nice place; I can't believe how run down it is,' Dicky replied.

They took a step forward out of the way of the coal cart as the jagger urged his horse onward. The man was black from head to toe from the coal dust, with only his eyes and teeth visible.

'Right, come on,' said Bobby, 'let's get this over with.'

30

Whilst the Cavenors were travelling the eight miles to Wednesbury, Seth was doing his best to comfort Alice. He listened patiently as she told him tales of her first meeting with Stanley in the park and how he had proposed twelve months later.

Seth toasted some bread on the fire in the range for them both and Alice was so busy reminiscing, she ate without realising.

McGuire arrived back from the yard and he too listened without interruption, but his heart ached, knowing it could so easily have been him she had married.

Alice paused before saying sadly, 'I'll have to let the boys know.'

'It's done, I sent the Cavenors this morning,' McGuire assured her.

'Thanks, Toby, I appreciate that. It won't make any difference to them,' Alice said, 'they still won't come and see me.'

'Possibly not, but they can't say you didn't tell them,' Toby said.

'It's their wives I hold responsible, pair of bitches that they are!'

Seth drew in a breath, surprised at the venomous remark from such a kind-hearted woman.

'It's true, Seth, Toby will bear me out. The moment my sons married, those sisters sealed my fate.'

'Two brothers marrying two sisters is very unusual,' Seth commented.

'Aye, it is, and I wish it had never happened. They begged money from us until we had nothing left. The boys bought a hotel in Wednesbury which they run between them, but when our savings ran out, their wives said Stanley and I were being spiteful by not giving them any more money.'

'How could you give what you didn't have?' Seth said sympathetically.

'Exactly, but the wives didn't believe us. So, they cut the ties between us and our sons. I haven't seen Marcus and Luke for years, and I've not yet met my grandson and granddaughter.' A dry sob escaped Alice's lips and McGuire closed his eyes tight for a second at her distress.

Looking around her, Alice said, 'Anyway, I suppose I should get on with making your dinners.'

'No, love, you just rest, we can manage that later,' Toby said. 'In fact, I'll put the kettle to boil, so I will.'

'Bloody hell, Toby McGuire making tea!' Alice said.

McGuire smiled, happy to see a little of the Alice he knew and loved peeping through her grief. 'I might burn the water, but I can make a cuppa.'

Alice managed a little smile of her own, then asked, 'I wonder how long it will be before I can bury Stanley?'

'The coroner said they'll let us know, but if you want to arrange a funeral package, I'll come with you,' Toby answered.

'I can't afford it,' Alice admitted quietly, her eyes on her hands twisting in her lap.

'I'll see to it, so don't you be worrying about that. All you have to do is choose what you want and leave the rest to me.' Toby poured hot water onto the tea leaves and placed the pot on the table.

'Thanks, Toby, I appreciate it,' Alice said as she automatically stirred the tea in the pot.

'We'll go whenever you're ready. There's no rush,' Toby said, and Alice nodded.

* * *

Back at the yard, Jared was enjoying himself immensely being in the boss's chair, literally and figuratively.

Going to stand in the doorway, he heard one of the sorters still grumbling.

'He's only a lad!' the man said.

'Maybe, but the boss chose him, not you, so I suggest you stop moaning and get on with your work,' answered another.

Jared was glad to have at least one man onside, but knew he would have to watch his back, otherwise there could be trouble. He found himself glancing towards the gates, hoping the Cavenors would return soon.

It was mid-morning when Seth arrived and explained why he was late in. 'Mr McGuire asked me to stay with Alice while he came to see you here.'

'I guessed as much and he did say you'd be in,' Jared acknowledged. Then he asked, 'Seth, how many folk come in for manure? The bags are piling up and it's stinking something terrible.'

'Not many and I agree it smells bad over by the gates.'

'Hmm, I wonder,' Jared said thoughtfully.

'What?'

'Could we exchange a bag of manure for rags to anyone who

wants it for their gardens? Maybe there's allotment owners who don't know we have it for sale.'

'The bags might pong a bit in the carts, but it might be worth a try. At least it will help shift some of it,' Seth replied.

'Right, let's try it tomorrow then, shall we? We'll let the boys know when they're back from their rounds.'

'If it doesn't go, the sorters might complain it's making the rags smell bad, though,' Seth said.

'Leave the sorters to me, I can deal with them,' Jared said with conviction he didn't honestly feel.

At lunchtime, Jared took an apple to Bess in the stables. 'Sorry, old girl, but I've been a bit busy,' he said quietly as the mare nuzzled him. 'You enjoy the rest because we'll be back on the road again soon enough.' After fussing her for a few moments, he went to speak with the grooms about his idea for the muck sacks.

'It'll be nice to get it moved, it's becoming a bit overpowering even for us,' one said with a laugh.

'We'll try it out and see how it goes.' Jared returned to the office just as a wagon pulled into the yard.

Seth was there to meet it, ledger in hand. Jared watched the interaction between the carter and Seth as they walked to the pile of sacks.

'I only want two, my allotment is tiny,' the carter said.

'That's fine, but what about the other allotment owners, won't they want some?'

'I ain't buying for them! I can't afford it.'

'I understand that but if you bought four bags, you could sell the other two for a penny each more than you paid for them. You'd be tuppence better off and you never know, they might come to you again.'

The carter lifted his flat cap and scratched his head. Replacing the cap, he nodded. 'Go on then, but if I don't sell it, I'm bringing it back, so have my money ready just in case.'

Jared grinned as he watched the two shake hands on the deal.

Once the carter had gone, Seth went back to the office to put the money in the tin box expressly put aside for the purpose.

'Well done, mate,' Jared said, 'that's a brilliant way to get that stuff gone.'

Seth grinned. 'Fancy a cuppa?'

Jared nodded with a smile of his own, his thoughts turning to how much tea was drunk in and around the Black Country. It was a panacea for all ills and was offered to visitors immediately on their arrival by way of a welcome. Seth and he seemed to be becoming friends and Jared was glad there was no more animosity between them.

Around four o'clock, Bobby and Dicky walked into the office and saw Jared sitting in McGuire's chair.

'I wouldn't get too comfortable,' Dicky said with a chuckle.

'How did it go? Did you find Alice's sons?' Jared asked.

'Not too badly, considering Bobby wanted to punch the twins' lights out,' Dicky answered.

'Ah, right,' Jared said with a wince.

'We'll go and tell the boss, then go home, unless you need anything here, lad?' Bobby said.

'Righto, when the tatters get back I'll lock up and make sure everything is secure before I leave.'

With a nod, the brothers left Jared wondering how bad their meeting with Alice's sons had actually been.

31

By six o'clock, all the tatters had rolled in. Leaving the carts in the usual line, they unhitched their horses and led them to the stables for feeding, watering and a rub down. The grooms and tatters chatted about their day and eventually everyone left so Jared could lock up.

Seth took his time walking back to McGuire's house, his ribs still very painful.

The other tatters waited for Jared and they all strolled away, Jared filling them in on the day's events.

'Well, I ain't calling you Boss,' Johnny said with a laugh.

'How long will McGuire be away?' Paul asked.

'I've no idea,' Jared answered truthfully.

'I'm glad he asked you and not me,' Sam put in, 'those sorters can be vile when they want to be.'

'One of them is definitely not happy,' Jared agreed.

'Which one? Never mind, don't tell me. I'm guessing it's Bill Cank,' Dan said.

Jared nodded.

'Just watch out for him, he's mates with Ned Watkins, I think,' Sam informed them.

'Oh, I will,' Jared answered but as they parted company, he wondered how he would deal with it if Cank stirred up trouble. At least the Cavenors would be on hand and that went some way to easing his mind.

* * *

Seth kept an eye open for any signs of his father as he carefully stepped over the cobbles. Suddenly he had a thought which made him stop in his tracks. When McGuire and the Cavenors had rescued him, Seth had left behind the picture of his mother he'd found in a drawer and kept hidden in his bedroom. It was all he had tying him to her and he wanted it back. His heart raced as he resumed his steady pace, trying to work out how he could retrieve the beloved photograph. Of course, he would have to wait until his father was out, but how would he know when that would be? Then another thought stabbed like a knife. If Ned was thrown out of the house for non-payment of rent, which was more than likely, then everything indoors would be put in the rubbish.

'I have to get that photograph back before it's too late,' Seth muttered to himself. Knowing McGuire had his hands full with Alice, Seth knew this was one problem he needed to solve on his own, unless...

* * *

The Cavenors explained briefly to Alice that they had delivered the sad news to her sons, and they were both relieved when she merely gave her thanks and asked no questions.

'I'll see you out,' McGuire said. 'Thanks, lads.' On the

doorstep, he quietly asked them how it had gone, desperate to make sure that Alice didn't overhear them. 'Well, how did they take it?'

'They were upset, Boss, as was to be expected,' Bobby said.

'But?'

'Well, their missuses were there and they started.'

'Go on.'

'They were rude, Boss, saying things like "Why should we care? Stanley and Alice haven't been to see us. They've not even bothered to visit their grandchildren!" I can tell you, Boss, I wanted to plant one on the boys and tell them to grow a backbone,' Bobby replied.

'I can understand that. It's strange how they both follow their dad being gentle and mild.'

'We said we'd let them know when the funeral would be,' Dicky added.

'Luke's wife said they didn't want to know 'cos they wouldn't be attending,' Bobby said.

'Did they now? We'll see about that. Alice's sons *will* come to that funeral, no matter what their wives say!' McGuire's temper was only just in check as he bid the brothers goodnight with his thanks again.

Going back indoors, he said cheerily, desperate to buck Alice up, 'Right, lady, what shall we have to eat?'

'Nothing you've cooked, that's for sure!' Alice spouted as she stood and walked to the pantry.

McGuire knew it was her way of dealing with her grief; she was keeping busy. The funeral would be the time she would suffer badly, and Toby would be at her side to help her through it all.

Before long, Seth joined them and passed on the news of the day including his own achievements and Jared's idea for the manure while Alice cooked their meal.

'I ought to be getting on home,' Alice said eventually.

'You should stay here with us, Alice, at least for the time being,' McGuire advised. 'You don't want to be on your own yet, there'll be time enough for that.'

'Thanks, Toby, I must admit I didn't fancy sleeping in that bed, it would be too much.'

'Well, you know where the spare guest room is, so make yourself at home.'

Alice bade them goodnight and retired, not sure she would be able to sleep.

Seth went to his bed not long after, but McGuire sat by the fire, staring into the flames. Alice, the love of his life, was staying in his house a few rooms away from his own, but he could not go to her. He knew she would be shedding more tears, not only for the loss of her husband but for the disrespect of her twin sons.

Toby closed his eyes but not through tiredness; his mind cast him back to an era when he had missed the opportunity of a lifetime. He saw again the images of a young woman with dark hair and sparkling eyes, the girl he should have married but didn't. Too busy building up his business, he had missed his chance when Stanley Crawford had stepped in and swept Alice off her feet. Every day since, Toby McGuire had regretted his decisions, but by asking her to housekeep for him, at least he could have her near for some of the time.

Now his Alice, as he thought of her, was a widow and was breaking her heart; he could do nothing to comfort her or lessen her distress.

Opening his eyes, Toby felt the lone tear roll down his cheek, then it was followed by another, until he cried silently as he had so many times before.

* * *

It was early the following morning when Seth arrived at the yard and once everyone was about their work, he spoke to Jared.

'Can I ask you something?'

'Yes, of course you can,' Jared answered, a quizzical look on his face.

'There's something at my dad's house that belongs to me and...'

'You want to get it back, right?'

Seth nodded. 'I just don't know how to go about it.'

After a moment's thought, Jared answered. 'I have an idea, but it will involve the other lads, if they're willing, that is.'

'Do you think they will be?' Seth asked anxiously.

'I'm guessing so, but we'll ask when they get back.'

'It will have to be soon 'cos I reckon my dad could be chucked out any day now.'

Jared sighed and chewed his bottom lip. 'Let me think on it some more, then we'll discuss it later when work's finished for the day.'

As Seth left the office with his thanks to see to a customer for manure, Jared's brain whirred into action.

32

Alice was surprised she had actually slept quite well and felt a little more refreshed. She had cooked breakfast and seen Seth off to work, and now she sat at the kitchen table with McGuire.

'Toby, I should go to the funeral parlour today and arrange a package even though the interment can't take place yet.'

'All right, love, if you're up to it.'

'I need to face it, Toby, as much as I'd like to put it off.'

'Come on then, let's get it done.'

After securing the house, Toby hailed a cab and told the driver their destination. Helping Alice inside, he climbed in beside her and the cab rolled away. They sat in silence for the journey, each lost in their own thoughts until the carriage came to a halt.

Toby asked the cabbie to wait and he led Alice into the shop where they would buy her husband's last resting place. The small room was stark, with a desk and chair on one side, and two upright chairs stood at the other side of the desk for customers. The walls, which had once been white, were now a dull grey, and the only attempt at cheer was a child's painting of a poppy which was on one of the walls.

'Good morning, how can I help you?' a middle-aged man asked, entering from another room. His short dark hair was shot through with grey, and he had a kind face, the crinkles at the corner of his blue eyes bearing testament to the fact that, away from his work, he was a jolly man.

'Good morning. We have a funeral to arrange and we're hoping you can help,' McGuire said.

'Please take a seat and I'll do my best.' The man flicked up his tailcoat before sitting at the desk.

McGuire explained the situation concerning the death of Alice's husband and the coroner's involvement. The funeral director, Mr Webb, said it would not pose a problem; it was more common than they would think and he'd dealt with the coroner on numerous occasions.

'As soon as you have word from the coroner's office, let me know and we can set a date for the funeral. Now, this is what we have on offer...'

'I want the best – of everything,' Toby interrupted.

'No, Toby, it will be too expensive,' Alice protested, 'let me choose.'

McGuire acquiesced and Alice glanced through the brochure handed to her. She pointed at a casket and the director made a note, before doing the same with the flowers that Alice chose. Next, Alice elected for a short graveside service and small headstone. The whole appointment lasted only half an hour and then they were in the cab on their way home.

Arriving at Ivy Lane, McGuire paid the cabbie and once they were settled with tea, Alice said, 'Thank you, Toby. That wasn't as bad as I expected it to be.' McGuire gave her a thin-lipped smile. 'I'll have to clear out Stanley's things, maybe one of your lads can come and get them.'

'There's time enough. No need to hurry yourself until you're ready.'

'No, there isn't time, Toby. I've decided to move out of the house.'

McGuire was shocked. 'Why? Where will you go?'

'I don't know as yet.'

'Is it that the place holds too many memories?'

'No, it's not that. I can't afford the rent on just my money and before you say anything, you've done enough already.'

'Alice, you have to let me help!' McGuire said as panic seized him. 'Look, I tell you what, why don't you move into the other end of this place? You can have your own key, that other front door still works. It will be like having your own house. That way you can keep your job as well.'

'Toby, you've paid for Stanley's funeral; I can't expect you to house me as well.'

'If it's drowning you're after, don't torment yourself with shallow water.'

'Here we go again – you and your bloody Irish sayings! What else am I to do?'

'Take my offer, Alice, for god's sake! This house would go to rack and ruin without you, and who would keep me fed?'

Alice thought for a few moments then said with a smile, 'It would make sense, I suppose.'

McGuire sighed with relief. 'That's settled then, you can move in whenever you want. We can move the furniture out if you want to bring your own, just do what you will with the place.'

'Toby, you're a saint.'

'Ain't I?' he answered with a grin. In his chest, his heart hammered; he had come too close to losing Alice and silently vowed it would never happen again. Once she was under his roof, there she would stay for the rest of her days.

'Stop that preening and get the bloody kettle boiling,' Alice said in her no-nonsense way, but beneath her hard carapace she was still grieving. She gave a little smile as Toby began to mutter under his breath as he did as he was told.

* * *

Over at the yard, Seth and Jared were discussing Jared's idea of the boys exchanging a bag of manure for bundles of rags.

'I don't think it will work because not many people have gardens, but I wanted to give it a go anyway,' Jared confessed.

'There's nothing lost in trying,' Seth said.

'Your idea was better, though, getting the man from the allotment to buy more than he needed.'

Seth beamed at the praise. 'I don't think the lads were too happy about it, though. The look on their faces when the grooms set the sacks in the carts was priceless,' Seth added with a chuckle.

'Yes, I've a feeling they won't be too happy with me when they get back.'

They both laughed but stopped abruptly when they heard Bill Cank's voice outside. 'It's all right for some, sitting in the office, having themselves a little party while we do all the work.'

Seth and Jared exchanged a glance and Jared sighed. 'I wondered how long it would take,' he said, getting to his feet. He descended the steps to the yard, followed by Seth.

'Do you have a problem, Mr Cank?' Jared asked.

'Now you mention it, yes, I do,' Bill said, his greasy hair falling over his eyes.

'If you'd care to discuss it, then come to the office,' Jared said as he noticed all work had stopped so the men could listen in.

'I'd prefer to *discuss* it here,' Bill said, looking around him.

'Fair enough. Please proceed.'

'You, with your high-fallutin' ways, sitting in McGuire's chair, actin' like a big boss man,' Bill went on, 'we ain't happy about it.'

'I see. Is this the consensus of you all?' Jared asked while he too cast a glance around. Seeing the puzzled looks, he asked again, 'Is this what you all think?'

Behind Bill, heads were being shaken vigorously, but stopped as soon as Cank turned to look at his colleagues.

'It looks to me that you are the only one unhappy with the arrangement, Mr Cank.'

Bill was fuming that his workmates had not only refused to back him up, they had positively hung him out to dry.

'You're cowards, the lot of you!' he bellowed.

'I explained to you what Mr McGuire had decided upon and I also told you that if you didn't like it, you could walk. Now, should you take that option, I suggest you think about how you would tell your wife and the consequences of that conversation,' Jared said calmly, but inside, he was shaking. If Bill became violent, Jared knew he would be no match for the big man.

Bobby and Dicky, standing guard at the gate, had heard the commotion and had come to stand behind Jared, neither saying a word.

'Oh, you're cocky with them by your side, ain't yer?' Bill pushed.

Jared glanced at the Cavenors as they stepped forward, proudly displaying a united front. 'This has nothing to do with Mr Bobby or Mr Dicky. This is about you running your mouth because the boss chose me to stand in for him and not you,' Jared said, feeling more confident.

'It should have been me! You're just a kid and you ain't been here long enough to know the business yet.' Bill pursued the argument but even he knew he was clutching at straws.

'I know enough, so much so, in fact, that my ideas are earning Mr McGuire more money,' Jared replied with a shrug.

'Maybe, but we ain't seen a penny of it, have we?' Bill gave a curt nod, thinking that with this crucial point, he was winning the contretemps.

'Not yet, but it was my intention to suggest to Mr McGuire that you all have a rise in your pay packets. Of course, you'll miss out on that if you choose to leave.' Jared raised his eyebrows in a take it or leave it gesture.

Bill cast another look around, knowing he was not only alone, but he was beaten. 'All right then, just make sure you remember.'

'I take it that you are staying?' Jared asked pointedly.

A single nod from Bill gave him the answer and Jared turned and walked back to the office. Seth went with him, followed by the Cavenors.

'Christ, Jared, that could have been very nasty!' Seth said in a loud whisper.

'It wasn't, though – thank goodness,' he replied.

'You ain't half pushing your luck,' Bobby said.

Jared grinned. 'I know.' Then, as an afterthought, he asked, 'Could you two gents spare me a few minutes after work? I could do with your help on another little matter.'

'Yeah, okay,' Dicky said before he and his brother returned to guard duty on the gates.

'What are you thinking?' Seth asked.

'I'll tell you later when we're all together, I just hope my plan works.'

'So do I, whatever it is you've got up your sleeve now,' Seth said with a shake of his head.

Jared grinned again as Seth went to the yard to cajole another customer into buying more manure than they actually needed. That boy was learning fast!

33

That evening, when the boys returned from their rounds, Jared saw that his idea to upsell the manure sacks had not worked, so by way of apology, he unloaded and stacked the sacks himself.

When the sorters and grooms had left, Jared asked his friends to join him, the Cavenors and Seth in the office where he explained about Seth's predicament.

'For Seth to retrieve the item in question, we're going to need Ned out of the way. Firstly, Ned needs to be out of the house for a while so Seth can run in and get what he wants, but might need time to search so...'

'Ned has to stay out for a significant length of time,' Dan said.

'Exactly,' Jared agreed. 'We'll need look-outs.'

'Sam and I can do that,' Johnny put in.

Jared nodded. 'I'll go in with Seth in case the item isn't where it should be,' he said.

'What about me?' Paul asked.

'Let me explain. You can come at Ned's house from four directions, so you, Paul, will be one end of High Street, Johnny on Heath Mill Lane, Sam by the bank on Gibb Street, and Dan on the other end of High Street, all keeping a keen eye out for Ned returning.'

'Erm – and us?' Bobby asked.

'This is the biggest favour – you'll need to get Ned into a pub somewhere and keep him there,' Jared said, waiting for the backlash. It wasn't long before it came.

'I ain't drinking with that mongrel,' Dicky said fervently.

'I was afraid you might say that, and I understand why you don't want to. Never mind, we'll just have to watch and wait, but thanks anyway,' Jared said.

'Hang on,' Bobby said, turning to his brother, 'if we get him sozzled... You know how Ned likes to fight when he's pis... drunk,' Bobby corrected himself, 'then who knows, he could end up in the gutter with a black eye.'

'I cannot condone any violence, Mr Bobby,' Jared said quickly.

'I was just saying we'll get him drunk and it could be somebody else might give him a pasting 'cos by that time we'll be long gone.'

Jared eyed the big man, who was looking the picture of innocence. 'All right, now the question is how we get Ned into the pub in the first place because it's my guess he has no money.'

'That's easy,' said Dicky. 'We'll call round for him and ask him if he wants to come out to play.'

Everyone burst out laughing at the remark before Jared quietened them down by saying, 'It has to be tonight, though, because Seth is convinced his dad is due to be evicted any day now.'

They agreed a time of eight o'clock to meet at the bank where Sam would stand his watch, and before they all went home, Seth gave them his grateful thanks. For the first time in a long time, Seth felt like he had real friends.

Jared locked up and as they strolled away from the yard, he asked Seth, 'How will you get out tonight?'

'I'll tell Mr McGuire I'm coming to your house.'

'Good on yer,' Jared replied, clapping Seth on the back, then muttered, 'Sorry,' when he saw Seth wince.

Before they went their separate ways, Jared added, 'When we're done, you and the boys should all come back to my house with me. We'll have a cuppa and play a game of cards. That way, if McGuire or anyone else asks, we can tell them truthfully what we were doing, we just don't have to tell them everything.'

Jared reached out his hand for Seth to shake; an accord had been reached.

* * *

At the allotted time that evening, the group of boys were hanging around on the corner outside the bank.

'How did your mum take it when you said you were coming out again?' Johnny asked Sam.

'Surprisingly well, actually, but she did say, "Don't you be back late,"' Sam replied.

All his friends chuckled.

'Here come the Cavenors,' Jared said, tilting his head in the men's direction.

'Blimey, they look different without their suits,' Dan said.

Bobby and Dicky approached dressed in dark trousers, white shirts, waistcoats and flat caps. 'All right, lads?' Dicky asked.

'Jared, why can't we just go in and hold on to Ned while Seth gets what he wants?' Bobby asked.

'As tempting as that sounds, I don't think it's a good idea for Seth to be seen by his father, Mr Bobby. It could cause all sorts of problems. Ned could lose his temper and go on the rampage, for one thing,' Jared replied.

'We could deal with him,' Dicky put in.

'I have no doubts on that, Mr Dicky, but it would be better all round if Ned doesn't know anything about it.'

'Fair enough. Right, if we're sticking to the original plan, let's get going then,' Dicky said, nudging his brother in the ribs.

As the two men crossed the road, the boys formed a circle around Seth, hiding him from view, and continued to talk quietly together. Jared stood facing Ned's house and watched Bobby knock on the front door. 'Shush, Ned's opened the door.'

The boys remained in their places but listened intently, their fingers crossed in their trouser pockets.

'What do you two want?' Ned demanded as he eyed the brothers on his doorstep suspiciously.

'Do you want to come for a beer?' Dicky asked.

Ned frowned and glanced up and down the street as well as at the group of youths by the bank. 'What, and be lured into a back alley so you can give me a beating?'

'Look, mate, what goes on between you and your boy is no business of ours, we just thought you might be a bit skint and could do with a drink,' Bobby said.

'You work for McGuire.'

'We do but that's got nothing to do with us having an ale together,' Dicky said, trying to hold on to his temper.

'It's time to settle the dust,' Bobby added.

Across the road, Jared muttered, 'Come on, Ned, take the bait.'

'Why should I trust you?' Ned asked.

Bobby sighed. 'Please yourself, but you can't say we didn't try. C'mon, bruv, there's a jack with our names on it.'

'No, don't give up!' Jared whispered. All the boys had heard the conversation and exchanged worried looks. Jared blew out his cheeks with relief when he heard Ned speak again.

'Wait! Is this on the up?'

'Yes, mate,' Dicky said. 'Get yer jacket 'cos the ales are on us.'

Two minutes later, the three men trudged down the street, looking for all the world like they were the best of friends.

As soon as they were out of sight, the boys scattered, each taking up their allotted posts as Seth and Jared went into Ned's house.

Once inside, Jared said, 'Hurry up, in case your old man changes his mind!'

Seth tottered upstairs and reappeared a moment later. 'Got it, let's go.'

'Wow, that was quick. Do you mind me asking what it is you wanted to get?' Jared asked as they left the house, hurrying just to be on the safe side.

'A photograph of my mum,' Seth replied as they returned to the bank.

Jared nodded and gave his friend a sympathetic pat on the back before giving a whistle; the sign for the others to gather together once more.

'All done? That was quick,' Paul asked.

'Yes, thanks, everybody,' Jared answered. 'Now, let's get gone. Who's up for a game of cards back at mine?'

'I don't know how to play,' Sam said.

'Oh, good, I take it we'll be betting then?' Johnny asked with a grin.

'Oh, bugger,' Sam muttered, and his friends all burst out laughing.

34

The Cavenor brothers entered the yard the following morning feeling a little worse for wear. They both had banging headaches and roiling stomachs, but had turned out for work nevertheless.

In the office, Bobby asked, 'So did our plan work?'

'Yes, it did, and it's all thanks to you,' Jared said. 'It would have been impossible without your help.'

Looking around, Dicky asked, 'Where's Seth?'

'On his way, I would imagine. He still can't walk very fast because of his ribs.'

Dicky nodded. 'What was it he wanted?'

'A photograph of his mum,' Jared informed him.

'We're suffering a hangover all for a picture?' Bobby asked incredulously.

'It's all he has to remember her by, Mr Bobby, I wish I was that fortunate,' Jared answered kindly.

'We'd do the same if it was our mum,' Dicky told his brother.

'I don't know how much you spent on ale for Ned, but we had a whip round and this is to cover your expenses,' Jared said, pushing a pile of coins across the desk.

'That's good of you, lad, but we don't want it. We were just happy to help,' Bobby said.

'Thank you both,' Jared answered, feeling humbled.

With gentle nods, the men turned to leave and were greeted by Seth standing in the doorway. 'Can I add my heartfelt thanks?' he said. 'You did a sterling job, and I'm ever so grateful to you both.'

'Keep that photograph safe,' Bobby said, patting Seth on the shoulder before they stepped past the young man.

'I will, you can be sure of that.'

The sound of the other tatters coming into the yard was a sign that a new day had begun and it was time to get down to work. Chatter and laughter rang out as they poured into the yard and on into the stables to fetch the horses and led them to be hitched to the carts. Thicker coats and scarves were donned as the chill tried to steal beneath their clothes, and gloves were in coat pockets ready to be pulled on before they set out on their rounds.

* * *

Meanwhile, back at Ivy Lane, Alice was feeling washed out as she stared into her cup, the tea long since having gone cold.

Toby watched her, unwilling to break into her thoughts. It was better, as he saw it, to give her time and just listen if she wanted to talk.

Without raising her eyes from the cup she held with both hands, Alice said, 'My boys won't come to the funeral.'

'They will, they wouldn't miss saying goodbye to their dad,' Toby said softly.

'I know you're saying what you think I want to hear, Toby, but I'd rather have the truth.'

McGuire drew in a long breath and answered with, 'It's the wives who won't come and, if you ask me, that's no loss.'

Alice nodded slowly. 'I have to agree with that. God, I wish they'd never married those girls!'

'I'm not going to argue with you there. But they did, sweetheart, so we'll have to find a way to deal with it.'

'Oh, Toby, everything is such a mess!' A tear rolled down Alice's cheek. 'Stanley's gone, I don't see my sons, Seth is walking wounded and I can't pay my rent!'

'That all may be true, but you still have a roof over your head and food in your belly. Seth is recovering well thanks to your ministrations and as for the twins, there's still time to mend the bridges,' Toby said. He saw the tears fall and was desperate to comfort Alice with a hug.

'I'd love to get to know my grandchildren, but I can't ever see that happening.'

'Why not? I know you're estranged, Alice, but one day you might get to see them,' Toby said.

'I won't because I have no money. All was well while Stanley and I were paying, but now...' Alice left the sentence unfinished.

'Nobody should have to pay to see their grandkids, Alice, it ain't right.'

'You're preaching to the converted here,' Alice responded with a big sigh.

'It will come right. Once Stanley is laid to rest, we will see what can be done.'

'I won't hold my breath.'

The two continued to talk in the same vein for a long time in between making and drinking tea, the Black Country remedy for everything.

Mid-afternoon, Toby draped Alice's shawl around her shoulders. 'Come on, let's go for a walk, the fresh air will do us both good.'

Toby and Alice strolled across the town, not noticing the grey clouds rolling above them, threatening rain. In the far distance, they could hear the town crier relating the news to the uneducated and although they couldn't make out his words, his voice was loud. The church bell then tolled the hour, drowning out the crier altogether. Carts and wagons rattled past and the tram horn sounded before the brakes screeched. Children's laughter and squeals of enjoyment were loud all around them and the aroma of cooking was carried on the air.

Turning into Park Street Gardens, Alice and Toby followed the gravel path, nodding greetings to other people who passed by. Coming to a bench, they decided to sit for a while.

Alice looked at the carpet of brown and gold leaves around the base of the trees. There was no doubting now that autumn had arrived in all her glory. A scratching noise drew her eyes to a squirrel scampering up the trunk of a tree.

'Toby, I can't thank you enough for all your kindness, but I need to go home,' Alice said sadly.

'Why?' Toby replied, desperate not to lose her.

'I need to take a bath and change my clothes, I've been in these for days.'

'Oh, Alice! Forgive me, I never thought... We'll go now. You can pack up your things and take them back with us.'

Getting to their feet, they made their way to Alice's house. Once there, Alice found an old suitcase and filled it with the few clothes she owned.

Toby realised just how badly off Alice was when he saw the single piece of baggage. It made him feel wretched for how much money she must have given to those ungrateful boys over the years. 'Is there anything else you need to take?'

'No,' said Alice with a quick look around the living room.

Picking up her luggage, Toby led her out of the house. 'When we get back, you can have a long hot bath,' he said.

'I'd like that.'

'Then tomorrow we'll go to the town and get you some new clothes.'

'There's no need.'

'I ain't having my friend doing without, so we'll have no arguments.'

Alice smiled, he could have said housekeeper, but he had called her his friend, and although she'd always known that was how he saw her, his voicing it gave her a warm feeling inside.

Finally arriving back at Ivy Lane, Alice felt different when she walked inside; it was as if she'd come home.

35

Everything in the McGuire empire appeared to be running smoothly until the next morning when Jared heard shouting coming from the yard.

Glancing across the office, he saw the colour drain from Seth's face. 'Oh, god, it's my dad!'

'You stay here and keep quiet, I'll deal with him,' Jared advised. Walking from the office and down the steps, Jared came face to face with Ned.

'Can I help you, Mr Watkins?' he asked as Bobby and Dicky came to stand either side of him.

'Yeah, you can get my lad out here!' Ned growled.

'I'm afraid that's not going to happen,' Jared replied, showing bravado he didn't feel.

'Where's McGuire?'

'Mr McGuire is indisposed at the moment.'

'Hah! Well, un-dispose him, 'cos I want to talk to the organ grinder, not his monkey!'

Jared bristled at the insult but managed to keep it hidden.

'Like I said, Mr McGuire is unable to speak with you at the moment as he's not here.'

'Left you in charge, has he?' Ned said with a sneer.

'That's correct.'

'Then I'll tell you again – fetch my boy 'cos I need...'

'Mr Watkins, go home and sober up!' Jared's tone was harsh. 'You will not be having a conversation with Seth today or any other day, so get yourself gone.'

'Why, you cheeky young...' Ned took a step forward, his clenched fists raised, but a shout stopped him in his tracks.

'Dad!'

Glancing towards the office with a look of thunder on his countenance, Ned spat, 'There you are, boy. Get down here!'

Jared sighed loudly as he exchanged a glance with the Cavenors.

Seth slowly descended the steps and walked towards Jared. The grooms and sorters had gathered around too in a show of support for Seth.

Bill Cank stood to one side and watched the confrontation. He had been a drinking pal of Ned's for many years, but even he could see Ned was asking for a severe pasting if he carried on like this.

'Billy, my mate, are you gonna help me out here?' Ned asked as he swayed from foot to foot.

'This ain't my fight,' Bill replied, feeling all eyes on him.

'Mr Cank is right,' Jared said.

'It ain't yours either,' Ned said forcefully.

'It becomes mine when you come into my workplace yelling and bawling the odds, so drunk you can barely stand,' Jared answered confidently. In his peripheral vision, he saw the Cavenors nod in agreement.

'It ain't your business…' Ned began.

'Dad, stop it!' Seth snapped. 'Go home.'

'I can't. That's what I came to tell you, I've been slung out!'

Seth looked at Jared and closed his eyes tight for a second.

Jared nodded in confirmation of Seth's unspoken words – they had retrieved the photograph just in time.

Looking back at his father, Seth said, 'I'm sorry for your problems, but I can't help you.'

'You can pay the rent so I can get back in. Give me some money and I'll pass it on to the rent man,' Ned said in a whiny voice.

'Don't do it,' Jared said under his breath.

'No, Dad. I don't have any money and even if I did, I wouldn't let you have it. You'd only spend it on ale.' Seth turned out his trouser pockets to prove his point, having left his wages in his room at McGuire's house.

'Aww, lad,' Ned said as he shook his head, causing him to stumble. 'I've tried to be nice but I can see it ain't worked…'

'Get ready,' Jared muttered to the Cavenors.

Seth stepped back into the safety of the crowd of sorters and grooms as Ned lurched forwards.

'Mr Watkins!' Jared yelled at the top of his voice, stopping the other man dead in his tracks. 'I think you'd better leave these premises and I suggest you do not return.'

'And go where? I ain't got a home no more!'

'That's not our problem, but if you refuse, I'll be forced to send for the constabulary.' Inside, Jared was shaking in his boots but did his best to maintain a calm exterior.

Ned drew a hand through his greasy hair and turned to go, knowing he was beaten yet again. 'I won't forget this. You'd best be on your guard, all of you!' A moment later, he staggered out of the gates and was gone.

Jared blew out his cheeks in relief, then turning about, he said, 'Thanks, everyone. Your support was much appreciated.'

Slowly the little crowd dispersed and Jared and Seth went back to the office, Bobby and Dicky trailing in their wake.

'I'm sorry, Jared,' Seth said.

'Don't be, it's not your fault, but I've a nasty feeling we've not seen the last of your dad,' Jared replied, but he could see the guilt written all over Seth's face. 'Well, he's gone for now, so let's get back to work, shall we.'

The mood in the yard was sombre for the rest of the day, and Jared guessed everyone was thinking the same as him – how long would it be before Ned Watkins came calling again?

Whilst Jared dealt with the upset in the yard, Toby had left Alice to take a bath in the upstairs bathroom.

'I'll stick my head in at the yard, then I'll be back to take you shopping,' he said.

'I told you, I don't need anything,' Alice replied.

'I have to go to the bank, so I'll leave you at the dressmaker, then we'll have lunch somewhere nice.'

'All right, that sounds like a lovely idea,' Alice finally agreed to Toby's gentle demands.

McGuire left the house, striding across the barren heath, a great open expanse of wasteland which, he had wondered more than once, he could extend his business onto. Something to think about again at a later date. He came to the gates of the yard and Bobby and Dicky stopped him to explain what had happened with Ned.

'That lad ain't gonna be safe while Ned Watkins is still breathing,' McGuire said quietly.

'That's the truth of it, Boss,' Bobby said.

'Then it's time we did something about it, to be sure.'

The Cavenors nodded at the seriousness of McGuire's statement, already knowing what he had in mind.

What they didn't know was that they would be too late.

36

Jared greeted his employer with surprise, happy to see him.

'How are you getting on?' McGuire asked.

'Good, Mr McGuire, everything is running well,' Jared responded honestly.

'The Cavenors have told me about your visitor,' McGuire said, casting a glance Seth's way.

'I'm really sorry, Boss,' Seth said, clearly still feeling wretched.

McGuire waved a dismissive hand. 'It's your man who's causing grief, not you, lad. Sure, he needs a good hiding, so he does.'

'Seth, would you give us a minute so I can fill Mr McGuire in on business matters? I wonder if you'd ask the others if they want to come to mine tonight for a game of cards. Tell them you'll be there.'

Seth's face lit up and he trundled out to the yard to pass on the invitation to the sorters and grooms.

'So what's to be done about Ned?' Jared asked.

'Me and my lads,' McGuire indicated the brothers with a tilt of his head, 'are gonna teach him a lesson tonight.'

'Do you want me to gather some of the boys to come along?'

'No, lad, you're doing the best thing keeping Seth occupied. It looks like you've become friends, am I right?'

'I suppose we have.' Jared thought for a moment before he smiled. 'I would never have believed it was possible when I first came here.'

'I'm glad to see it, 'cos it's changed him for the better. Right, if there's nothing else you need from me, I have to take Alice shopping. I'll leave you to it.'

'How is she doing?' Jared asked.

'She's coping at the moment, but we have the funeral yet. Only then we'll truly know.'

'If you need anything, Mr McGuire, just get a message to me. But before you go, there was one thing I wanted to talk to you about. I hope you don't mind, but I told the workers I'd ask for them to have a raise as the yard is doing so well now. They've all been working extra hard with all these new ideas we've introduced, so I hope you would be amenable to considering it.'

'Fair enough. Let me have a look at the figures and I'll see to it as soon as I can.' And with a nod of thanks, McGuire left the office. He needed to go to town before returning home, there was something special he wanted to purchase.

A few minutes later, Seth returned to the office and told Jared he would have a houseful that evening. 'They're all bringing something to help out, though, so don't you be worrying about anything. They'll bring bread, cheese, that sort of thing, but I said definitely no alcohol. I hope you don't mind.'

'I agree, thanks, Seth. We don't want any thick heads tomorrow.'

When the tatters returned to the yard later, they too were asked to join the little party to play cards.

'This is becoming a regular thing,' Dan said, 'and I have to say I ain't complaining.'

'You're only glad because you won all of our matchsticks last time,' Johnny said with a feigned look of misery.

Sam and Paul burst out laughing.

Tom asked, 'Sam, what about your mum? What will she say?'

'I won't be asking, I'll be telling. I'm out with my friends – don't wait up!' Sam replied with his chest puffed out.

Laughter and chatter filled the yard once more as they went to feed their horses.

* * *

Back at Ivy Lane, Alice asked, 'Did you get your business done?'

'I did,' McGuire answered, subconsciously touching a little box nestled in his jacket pocket. Changing the subject quickly lest Alice ask further questions, McGuire told her about Ned's visit to the yard.

'Bloody hell, Toby! When will that man stop terrorising his son?'

'Very soon, Alice, if I've got anything to do with it,' came the reply.

Alice looked at him and she knew what was in his mind. She simply nodded her approval. Whatever was coming to Ned Watkins, he more than deserved it. 'I've been meaning to ask, is there any more news about Molly Watkins? That poor boy needs at least one good parent,' she asked.

'Not as yet, but once I'm back at work, I can send the Cavenors out again.'

'Somebody must know where she went. I know it's been years, but even so, someone is harbouring a secret.'

'I agree, Alice me darlin', but finding that person is the problem,' Toby said.

'Making them talk won't be, though, will it?' Alice asked, knowing Toby would get the information out of the person one way or another.

'Shouldn't be,' Toby said with a grin.

With a loud sigh, Alice pushed herself up from the kitchen chair. 'I'll make a start on tea, Seth will be hungry when he gets in.'

'What about me?'

'You're always bloody starving. I don't know where you put it, you must have hollow legs.'

'I must indeed for it ain't here,' McGuire said, patting his flat belly.

'Oh, will you look at yourself, bloody Adonis!'

McGuire chuckled. 'You got that right.'

'Where's that bucket?' Alice asked, looking around.

'In the scullery, why?' McGuire asked with a frown.

''Cos I'm gonna throw up in it!'

They were still laughing when Seth arrived home, excited to be spending some social time with his new friends. 'I'm playing cards at Jared's tonight,' he told Alice.

'I'm pleased for you, lad,' she replied.

'I'll be out for a while later too,' McGuire added as Seth went to his room to wash and change.

'Just you be careful, Toby, I don't want you hauled off by the coppers. I couldn't bear to lose you an' all.'

The two shared a look that lingered, and in that moment, both were thinking the same thing. Alice and Toby were in love, and had been for a very long time.

37

The Cavenors arrived at Ivy Lane and before they had a chance to sit down, McGuire was all business. He asked, 'Where's Ned likely to be now he has no home?'

'He's been banned from most of the boozers and having no money, my guess would be he'll be at one of his mates',' Bobby answered.

'And Ned only has one of them as far as I know – Bill Cank,' Dicky put in.

'Right, we'll start there then,' McGuire said.

Nodding at Toby, Alice said, 'You look after him,' concern written all over her face.

'We will,' the brothers spoke in unison.

Leaving the house, they walked determinedly down the street.

'If he ain't at Bill's, we'll have to search the pubs,' Bobby puffed as he tried to keep up with McGuire's fast pace.

'Blimey, do you know how many there are in this town?' Dicky asked.

'I do, having drunk in most of 'em,' Bobby said with a chuckle.

'I'm not trawling the town for him, I have better things to do,'

McGuire growled. 'Cank lives in Bromley Street, doesn't he? Which house is it?'

'Number ten, I think,' Dicky said.

The three men walked on as darkness began to fall. The chill wind had driven many people inside where they closed their doors and lit their fires. Coming to Bromley Street, McGuire looked at the houses packed tightly together, the brickwork grimy and windows dirty.

McGuire knocked on the door of number ten and waited. A moment later, it was opened by a tired-looking woman. 'Mr McGuire!' the woman said, surprised to see her husband's employer on her doorstep.

'Evening, Mrs Cank, is Bill in?'

'No, he's gone to the Old Red Lion in the Bullring. Is he in trouble?'

'No, no. I have a favour to ask is all,' McGuire said.

Mrs Cank was visibly relieved, then she turned around and screeched over her shoulder, 'Shut up, you lot!' Turning back to her visitors, she said more quietly, 'Sorry, bloody kids are driving me up the wall.'

'Thanks, my apologies for disturbing you.' McGuire tipped his cap and strode away, with the Cavenors in tow.

'That was easy, I expected her to get arsy with us,' Bobby said.

'To be sure, that was simple, but we ain't found him yet,' McGuire answered.

A few minutes later, they reached the pub and stopped short. Outside, a crowd had gathered, and a police constable was trying his best to keep order.

'Looks like there's been a punch-up,' Dicky said.

McGuire rubbed his stubbly chin. 'We could do without this.'

'Should we leave it for tonight then?' Bobby asked.

'Let's see if we can get in first,' McGuire answered as he pushed through the group of men who were all speaking at once.

'Move back!' the young constable shouted over the melee.

The clatter of boots on the cobbles made everyone turn to see two more policemen arrive on the scene. A whistle sounded loud and shrill, and the crowd parted to allow the bobbies through. It was then that McGuire saw a man lying on the ground. His eyes then moved to another man in handcuffs being held by the policeman. The cuffed man was sobbing openly.

'What happened?' McGuire asked the person next to him.

'He was drunk as a lord,' the fellow pointed to the dead man on the ground, 'and he picked a fight. The next thing we knew, it had spilled out here and that's the result.'

McGuire turned away. 'Come on, lads, let's go and find a quieter place for a drink,' he said, making sure those closest to him heard his words. 'Thanks, pal.'

'You're welcome, Mr McGuire,' the man said.

That brief exchange would be his alibi when the bobbies came calling, as he knew they would, if only to tell him one of his employees, Bill Cank, was in their custody. McGuire was known to be a hard man and rumours were rife about him sorting out disputes with violence. Therefore, he could not be held responsible for what had happened.

Bill Cank was destined to spend a night in the cells before appearing before the magistrate in the morning.

Ned Watkins was not so lucky – he would soon be on his way to the morgue.

* * *

Seth, as yet unaware of his father's demise, was enjoying the company of his friends over at Jared's house. All the boys were sitting on the floor, snacking on the foods they had brought as they played card games. Using matchsticks in lieu of money, Sam was on a winning streak. The room was noisy with laughter and some groans as their fortunes ebbed and flowed. Candles cast a shimmering light on the players and a fire in the grate burned brightly.

The last round came to a close and the boys said goodnight and gave their thanks before leaving.

Once he was alone, Jared tidied up the living room, wondering how McGuire's evening had gone, but more to the point, how Ned had fared. Sitting by the fire, Jared felt complicit in what must have happened to Ned by now, and he couldn't stop himself worrying about that. He was aware of what McGuire had set out to do and that made him an accessory in his eyes. His heart was heavy about the whole sorry tale, and he guessed Seth would be angry with him when he found out.

Another question that tormented him was how would the others react when they found out? Although it was not his idea in the first place to teach Ned a lesson, Jared had been told about it beforehand and he hoped his friends would see it for what it was. McGuire was intent on sorting this out once and for all, and nothing Jared could have done could have prevented it.

With a sigh, Jared placed the guard around the fire and extinguished all but one of the candles. Locking the door, he made his way to bed by the flickering light, feeling tired to the bone.

38

It was mid-morning the following day when a constable arrived at the yard, seeking Toby McGuire. Jared explained why the tatter king was not there. 'He's looking after his housekeeper who has recently lost her husband. I'm standing in for him until he comes back.'

The bobby frowned. 'You're a bit young, ain't you, to be running this place?'

'It was Mr McGuire's decision, officer,' Jared said respectfully.

With a shrug of his shoulders, the policeman said, 'I'll try him at home then.'

'Is it anything I can help with?' Jared asked, not completely surprised that the police needed to see McGuire but worried nonetheless.

'No, lad. I'm sure if you need to know then Mr McGuire will tell you.' With that, the constable left a concerned Jared. Did the police need to see his boss because of his plans for the previous evening? Had the policeman come to arrest McGuire? If so, he couldn't help but notice that the constable seemed very relaxed about it. Jared's thoughts were interrupted by the Cavenors entering the office.

'Do you want to tell me what all that was about?' Jared asked, pointing to the retreating constable.

The brothers shuffled their feet, unsure whether they should say anything, especially as Seth sat there listening.

Jared noted their unease. 'Seth, would you mind going to see if Bill Cank has turned up yet, please? He's been trying my patience recently by turning up later and later.'

With a nod, the young man did as he was bid.

'Well?' Jared asked.

'Look, we ain't said a word, right?' Bobby said.

'My lips are sealed,' Jared replied.

'Bill Cank is in jail!' Dicky blurted out.

'What for?' Jared asked, a shocked look spreading across his face.

'Seems he got into a fight with Ned Watkins,' Bobby explained.

'And now Ned's dead!' Dicky added.

'Oh, hell!' Jared gasped. 'So you didn't...?'

'No, we d'aint get the chance,' Bobby answered.

'It was all over when we got there,' Dicky added.

'Why didn't that bobby tell Seth about Ned, though?' Jared asked more to himself than anyone else.

'P'raps he doesn't know Seth is Ned's lad. If it was me in his shoes, I wouldn't say a word either.' Bobby shook his head as he spoke.

'I agree. It's not our place, especially as we don't, as yet, know the details. I expect Mr McGuire will come and speak to Seth, until then, we keep quiet.'

The Cavnors nodded and left to take up their positions guarding the gates.

'Bill's still not in,' Seth said as he came back into the office. 'Maybe he's overslept.'

'Probably. Not to worry, there are enough sorters to manage.' Jared felt awkward knowing what he did and being unable to say anything. Today was going to be very difficult for him, but also he was concerned about how Seth would react to the news of his father's death.

* * *

Over in Ivy Lane, Alice's face lost all colour when she opened the door and saw the constable standing there.

'I'm looking for Mr McGuire.'

'You'd best come in then,' Alice replied and after closing the door, she led him into the kitchen.

'Ah, Mr McGuire. I'm sorry to bother you but they told me at the yard that you were here.'

'Morning, constable, do have a seat,' McGuire offered.

Removing his helmet, the constable laid it on the table as he sat down. 'I believe you have a man in your employ called Bill Cank.'

'To be sure,' the Irishman replied.

'I'm here to tell you that Mr Cank was apprehended last evening and has been charged with murder.'

'Oh, my god!' Alice gasped.

The constable went on, 'It appears he got into an altercation with Ned Watkins, who died of his injuries at the scene. I believe the deceased was recently evicted and we are trying to locate his family.'

'Ned's son, Seth, is residing here; he also works for me. We brought the lad here after Ned beat him half to death,' McGuire informed him. 'As for Molly, Ned's wife, she ran out on him many years ago after she also took a bad beating. No one knows where she is. In fact, we have been searching for her ourselves.'

'And why would that be, sir?' the constable asked, a frown forming.

'We thought if we found her then Seth could possibly rebuild a life with her – away from Ned's cruelty.'

'I see, well, if we hear anything we'll be sure to let Seth know. However, for now, I need to speak with Master Watkins.'

'He's at the yard. I'll come with you because Seth will need some support when you tell him the sad news.'

Making sure Alice would be all right alone, McGuire and the constable left the house to return to the yard once more.

Alice breathed a huge sigh of relief when she was alone. She had felt sure the copper had come for Toby and her heart had been beating out of her chest. Flopping onto a kitchen chair, she covered her face with her hands and wept. She cried for Stanley and the fact she would never see him again; her tears fell for her sons who never bothered with her any more, and she bawled for Toby, who she'd thought might be taken from her.

When eventually her sobbing ceased, Alice stared at nothing as she whispered, 'I'm sorry, Stanley. I did love you in my own way. We really shouldn't have wed, you and I, but I stood by your side until the end. I know how much you loved me despite knowing my heart lay elsewhere and I'll always be grateful for that. I hope you can forgive me and that you'll be able to rest in peace soon.'

Feeling a little better now, she rose from her seat to begin preparing the evening meal.

* * *

McGuire and the policeman arrived at the yard and walked up to the office, where Jared and Seth were going over the week's figures. Both looked up as the men entered.

'Seth, the constable here needs to be having a word with you,' McGuire said.

'Seth, lad, I'm afraid I have some bad news. I'm very sorry to have to tell you that your father was killed in a bar-room brawl last night.' The constable spoke quietly, his helmet tucked under one arm. Knowing Ned Watkins of old, he wasn't at all surprised when he heard Seth's reply.

39

Jared's jaw dropped open in feigned surprise when he heard the news and he stared at Seth when the reply came quietly from his friend's lips.

'Thank god!'

The policeman gave a little cough before saying, 'I'd best get back to the station; my condolences.' The constable nodded to McGuire and left the office.

Jared and McGuire exchanged a glance then watched Seth, expecting the boy to burst into tears. When he didn't, Jared placed his hand on Seth's shoulder. 'I'm sorry, mate,' he said.

'Thanks, but it was bound to happen sooner or later.' Looking up at McGuire, he asked, 'Where is he?'

'At the morgue, son. He'll need to be buried.'

'I've no money for that, so he can have a pauper's burial,' Seth replied.

'I can help...' McGuire began.

'No! Thanks, Mr McGuire, but he doesn't deserve help, not after what he did to my mum and me.'

McGuire nodded, feeling Jared's eyes on him.

'Who did it?' Seth asked.

'It seems your dad and Bill Cank got into an argument which spilled out into the street.'

'I thought they were pals,' Seth said shaking his head.

'Even friends fall out sometimes, look at you and me,' Jared put in.

Seth gave a tight-lipped smile at being called Jared's friend. 'Mr McGuire, would it be very wrong of me to say I'm relieved?'

'In your case, I would say not,' McGuire answered.

'You won't have to look over your shoulder any more, Seth,' Jared added.

Seth drew in the longest breath then let it out in the biggest sigh Jared had ever heard. 'I'm free at last,' he said, 'now I just have to find my mum.'

'Why don't you come home with me? I know Alice would love to look after you and you could comfort each other,' McGuire suggested.

'If it's all the same to you, Mr McGuire, I'd rather stay here and work,' Seth replied.

'I'll look after him,' Jared said as McGuire nodded.

'Fair enough, I'll be on my way then. I don't want to leave Alice on her own for too long.'

Once McGuire had gone, Jared stared at Seth.

'I feel guilty,' Seth said suddenly.

'About what?'

'I feel guilty that I don't feel bad about my dad's death,' Seth replied.

'Well, you shouldn't. Just remember how he treated you and your mum; the beatings you both took. He drove your mum away. If it was me, I wouldn't feel bad either.'

'Thanks, Jared. I'm glad we're mates at last. It took a while because of the way I was with you and the lads, but I'm happy that's behind us now.'

'Me too. I remember when we first met and you shouting, "Oi, you!"'

The two laughed together before Seth asked, 'Do you think McGuire will put me back on the rounds?'

'I don't know. If he does, then Tom will have to return to sorting.'

'Oh, yes, I forgot about that. Tom should stay on the cart, he loves it. As for me, I'm not sure what the boss will decide because there's not enough for me to do here.'

'Mr McGuire will come up with something, I'm sure of it. He won't sack you, if that's what you're worried about,' Jared said confidently.

'I hope not, but I'm more concerned about finding my mum, to be honest.'

'Right, let's get our thinking caps on then and see what we can do about that.'

* * *

Whilst Jared and Seth put their heads together, over in Ivy Lane, McGuire and Alice were discussing Ned Watkins's demise and the fate of Bill Cank.

'He'll go to jail without a doubt,' McGuire answered Alice's question of what would now happen to Cank.

'It's Mary Cank I feel sorry for. She's got six kids to feed as well as rent to pay.'

'Don't you be worrying about that, *cailín*, I'll see them right,' McGuire said.

'Bless you, Toby, but you also have to decide what to do with Seth. He can't live here for the rest of his life, we both know that.'

'To be sure, but it might be easier to trace Molly now Ned's out of the way.'

'How?'

With a sigh, McGuire shook his head. 'In truth, I haven't got a clue.'

'Well, hopefully the coppers are looking for her as well.'

'They are but I suspect it will be half-heartedly.'

'Why do you say that?' Alice asked, perplexed.

'It's not exactly urgent, is it? Ned's dead, so he's going nowhere. Seth has a home and a job, so there's no worries there. Discovering Molly's whereabouts won't be a priority for them,' McGuire answered.

'I suppose not when you put it like that.'

'No, Alice, it will be up to us to find Molly Watkins and just how we do that eludes me for the moment.'

'You'll manage, I've never known anything beat you, Toby McGuire.'

Except Stanley – he beat me when he got to you before I did.

Toby smiled, but inside his heart ached. His love for Alice had begun when they were at school together and had grown stronger over the years. Yet again, he silently berated himself for not proposing to Alice when he had the chance. He had waited, wanting to build up his business so he could give her the life she deserved. He needed to ensure she wanted for nothing, but he had left it too late. Stanley had breezed in and married her.

'Here's a thought, why not put a notice in the paper about Ned's death. You could word it saying you're searching for Molly to let her know!' Alice said excitedly.

'Ah, Alice, may the most you wish for be the least you get!'

There's only one thing I wish for now, Toby, and that's to become Mrs McGuire, but I doubt that will ever happen.

'Go on, then, get yourself down to the newspaper office. They'll help you with what to put in print.'

Toby stood and he kissed Alice on the cheek, then he was gone.

Staring at the doorway through which Toby had disappeared, Alice lifted a hand to her face. The physical pain in her heart stabbed like a knife as she realised how long she had waited for his kisses.

40

McGuire placed his notification in the newspaper for one week requesting members of the deceased Ned Watkins's family to get in touch with him at the yard. He didn't want people turning up at his house purporting to be related to Ned and hoping for a handout from a will. Returning home, he explained to Alice what he had done and why.

'Then you should be at your work, Toby, in case Molly does come,' Alice said.

'I don't want to leave you alone yet, Alice, not until...'

'Ah, go on with you, I'll be fine here. I have to get used to it, so the sooner the better.' Despite his protestations, Alice ushered McGuire out of the house, telling him not to come back until teatime.

Striding out, McGuire headed for the yard to tell Seth about the article in the paper. When he arrived, it was to hear laughter coming from the office. 'Somebody's happy in their work,' he commented to the Cavenors as he approached the gates.

'Yes, Boss,' they chorused.

Tilting his head as an indication for them to follow, McGuire walked through the yard, up the stairs and into the office.

'Mr McGuire, it's nice to see you,' Jared said, surprised at the unexpected appearance of their employer.

McGuire explained to them all about the piece he'd put in the paper. 'Hopefully we might hear something about your mum, Seth. So I'll be here this week, just in case.'

Jared and Seth exchanged a hopeful glance. 'That's great news, Mr McGuire,' Seth said and Jared nodded his agreement.

'So tell me, how's the business doing?' McGuire asked.

'Everything is running smoothly. The rag piles are going out every day, as are the manure sacks. The washed clothes are coming in regularly and we have quite a lot now. I was going to suggest it might be time to move them on.'

'I'll see if any of the laundry women want to stand a stall on the market. Bobby, would you be good enough to put the word to the sorters?'

The big man nodded and went to do as he was bid.

'If you're back, Mr McGuire, what do you want me to do?' Jared asked.

'I'd like you to get Bess back on the road, I think she's had enough rest.'

'Yes, sir!' Jared was delighted to be going back on the rounds.

'Mr McGuire,' Seth said tentatively, 'I'm really grateful for what you have and are still doing for me...'

'But?' McGuire enquired.

'Well, Jared and I have been talking and he said I could go and live with him if I want to and...'

'Was that what all the laughter was about when I arrived?' McGuire asked.

'Yes, Boss, we were discussing how not to get on each other's nerves,' Jared put in.

McGuire nodded. 'I think it's an excellent idea if that's what you both want.'

'It will be company for me and it will get him out from under your feet,' Jared said with a little laugh.

'It's nice to see the turn-around in your relationship, lads, and I wish you luck. You have my blessings if that's what you'd both like. Right, let's get to work.' McGuire flicked a hand, dismissing Dicky, leaving only Seth and Jared behind. 'I have to say I'm a little surprised about you and Jared sharing a residence,' McGuire said.

'I was too when he suggested it,' Seth answered with a glance at his friend.

'I think it will be good for you, Seth, it will help you to stand on your own two feet. You'll be better off with someone your own age too instead of being with us old 'uns.'

Seth smiled. 'I wonder if you'll get any response to your request for information on my mum.'

'Time will tell. Until then, we just have to wait and hope.'

McGuire, Jared and Seth were all thinking the same thing – how marvellous it would be if Molly Watkins turned up at the yard.

Bobby trudged back up the stairs to report that the sorters would discuss the market stall idea with their wives that evening and send their answer the following morning.

McGuire nodded before turning to Jared.

'Now then, Jared, let's have a look at the books and decide how much we can up the wages as per your promise to the workers,' McGuire said with a wry grin. Once the decision was made, sixpence a week to be added to the pay packets, Jared thanked his boss and left to take Bess out on the road. McGuire and Seth then settled quietly to their work.

Seth and Jared were given permission to leave work earlier

than usual so Seth could say thank you and goodbye to Alice before taking the few clothes he had collected together from the good pile, along with his beloved photograph. He left a tearful Alice on the doorstep as he strode on to move in with Jared.

When he arrived, the two of them ran to the pawn shop, which was just about to close its doors. After begging the owner to allow them inside, they purchased an old bedstead and mattress along with two thick blankets. Between them, they brought the items home on Jared's cart he had used for tatting when he first started out. They chatted excitedly about sharing the house and how they would have a kitty for buying food and coal.

Having manoeuvred the bedstead into place, Seth being very careful of his aching ribs, Jared dragged the mattress upstairs and manhandled it onto the springs. Seth carried up the blankets and a candle-holder complete with candle and matches.

Downstairs once more, Jared lit the fire and then together they prepared a meal of liver and bacon with fried onions. Seth made tea while Jared washed up, then with cups in hand, they sat on the old settee, watching the dancing flames in the hearth. Comfortable in each other's company, neither felt the need to speak, but they both marvelled at how things had turned out; that they were now living together as friends. Both slept well that night and rose bright and early the following morning.

Arriving at the yard at the usual time, everyone was taken aback when McGuire informed Seth he would be back on the rounds.

Tom's face had fallen. Although he had expected to return to the sorting eventually, he was disappointed it had happened with no warning. But McGuire had a surprise for them all.

'Seth, your new mare is in the stables, so you'd best get to know her. Tom, you stick with your round. You've done a great job and I'd like you to stick to it if you'd like that,' McGuire said.

'Oh, yes, please. Thanks, Mr McGuire!' Tom said, the grin once more on his face.

Seth nodded his thanks too, swallowing the lump in his throat.

The chatter was loud as everyone bustled out to the stables to meet the new horse.

McGuire had been up and out early to see a man about a horse. The man he always dealt with was glad to see him about buying the mare, and a lad had led it along the streets to the yard. A tanner in his pocket for his efforts and the boy left, happy to have been of service. The grooms were already hard at work building another stable onto the end of the row. Eventually the wooden structure would be replaced by a brick-built one, but for now, a shelter was needed quickly for the new addition to the equine family.

Everyone gathered in the stables to see the new mare assigned to Seth. She was a good size and her brown coat shone in the light coming through the doorway. Seth walked up to her, talking quietly. Her eyes rolled around to him as he approached and he stroked her neck. 'Hello, beautiful,' he whispered before breathing into her nostrils. A snicker came by way of reply. 'Now what shall we call you?'

A few names were called out by the others, but the horse made no movement. It was when Seth said, 'You need to have a name, beautiful,' that she snickered again. 'All right, Beautiful it is, then. I think we will be great friends.'

'A couple of the sorters' wives said they'd be more than happy to stand a market stall,' Dicky said as the brothers followed McGuire back into the office from the stables where they had witnessed Seth and his new horse meeting for the first time.

'Excellent. I'd be obliged if you could arrange a pitch with the market manager then.'

Dicky nodded.

'We're still two short on the sorters, Boss,' Bobby said.

'I know. I'll get down to the nearest bread line later and see about filling the jobs,' McGuire answered, then as an afterthought, he added, 'In actual fact, I think I'll go now.'

At the intersection between Westley Street, Bolton Street and Watery Lane, a group of men stood, leaning their backs against the brick wall of a large building. Hands in their trouser pockets against the cold, they were grumbling loudly about having no work and the fact that winter was on its way.

'It gets colder every day,' one said.

'And wetter, the damn rain falls almost all the time,' said another.

'Judging by those clouds, we're in for some more an' all,' the first replied.

'It won't be long before it freezes,' said a third man.

'Then we'll need more coal. How are we supposed to buy it when we have no bloody jobs?' said the first.

Walking towards them, McGuire heard their grumbles before he introduced himself. 'I'm Toby McGuire and I own the tatters' yard over on the heath.'

The men nodded a greeting, some standing up straight in the hope of work, others not bothering, their enthusiasm for life drained away by the cold and the hunger.

'I have work for two sorters if anyone is interested.'

Hands flew into the air like children in class as the men scrambled to be chosen.

'Who of you have family?' McGuire asked. Again, lots of hands shot up.

'I've got a wife and six kids, gaffer,' one man said.

'I've a wife and four boys,' said another.

'Right, you two come along with me.' The other men all

groaned with disappointment and McGuire added, 'Sorry, fellas, I've only work for two right now. But good luck to you all.' With that, he turned and walked away, the two new recruits hurrying along behind him.

Back at the yard, McGuire took the details of his new employees before Bobby and Dicky led them to the sorting area. Here they were shown the ropes by the other sorters and they quickly slotted into the work regime, ecstatic to finally have work.

When they returned to the office, McGuire gave the Cavenors the task of taking some money round to Mrs Cank to enable her to feed her children. She was told she would receive a little each week to help out until her children were old enough to work or Bill returned home, whichever came first.

Mrs Cank sent back her thanks with a message that the magistrate had ordered her husband to appear at quarter sessions and would then go on to the Assizes. Bill was at present incarcerated at Stafford Gaol.

'What do you reckon, Boss, will they hang him for murder?' Dicky asked.

'Depends on the outcome of the trial, but somehow I doubt it. He'll probably stay in jail for a while, for surely it was an accident.'

'That's what we've heard. It seems the fight took Bill and Ned out into the street, and after a few punches, Bill pushed Ned, who fell and hit his head against the corner wall of the pub,' Bobby explained.

'Well, there were enough witnesses, so we'll have to wait and see what the court decides,' McGuire said.

The brothers wandered away, discussing the gruesome details of what a hanging would be like.

'You would feel your throat tighten and be unable to breathe,' Bobby said.

'Nah, you wouldn't, 'cos your neck would break with the drop,' Dicky countered.

'I wonder if people would hear that,' Bobby asked.

'Sure to, it would go with a hell of a crack,' Dicky answered.

McGuire shook his head and muttered, 'I worry about those two sometimes, I really do.'

41

Later that day, McGuire arrived home to find Alice sitting in the kitchen, staring at an unopened letter on the table.

'Alice?'

Looking up at him, her eyes held what he could only describe as fear. Pushing the letter away from her, she whispered, 'I can't. Can you open it for me, Toby?'

McGuire sat opposite her and opened the letter. After a moment, he said, 'It was his heart, love. Stanley's ticker gave out. Now we can lay him to rest.'

Alice drew in a big breath and exhaled slowly. 'I'll go tomorrow and let Mr Webb know at the funeral parlour.'

'If you're up to it,' McGuire said, laying his hand on hers across the table.

'I am. And while I'm out, I need to replenish the larder as well; a bit of shopping will take my mind off things.'

McGuire nodded. Pulling out the drawer in the table, he said, 'You'll need more housekeeping money then.' Taking his wallet from his pocket, he put the cash in the drawer and shoved it to quietly.

'How can an apparently healthy man die just like that? He'd never complained about any pain or anything,' Alice asked, snapping her fingers.

'I don't know, sweetheart, sure, maybe his heart was tired.'

'That's a nice way to think of it,' Alice said with a tight smile. Getting to her feet, she added, 'Suet pudding for tea.'

McGuire watched as she plated up his meal. 'Where's yours?'

'I'm not hungry.'

'Oh, Alice, you have to eat, otherwise you'll be ill.'

With a sigh, she nodded.

In the dining room, McGuire ate while watching Alice pushing the food around her plate, occasionally taking a small bite. It was Toby who took the plates back to the kitchen, telling Alice to go and sit by the fire. After a moment, he joined her. 'Talk to me, *colleen*.'

'I don't feel like a girl any more, Toby, some days I think I'm an old woman.'

'You'll always be a girl to me,' he said softly.

A small smile etched her face as she looked into the heart of the fire.

Toby so desperately wanted to tell her how he felt, that he loved her with all of his being, but he knew now was not the time. Once Stanley was laid to rest and Alice had had a suitable grieving time, maybe then he could voice his true feelings.

'Stanley always knew, you know.' Alice's words were barely more than a whisper.

'Knew what?'

'That I didn't love him like a wife should.' Toby's heart almost stopped, he was so taken aback. 'I told him before we wed,' Alice went on. 'I said as how my love belonged to another and always would.'

Hardly daring to hope, Toby asked, 'Then why did you marry

him?'

Alice looked up from the flames. 'Because you never asked me,' she said simply.

Toby released the breath he didn't realise he'd been holding. 'Oh, *mo-shíorghra*!'

'Why can't you speak bloody English?'

'It means my soulmate – my eternal love,' he whispered.

'We've wasted so much time, Toby,' Alice said, a tear on her cheek glistening like a crystal in the firelight.

'I've loved you all my life, sweetheart. I needed to build up the business before I proposed to you so you could have your heart's desires and want for nothing.'

'You're an idiot, Toby McGuire. How could you not know all I wanted was you?'

'I'm so very sorry, Alice. I've suffered agonies over the years watching you wed, having your twins, living with Stanley. He was a good man, don't get me wrong, and he adored you, but I so desperately wanted to be in his shoes.'

'He knew that too. We talked about it before our wedding and he said if you asked, he would step aside.'

'Oh, my god! Alice, I feel wretched now. Stanley was a saint.'

'He was, and I made sure to stand by him until the end because he was good to me and the boys.'

'Alice...' Toby began, his hand touching the little box in his pocket.

'Not yet, Toby. Give me time. Then, if you still want to, you can ask your question,' Alice said gently.

McGuire nodded and as he watched her gaze into the fire once more, the melange of feelings threatened to overwhelm him.

Going to the sideboard, he poured two whiskies and, handing one to Alice, he said, '*Sláinte*.'

Alice clinked her glass to his, returning the toast in English.

'Health.'

* * *

The following morning, Alice walked to Webb's Funeral Parlour. Showing him the letter, she nodded when Mr Webb said, 'We've allocated a plot already, Mrs Crawford, so how does Monday sound?'

'Thank you, that's fine.'

'We will collect Stanley and lay him to rest at two o'clock. He will sleep soundly beneath the largest oak tree at St Bart's.'

Alice swallowed the lump in her throat and, giving her thanks again, she left quickly. As she walked away, her tears fell; she could no longer hold them back. Now she could bury her husband. Relief at no longer having to wait to hear from the coroner mingled with sadness and a scintilla of guilt which raged through her mind. *I'm sorry you've left me, Stanley, and I pray you can forgive my loving another all our married life.*

Stepping into the market, Alice wiped away her tears with the back of her hand. She knew she had to take things one day at a time and today she needed to fill Toby's larder. Coming to the bread stall, she pointed to a fresh loaf.

'I was sorry to hear about your Stanley,' the vendor said, and Alice nodded, not trusting herself to speak for fear of her tears falling once more.

Moving on, she bought fresh vegetables and potatoes, then on again to the meat stall where she purchased sausages, bacon and a pork joint. At each stall, the saleswomen gave their condolences and Alice muttered her thanks before turning swiftly on her heel and fleeing back to Ivy Lane.

* * *

Whilst Alice had been trawling the market, Jared and Seth walked to work together and Jared asked Seth, 'Do you want to find out about when and where your father's funeral will be?'

'No, I couldn't care less,' Seth answered firmly. 'I'm sorry if that sounds shocking but he's gone, Jared, and good riddance as far as I'm concerned. It's Bill Cank and his family I feel sorry for. They were friends for years, but my dad had to ruin even that.'

'I'm sure he'll be found innocent, Seth, the court will see the truth of it.'

'I hope so, it will be nice to have him back at work 'cos he has kids to feed.'

'He might not come back, though, Seth. He may feel awkward and guilty working here with you,' Jared said quietly.

'I'll make sure that doesn't happen. I'll tell him I don't hold him responsible and that my dad was at fault. If it hadn't been Bill, it would have been someone else. It was bound to happen sooner or later, it was on the cards. He'd never have made old bones.'

When they arrived at the yard, Jared was surprised to realise there was no sign of the Cavenors. Maybe McGuire had sent them on another errand.

'Jared!' McGuire's voice sailed across the yard.

'Coming, Mr McGuire,' Jared called back, shrugging his shoulders at the quizzical looks directed at him from the other tatters. Going up to the office door, Jared knocked and walked in.

'Jared, there's someone here to see you,' McGuire said.

Jared frowned. Who would come to the yard to visit him?

'Well, lad, I'm not sure how to tell you this, but this man here tells me he's your father.'

Jared's mouth dropped open as he faced the other man, who was smiling at him widely. Shock had Jared rooted to the spot as he searched the face for anything that might put proof to the claim.

42

That same morning, the Cavenors had taken a cab and, as instructed by McGuire, had gone to his house to see Alice and find out the details of Stanley's funeral. From there, they were to travel to Wednesbury to inform Marcus and Luke of the date, time and place their father would be laid to rest. Armed with the information, they set off.

'I hope their wives won't be there,' Bobby said as the cab rattled along.

'They're sure to be,' Dicky replied, 'and it won't make for a nice meeting. It's bad enough having to pass on the arrangements without those vixens kicking off.'

'We just do as we're told, bruv. We explain that Mr McGuire ain't taking no for an answer and those boys *must* attend or else,' Bobby said.

'It's times like these I wish I was a sorter.' Dicky's voice was quiet as he shook his head.

'Me an' all,' Bobby concurred.

Eventually, the cab halted and the brothers alighted.

'Here we are again. Ready?' Bobby asked, looking up at the

dilapidated building. The green paint on the double doors was cracked and peeling, and the windows were grimy. The chimney needed re-pointing and the whole establishment had a shabby look.

Dicky nodded and the men pushed in through the doors of the hotel. At the reception, they were greeted with an acerbic welcome. 'What do you two want now?'

'Hello to you an' all, Luke,' Dicky said sarcastically.

'Fetch your brother, and do it quickly,' Bobby instructed.

'He's busy,' Luke replied.

Dicky grabbed the young man by the lapels of his jacket and snarled, 'Get him – now!' Pushing Luke away from him, Dicky brushed his hands on his jacket, smoothing the crumpled fabric back into place.

Realising it would be unwise to disobey the big man, Luke fled from the small foyer and reappeared a moment later with Marcus in tow.

Bobby gave them the information about Stanley's funeral that they'd gleaned from Alice earlier then said, 'Mr McGuire will expect to see you both there to support your mum.'

The twins glanced at each other, both thinking the same thing – *our wives won't be happy about that!*

'I'm not sure we can spare the time,' Luke said.

'This is not open for debate!' Dicky snapped, his temper rising rapidly.

'Your dad made sure he had all the time in the world for you two, as did your mum,' Bobby put in a little more calmly. 'A few hours to see your father off and make your mum happy, that's all it will take.'

'We should,' Marcus said to his brother in a whisper as he glanced around furtively.

'I know, but...' Luke began.

'For god's sake, grow a backbone! Tell your wenches you're going and they can like it or lump it!' Dicky was fuming now. 'I'll tell you what, though, if you're not there, Mr McGuire will come and get you and believe me, you don't want that.'

Luke rubbed his chin and Marcus dragged a hand through his hair. Then, from another room, they heard a screech and both men visibly paled.

'We have to go,' Luke said, fear showing clearly on his face.

'Remember what you have to do,' Bobby said.

'You have been warned. Don't make me have to come back here again!' Dicky added over his shoulder as they strode from the premises.

In the cab once more, Bobby asked, 'Do you think they'll come to the funeral then?'

'Buggered if I know, bruv, but I'll enjoy dragging 'em by the ears if they don't.' Dicky chuckled when his brother shook his head with a grin plastered all over his face.

* * *

Whilst the brothers travelled homeward, back at the yard, Jared stared at the man claiming to be his father. Tall and skinny, with dark hair and eyes, he was dressed in old, tatty working clothes.

'Hello, Jared.' His smile broadened as he stepped forward and held out his hand to be shaken.

Jared scowled, glanced at the calloused hand then back at the man's eyes. 'Who are you?' he asked.

Dropping his arm to his side, the man answered with a frown. 'I'm Timothy Johnson, your father.'

'I doubt that very much. Who are you really and what do you want with me?'

'I've come home, son...'

'Don't you dare call me that! You have no right!'

McGuire and Seth both looked at each other from beside McGuire's desk as Jared's words pierced the silence.

'Look, lad, this is not the place…' the stranger began.

'Then why come here?' Jared interrupted. 'I don't know who you are or why you sought me out, but I do know this – I want nothing to do with you!' Shaking with anger, Jared turned and walked out of the office.

'Jared…' came the plaintive call from behind him.

'Sure, you heard the boy, so I'll be asking you to please leave my premises,' McGuire said as he got to his feet and pointed to the open doorway with his cigar.

With a nod, the man did as he was bid.

'Blimey!' Seth gasped.

'I'll second that, so I will.'

'Do you think he's really Jared's dad?'

'I've no idea, Seth, but your man there has a lot of explaining to do either way.'

Seth blew out his cheeks and turned to leave the office so he could go and hitch the mare to his cart.

McGuire narrowed his eyes as he puffed on his cigar. If that man *was* Timothy Johnson, why had he suddenly appeared from nowhere? Clearly, he was not well off as could be seen by his attire, unless he had taken time off from his work to make the visit. If it transpired he was *not* Johnson, then what was he after with Jared? In all probability, it would be money.

McGuire hoped and prayed Jared would not end up in the same situation that Seth had been with his father. Only time would provide the answer.

Jared was furious as he led Bess out of the gates, leaving behind him the puzzled stable boys. He didn't trust himself to speak to anyone lest his ire burst its banks.

Who the hell was that man purporting to be his father? Jared had searched the face for any signs of likeness to himself but had found none. There was nothing about the man that conjured up any memories and therefore Jared considered him to be a charlatan.

The question that nagged in his brain was, why? Surely the man would know that Jared had little money working as a tatter, so what was the true reason behind the visit?

As the morning wore on, Jared tried his best to be his usual jovial self but the questions, of which there were many, were eating away at him. He realised on reflection that he should have arranged a meeting after work with the fellow when he could have had some answers, but it was too late now. He had sent the man packing before hearing what he had to say, and now he might never know who it was had sought him out or the reason for it.

Jared's anger stayed with him for the rest of the day; unable to shake it, he turned Bess for home. Maybe McGuire might have a few pearls of wisdom to share on the whole debacle.

43

Once back at the yard and having seen to Bess, Jared requested a meeting with McGuire. They discussed at length the question of who the stranger was that had visited that morning. What he could gain by declaring he was Jared's father, where he had come from and why he was here now.

It was McGuire's contention that if the man was serious about being Jared's father, then he would be back. That then would be the opportunity for Jared to arrange to sit down with the man and get some answers. McGuire also suggested it might be wise for Jared to have some of his pals around him at any meeting, for they might have questions Jared hadn't considered.

Strolling home with the other tatters, Jared explained to them the reason for his angst. They told him they understood why he was so worried, for the man had turned up out of the blue. They agreed they would be at his side in unified support should he decide to meet with the man and have his questions answered.

'I really thought you were going to throw a punch,' Seth said.

'I came close to it,' Jared replied. 'I was absolutely livid that this bloke, if he is my father, would have the gall to turn up out of the blue after all these years. And if he's not my father, then what kind of lowlife would spring that trick on an innocent stranger, and why?'

'All we can do now is wait and see what comes of it all,' Dan put in wisely.

'At least you know we have your back,' Sam said as he patted Jared's shoulder.

Giving a wave, Jared and Seth parted ways with the group and as they reached the cottage, Seth said, 'Fathers, who'd have them?'

* * *

A little while later over in Ivy Lane, McGuire was telling Alice all about the unusual visitor.

'What the bloody hell...?' Alice was aghast. 'First Seth, now Jared!'

'I know, would you credit it? Whatever the truth of the situation, it will work itself out eventually, and I'll be there if the lads need me,' McGuire answered.

Alice nodded. 'Talking about lads who might need you, Bobby and Dicky went to see my boys this morning to tell them that the funeral is on Monday.'

'Aye, at least the twins know now.'

'I suppose so, but I'm not expecting to see them,' Alice said sadly.

'We'll see.' McGuire was certain the twins would be attending one way or another, he just hoped they would behave themselves and be kind to their mother. The last thing he wanted was for Alice to be any more upset than she already was.

* * *

A few days later, McGuire and Alice readied themselves for Stanley's funeral. Alice was quiet as she pinned her black hat in place, then she pulled on her gloves and collected her bag.

'You ready, love?' McGuire asked. Looking smart in a black suit, he donned a bowler and grabbed his umbrella. His shoes shone brilliantly as he walked towards her.

Alice nodded sadly.

Leaving the house, McGuire hailed a cab and Alice stared out of the window as they travelled to St Bart's. Alighting at their destination, they looked around them. There were trees all around the edges of the site and a small gravel path wove across the centre leading to the cemetery. Mr Webb walked towards them, holding out a hand in greeting before he led them to the grave site. Then he left them so he could lead the coffin procession.

McGuire glanced around at the mourners arriving. Bobby and Dicky plus their mum walked towards him, and Alice greeted them, pleased that they could join them. Then the sound of crunching boots on gravel made Alice turn and she gasped as she saw her beloved sons walking towards her. Glancing at Toby with eyes sparkling with tears, Alice gave a tiny nod of thanks. She knew this was McGuire's doing and she would forever be grateful for it.

The twins approached and each man in turn wrapped his arms around their mum. Alice was undone and sobbed, quite unable to speak.

McGuire and the Cavenors exchanged a knowing look, clearly the threat had worked. Everyone took their places as Mr Webb, the conductor, preceded the coffin carried by four strong young men all dressed in black. As the casket was placed gently onto the ropes laid out on the ground, the vicar began the service.

Alice heard none of the words spoken but glanced around the

congregation before looking up at her sons in turn. They shed no tears but were listening intently to the vicar. Maybe they're in shock, Alice thought. Then her eyes rested once more on the box which contained the body of her husband.

All too soon, the coffin was being lowered into the ground and each of the mourners threw in a handful of dirt as they passed by.

Alice and Toby were the last and, overcome with emotion, Alice's knees buckled and she collapsed. Toby was quick to catch her and lift her gently to her feet once more.

'Come on, my love,' he whispered.

The vicar shook hands with each person as they left the graveside to walk to the Red Lion at Dalend. A room had been set aside for the wake as requested by McGuire, and there was a buzz of quiet chatter as the mourners piled inside.

Alice was having difficulty holding back her excitement at seeing her sons, despite the solemnity of the occasion.

McGuire stood at the bar with Bobby and Dicky, watching Alice enjoying her time with her boys.

Mrs Cavenor sat in the corner, talking animatedly with two other women.

'That's nice to see,' Bobby said, nodding towards Alice, who sat between the twins, her head snapping from side to side as they talked.

'Aye, it's eased her grief no end. Thanks, chaps.' McGuire held up his glass in a toast to the brothers, who returned the gesture with a little clink as the glasses came together.

With gin for the ladies and beer for the gents flowing freely, the rest of the afternoon passed in an alcohol-induced celebration of Stanley Crawford's life. Many extolled the virtues of the deceased man as they drank copious amounts of beer, and before long, someone began to tinkle on an old piano. Sad refrains were soon lost to rip-roaring tunes and feet tapped along with the music. Alice hardly noticed, so deep in conversation with her sons was she, hearing all about her growing grandchildren.

* * *

Meanwhile, over at the yard, Jared had again been put in charge for the day whilst McGuire was at the funeral. Sitting in the office, he looked up from the ledger on the desk when there was a knock on the open door.

'Lady to see you, Jared,' a sorter called before disappearing back to the yard.

'Mrs Shipton! How lovely to see you,' Jared said, surprised to see the woman to whom he had returned the box of photographs some weeks earlier.

'Hello, Jared.'

'How can I help you?' Jared asked, assuming the lady might have more junk she wanted moving.

'I'm looking for Mr McGuire.'

'I'm sorry, he's not here today, he's at a funeral,' Jared replied as he indicated the lady take a seat.

Shaking her head, she said, 'In that case, I'll have to come back another day.'

'Is there something I can do for you?' Jared pursued.

'No, I don't think so,' the woman said, shaking her head again. 'It's to do with the piece Mr McGuire put in the paper.'

'Oh, about Mr Watkins's demise?'

'Yes. I really need to talk to Mr McGuire.'

Clearly Mrs Shipton was not going to say any more, so Jared nodded, saying, 'I'll tell him you called.'

'Thank you, Jared.' Mrs Shipton turned and left the office.

Jared sat down and rubbed his chin as he considered whether the lady would in fact visit again. He wondered if she might have information about Seth's missing mother, or if it was something to do with Ned Watkins. He hoped with all his heart she would return tomorrow but if she chose not to, Jared remembered where she lived so could lead Mr McGuire there should he decide to visit the lady instead.

44

That same evening, after eating their meal, Jared and Seth sat before a roaring fire. Over supper, Jared had told Seth about Mrs Shipton's visit to the yard and had explained that she had been looking for McGuire.

'Well, if you know where her house is, we should go and ask her what she wanted with the boss!' Seth could hardly conceal his excitement at the prospect of the lady possibly having information about his mother's whereabouts.

'We're not sure, Seth, it may have nothing to do with your mum.' Jared too was intrigued and hoped the woman could shed some light on the situation, but was worried about Seth getting his hopes up.

'I've waited all these years for word of my mum and now we finally have a thread to follow.'

'Look, mate, I know how you feel, but let's wait and see what Mr McGuire says,' Jared said, trying to calm his friend's agitation.

Seth sighed loudly but acquiesced with a nod. 'So close yet still so far.'

'I think by this time tomorrow we'll know more.'

'What about you, Jared, do you think that bloke could be your dad?' Seth asked tentatively.

'I'm buggered if I know, but if he is, what does he want with me after all this time?'

'Well, I suppose he could have come back for one of many reasons. Maybe he wants to build bridges with you.'

'It's more likely he's after money, whoever he is,' Jared spat.

'What a pair we are; me and my missing mother and you with your father returning,' Seth said, trying to soothe Jared's rising temper.

'You know what, Seth, if it turns out he ain't related to me, then I'm gonna kick his arse all the way to Wednesbury!'

'What if he is, though?'

'Well, I'll get the answers to my questions, then I'll kick his...'

'Arse to Wednesbury,' Seth finished Jared's sentence before they both burst out laughing.

'I thought you would have gone to the funeral today,' Jared said.

'I didn't know Stanley, so it wasn't really appropriate, besides, I'm not sure the boss would have given me time off work. I do feel for Alice, though. She was really kind to me.'

'She's a lovely woman, isn't she? And it just shows; live each day to its fullest because you don't know what tomorrow holds,' Jared said wisely.

The boys yawned simultaneously, both feeling the tiredness of the day settle on them. Jared locked up and Seth set the guard in front of the dying fire then, each with a candle, the boys headed for their beds. Whether either would sleep was another matter. They both had so many thoughts cluttering up their minds.

* * *

Outside the Red Lion, McGuire bundled a very drunk Alice into a cab. She was singing at the top of her voice, much to the amusement of the cabbie. 'Stop your catterwaulin', you'll wake the town,' McGuire said with a grin.

'Do I look like I care?'

'No, woman, you don't,' Toby replied with an amused smile.

Alice began singing again, the rattle of the carriage wheels on the cobbles her accompaniment.

Arriving at Ivy Lane, Alice stumbled from the cab, trying her best not to fall over. McGuire unlocked the door and Alice staggered inside. Going back to pay the cabbie, Toby then followed Alice into the house, turning up the gas lamps as he went. He found Alice sprawled out on the big settee in the living room, still humming to herself.

McGuire laughed and went to the kitchen to make tea. By the time he returned, Alice was sound asleep. Going upstairs, he pulled a blanket from the cupboard on the landing. Back in the living room, he shook out the blanket and draped it over Alice. Sitting in an armchair, he drank his tea, his eyes never leaving Alice. Finally, after propping his feet up on a stool, McGuire allowed sleep to claim him too.

The following morning, a bleary-eyed Alice packed McGuire off to work, making no bones about the fact that she was going to bed to sleep off her banging hangover.

When Jared arrived at the yard, he went straight to McGuire to let him know about Mrs Shipton's visit. 'She's the lady who asked me to shift that box of junk,' he explained.

'Hopefully she'll come back today and we'll know more about what she wants,' McGuire said.

'If not, I can remember where she lives.'

'Good lad, that's useful to know.'

Jared left the office to ready Bess for another day on the road.

McGuire's thoughts turned to Alice and the corners of his mouth lifted when he recalled her singing last night. She had coped with Stanley's funeral in the only way she knew how, to get blind stinking drunk after saying a tearful goodbye to her sons.

He then let his mind turn to the reason for Mrs Shipton's visit. Could it have anything to do with Molly Watkins? It must do because Jared had told him she said it was concerning the article he'd placed in the paper. Puffing on his cigar, McGuire sent up a silent prayer that Seth was one step closer to meeting up with his mother.

Out on his round, Jared was thinking much the same thing. When he first met Seth, even a blind man could see they disliked each other intensely. Over time, however, and with Seth's terrible beating and his subsequent apology to the boys, they had slowly become friends. And no one was more surprised than Jared that they now shared a house. Jared wondered if before long he would be living alone once more. Surely if Seth's mother could be found then they would want to reside together again.

A thought stabbed his mind. Was that what Timothy Johnson wanted? If it could be proved he was Jared's father, would the man want his son to live with him or indeed wish to move in with Jared?

As Bess clopped along, Jared shook his head. *I don't bloody think so, matey!*

45

A couple of days earlier, Tim Johnson had left the tatters' yard as requested by the boss. He'd gone back to his lodgings, a room rented out by an old spinster, to consider his options.

It had taken him a while to find Jared but finally, after asking many questions of many strangers, he had succeeded. Returning first to the house in Watery Lane, he had been told by the neighbour about the death of his wife, Iris, and his daughter, Maisy. Of Jared there was no news, other than that he had left the house after caring for his family as best he could.

Subsequent enquiries at the market proved a little more fruitful, the vendors having helped the boy when he scavenged for food. Then it came to light that Jared had become a tatter and so McGuire's had been the place to start his questioning once more. As luck would have it, it was a wise choice.

Sitting now in his room by a meagre fire, Tim thought again about Jared's reaction to his visit. The boy was furious and was it any wonder? Tim had left when Jared was six and Maisy was four after a blazing row with Iris. Unable to find work, there was no money coming into the household; his family were starving. His suggestion to look for a job further afield had not gone down well with Iris, which he hadn't blamed her for. She had her hands full with two young children and a house to take care of, so the idea of her husband deserting her had upset her greatly.

Nevertheless, Tim had left in search of any work he could find and his intention had been to earn a few bob which he could take home. Unfortunately, things had not worked out according to plan.

Fortune had smiled upon him at the outset and Tim had found a job as a barman in nearby Walsall. However, one fateful night, his luck ran out. An altercation with a customer over payment for ale had ended in punches being thrown. The police had been called and Tim and the punter were both arrested. As the constable had tried to restrain Tim, who was struggling, Tim's arm came about and caught the policeman on the nose, resulting in blood pouring over his nice clean uniform. Both Tim and the other man had been thrown in Stafford Gaol. There Tim had languished for eight years because of the accident with the copper at the time of his arrest; the magistrate having seen it as an assault on a police officer. Tim had been released a week ago with nothing but the little money he'd earned in jail for sewing mail bags.

After securing a room at the boarding house, Tim had set out to find his family, only to discover they had perished – all but Jared. Now he just wanted to get to know his son before his time came and he joined his wife and daughter in the afterlife.

Jared, it seemed, had other ideas. He was mistrustful of the man who turned up out of the blue claiming to be his father, and who could blame him?

Tim shook his head as he watched the flames lick around the small coal nuggets. The room was cold and damp, and he shivered. Dragging the blanket from the bed, he wrapped it around his body before sitting once more in the old chair by the fire.

What money he'd had was now spent on room and board, so it was imperative he find a job soon. At least he was fed here, albeit sparingly. But that small comfort would soon be snatched away unless he found a way to support himself. He surmised Jared may have thought he was looking for a handout and that, along with not knowing him from Adam, was why his son was so angry.

What a complete mess you've made of your life and those you left behind! The question now was – how could he put it right again? The only solution he could see was to visit Jared again and try to engage him in conversation, which would then allow him to explain what had befallen him. Then, if Jared still rejected him, at least he could try to move on with his life.

The sound of the dinner gong broke his thoughts. Replacing the blanket on the bed, Tim banked up the fire and set the guard in place. Donning his jacket, he left his room, wondering what his landlady had conjured up to tease his palate with today.

46

Hearing the steam train whistle, Jared drew Bess to a halt. The boy and his horse waited patiently for the great iron beast to rush past above them before moving on beneath the viaduct of the Grand Junction. Then, further along their route, they passed under another railway junction before turning into Belmont Row. Jared noticed Ashted Locks was busy with boat traffic coming and going from the basin. His round took him along Cardigan Street, Gospel Street, Howe Street and Curzon Street alongside the tramway. Passing the railway goods station, he then passed by the schools and up towards Midland Brewery. The smell of hops was strong in his nostrils as the cart rolled past. He noticed the Gaiety Palace, its doors closed at this time of day, and thought how nice it would be to be able to afford to visit. Before long, he was busy weighing bundles and giving out pennies.

As the day wore on, Jared's thoughts flitted from Mrs Shipton's visit to the yard to Timothy Johnson proclaiming he was Jared's father, all the time wishing he was still minding the office for McGuire, especially as the weather now held a winter chill. He had begun to realise recently how much he really wanted to be the boss, to run his own business and be beholden to no one. He knew, however, it would take many more years of hard work for that to happen, but he was determined to try, at least.

Jared focused on McGuire and wondered how long it had taken for *him* to build his little empire; and what McGuire might have missed out on over those years. Seth had told him about Stanley proposing to Alice before McGuire had the chance – and clearly this was a real regret Toby still felt. McGuire had never married, he had no children and had lived alone virtually all his life.

Jared decided that striving to be the gaffer was what he wanted to do, but not to the detriment of living a full and wholesome life. He liked the idea of being wed, with his children playing by the fireside of the house he owned. With a deep sigh, Jared clucked to Bess to move on. One day, maybe, all his dreams would come true.

* * *

In the meantime, over at the yard, McGuire settled Mrs Shipton in his office with a cup of tea.

'I'm sorry I wasn't here yesterday but I was attending a funeral,' he said.

'Yes, Mr McGuire, Jared told me.'

'So what can I do for you, Mrs Shipton?'

'Is it true? Is Ned Watkins really dead?'

'That he is.'

Mrs Shipton dipped her chin as she chewed her bottom lip, then she said, 'The notice in the paper said you're searching for Molly Watkins in order to notify her of her husband's demise.'

'To be sure, can you help me with any information?' McGuire replied.

'Well, I know where she is,' Mrs Shipton said. 'She's safe and well and not too far from here.'

'Thank the lord! Would you be willing to share her whereabouts for her son, Seth's sake?'

'Aye, I would. She's been worried sick all these years but couldn't come forward for fear of Ned.'

'I can understand that, for he had a black heart, and she would have put herself in mortal danger.'

'I'll write down the address, what you do with it is up to you.'

'Thank you, Mrs Shipton, I know Seth will be very grateful.'

While she jotted down the address on a scrap of paper, McGuire asked, 'Have you been in touch with her all this time?'

Mrs Shipton nodded as she pushed the paper across the desk. 'Molly and I have been friends since our school days. Many times, I begged her to leave Ned, to take Seth and flee, but the opportunity never arose until that night. Her one regret was having to leave Seth behind.'

McGuire nodded as he refilled her teacup.

'We've been writing to each other ever since. She's aware of what you've done for Seth and now she'll be able to thank you herself.'

'I need no thanks, I just want to see mother and son reunited.'

'So do I, Mr McGuire, and God willing, it will come to pass very soon.'

McGuire stood and walked to the doorway, where he let out a whistle and watched as Bobby crossed the yard. 'Would you kindly hail a cab for Mrs Shipton, please?'

Bobby doffed his cap and returned to the gate.

McGuire pulled out a five-pound note, handing it to the woman, who finished her tea and got to her feet.

'There's no need...' she began.

'My dear lady, there is every need. It's to show my appreciation for all you've done, so it is.'

The two shook hands and as Toby watched Mrs Shipton leave the yard, he thought, *Please God let this all turn out well.*

That evening, as the boys slowly returned one by one, McGuire yelled Seth's name.

'You wanted me, Boss?' Seth asked, wondering if he was in trouble for something.

'Yes, lad, take a seat.' McGuire passed over the piece of paper with a grin and waited.

Seth frowned. 'Is this my new round? It's miles away, I won't get there and back in one day.'

McGuire shook his head. 'That,' he said, pointing to the paper in Seth's hand, 'is where your mother lives.'

Seth's mouth fell open as he stared at McGuire, then he burst into floods of tears.

McGuire got up and called out for Jared, saying, 'Seth here needs a friend at the moment.'

Jared ran up the stairs and went to the sobbing boy with a perplexed look on his face.

'We've found his mother, Jared, and Seth here's in a bit of shock. Look after him for me, will you, because tomorrow we're taking him to Darlaston to meet her if that's what he'd like.'

'That's great news, Mr McGuire!' Jared said, feeling excited for his pal. 'Come on, Seth, let's go home and have some supper, then you can have a bath and shine your boots.'

McGuire nodded, taking back the paper Seth held out to him. He was taken aback as Seth flung his arms around him, hugging him tightly. He patted Seth's back, then said, 'Away home, lad, and be in bright and early in the morning, we have a surprise visit to make.'

Seth let go of the big man. 'Thank you, Mr McGuire, I'm never going to be able to thank you enough,' he muttered between sniffs.

'Mrs Shipton is the one to thank, which I'm sure you'll do in time,' McGuire said, raising an eyebrow.

'He will, I'll make sure of it,' Jared said as he and Seth left the office.

Down in the yard, a cheer broke out as Seth shared his good news and McGuire felt a tear prickle the back of his eye.

Returning to his seat, McGuire whispered, 'All we need now is for Molly to be in when we call – and for her to welcome her son with open arms.'

47

The following morning, after having had little sleep, Jared and Seth arrived at the yard looking very dapper. A cab was waiting and they climbed aboard with McGuire. Bobby and Dicky had been left in charge of the yard.

McGuire smiled as they set off, the two boys chattering nineteen to the dozen. He stared out of the window as the miles slipped by, his mind on how they would be received when they finally arrived.

Setting out on the eleven-mile journey, they crossed heathland, travelled over bridges, beneath tunnels and traversed streets unfamiliar to the cabbie. They could, of course, have travelled by train, but a cab would have been needed at Darlaston anyway. They passed hotels and houses, all in need of some repair or at the very least some redecoration. Foot traffic was heavy as people milled about, looking into shops longingly, knowing they couldn't afford what was held inside. Children kicked a leather ball around in the roadway, dodging carts and horse riders as they squealed and yelled to each other.

Eventually, coming into the town, the cabbie stopped to ask directions.

'You can't get there from here, cocka,' an old woman told him. 'You have to go back to the Bull Stake and go from there.'

The cabbie sighed with frustration before the cab rolled on. At the Bull Stake, they travelled up King Street before turning into Cook Street. Backing onto the graveyard ensured the street was very quiet. Here the cab halted and the cabbie jumped down to open the door.

'Thank you, please wait, if you'd be so kind,' McGuire said as he alighted, the boys tumbling out behind him.

The cabbie knuckled his forehead, closed the door, climbed into the driving seat and proceeded to light his pipe.

McGuire led the boys to the house they sought and banged on the knocker.

Seth shuffled from foot to foot as they waited, clearly bursting with nerves. 'Come on!' he muttered.

McGuire banged again.

'I'm coming, just a moment,' a voice came from within.

Jared and Seth exchanged a grin, then looked back at the door.

'Who is it?'

'Toby McGuire. I'm here to see Molly Watkins.'

Slowly the door opened a crack and a pretty face peered through the gap. 'Toby?'

'Aye, Molly. Will you be letting me in then? I have someone here who wants to meet you.'

The door opened further and Molly's green eyes sparkled as she caught sight of the boys. 'Seth, is that you? Is it really you?'

Seth nodded, tears coursing down his face.

'Oh, my god!' Molly flung out her arms and Seth stepped into them. 'Come in. Oh, my boy – my son!'

The three visitors entered and McGuire closed the door

behind them. He followed the woman into the living room and stood next to Jared, where they watched Molly and Seth hugging and crying.

'How did you find me? Oh, I don't care, you're here and that's all that matters,' Molly sobbed.

'I've missed you, Mum, more than you can ever imagine,' Seth managed at last.

'Me too, sweetheart. I can't believe how you've grown.' Then, collecting herself, Molly said, 'Sit, everyone, I'll make tea. Oh, it's so lovely to see you, Seth. Thank you, Toby. Let me...'

'Molly, make the tea, then there'll be time enough for you to explain everything,' Toby said with a little laugh.

'I'll help,' Seth said.

As they disappeared into the kitchen, Jared whispered, 'I'm glad she's happy to see him.'

'To be sure, so am I,' McGuire whispered back.

Over tea, Jared was introduced.

'Jared's my best friend, Mum, one I never thought I would have,' Seth said proudly.

Then Toby told her of Ned's death. 'He got into a contretemps with his friend, Bill Cank, who I'm sure you remember.' Molly nodded. 'Ned was drunk out of his mind and started throwing punches; Bill retaliated by pushing Ned and he hit his head on the pub wall from all accounts. According to the bystanders, there was no saving Ned, and he died at the scene.'

Molly was not in the least surprised to hear Ned had met a violent end, but she was visibly relieved. Toby continued by explaining how he had advertised for information and about how Mrs Shipton had come forwards and given them the address. 'She kept your secret these long years, Molly,' McGuire said.

'I knew she would, that's why I told her where I was going.' Turning to Seth, she said, 'I'm so sorry – I tried to take you with me, but Ned would have none of it. I had to flee before he... anyway, Irene Shipton has kept me up to date with everything as best she could, but I'll never forgive myself for not being able to give you a better life. I can never thank you enough, Toby, for taking my boy in and caring for him, and also you, Jared, for being his friend.'

'I have lots of friends now, Mum, but Jared is my best mate.'

The woman sobbed. 'I've waited so long to hear you call me Mum, I've dreamt of it every night. I never stopped loving you, Seth, and I'm so excited to see you at last.'

The chatter went on, Molly explaining that she worked in a dress shop so was able to rent the property she lived in. 'I like it here, people are kind and thoughtful and I've made some good friends. They know I have a son because I was proud to tell them that, saying he worked over in Birmingham, which is the truth. I kept the rest of my past secret – they don't need to know about Ned.'

McGuire nodded, then said, 'Forgive me, Molly, but I must get back to the yard.'

'Of course, I'll always be in your debt, Toby.'

'Can I come again, Mum, please?' Seth asked.

'Yes, my darling, you can visit any time you want. I tell you what, why don't you come on Sunday and we'll spend the whole day together? I'd love that.'

'I'd love that too!'

Seth and Molly hugged one last time before she saw them out to the cab. She waved until they were out of sight and when she went back indoors, she said quietly, 'God bless you, Toby McGuire, for bringing my son back to me.'

McGuire dropped the boys at home, saying they could have the rest of the day off, with pay, because he felt sure they would have lots to talk about and, furthermore, he was in a good mood.

It had warmed his heart to see mother and son reconciled, and he returned to the yard with a spring in his step, eager to tell Bobby and Dicky how well it had all gone.

* * *

That evening, Paul, Dan, Johnny, Sam and Tom all piled round to Jared's house on the pretext of having a game of cards. In truth, they wanted to know what was going on that they were not party to. Jared and Seth being away from work all day had set tongues wagging and they were desperate to know all about it. Seth regaled them with the tale of him meeting his mother for the first time in years and how welcome she had made them.

'I was choked up, I can tell you,' Seth said, even now having a tear glistening in his eye.

'We all were, mate,' Jared added.

'She was just the way I remembered her, she had hardly changed a bit from how she looked on the photograph!' Seth went on.

'We're all glad it went well, Seth,' Dan said.

'Yeah, we are pleased you and your mum are back together again,' Sam added.

* * *

While the boys were enjoying Seth's story, at the same time over in Ivy Lane, McGuire was sharing the same news with Alice.

'Alice, I wish you could have seen it. Molly was made up to have her boy in her arms again.'

Brushing away a tear, Alice sniffed. 'I'm really glad for them both; it's been a long time coming.'

'Aye, now all we have to sort out is young Jared and the fella purporting to be his father.'

'I'm not sure how he can prove whether he is or he isn't to the lad,' Alice said as she pointed to the salt and beckoned with her fingers.

McGuire pushed the salt cellar across the table and Alice sprinkled the condiment liberally over her steak and kidney pudding, potatoes and vegetables.

'I don't know either,' Toby concurred as he poured the wine, 'but he must be very sure of himself to come and announce it as he did.'

Alice nodded. 'I'm not surprised Jared told him to bugger off, though, I would have an' all.'

'Yes, I can understand it too, but perhaps Jared would have discovered answers to his questions had he not been so hasty.'

'Well, the bloke ain't put in an appearance since, so it sets the mind to wondering if it's true or not. Then again, what does he stand to gain if he's a charlatan?'

'It beats me, *mavourneen*.'

Alice smiled at the endearment and hoped he would always call her his darling. 'You know, I wish Stanley could have seen his sons one last time before he died,' she said a little sadly.

'It would have done the skinny devil good, to be sure.'

Alice laughed fondly. 'At least they came to see him off. I still don't know how you managed it, but I'm grateful you did.'

'They're good lads really, or they are when you get them away from the harridans they married,' McGuire answered.

Toby's mouth fell open at Alice's next words.

'Speaking of which, wasn't there a question you wanted to ask me?'

48

The mood in Jared's house was one of joviality as the boys listened to Seth's tale of reuniting with his mother again.

'You should take Mrs Shipton some flowers to say thank you,' Sam suggested.

'But be careful she doesn't think you're trying to court her!' Johnny said with a laugh.

'It's a nice idea, though, because if she hadn't come forward, you might not have met your mum again,' Dan put in.

'Can you still remember where she lives, Jared?' Seth asked.

'Yes, we could go tomorrow after work if you like.'

'Righto, we'll do that. I'll get some flowers from the market on the way,' Seth said.

'Okay, who's up for a game of cards?' Tom asked.

'Only if we're playing for matches and not money,' Paul answered.

With the bread, cheese and pickles brought by his friends spread out on the table, Jared added some ham off the bone and a huge pot of tea. Nibbling as they played, the boys enjoyed a few rowdy hands of poker before it was time for them to leave.

When the others had gone, Jared and Seth sat on the old settee by the fire, still too excited by the events of the day to go to bed. 'I'm so glad you found your mum again,' Jared said quietly as images of his own family floated around in his mind.

'Me an' all. I never thought to see the day. You know what, though, I think now we should find that bloke who said he was your dad and wring some answers out of him. I'd like you to have the peace of mind I do now.'

'I wouldn't know where to look, though, Birmingham is a big place. We could search for years and never find him.'

'True, but...'

'Nah, forget it. If what he said was true, wouldn't he have come back?' Jared asked.

'I suppose.'

The two settled into a comfortable silence, each with their own thoughts milling around in their heads.

So the following morning, no one was more surprised than Jared to see Tim Johnson standing outside the yard gates.

'You're back then?' Jared asked tersely.

With a nod, Tim asked gently, 'Could we meet up after you finish work, lad? There's a lot we need to discuss.'

'All right, but if you're pulling my tail...'

'I'm not, I swear,' Tim replied in earnest.

'Don't we all,' Seth mumbled.

'Fine. Five o'clock tomorrow. I won't wait if you're not here.' With that, Jared walked through the gate into the yard, Seth by his side. Without looking at his friend, Jared said, 'Don't you say a word!'

Seth grinned and began to whistle a little tune.

'The boss ain't in this morning,' Dicky said as the boys walked towards the stables.

'Why not?' Jared asked.

'He's not said as such, just that he has summat to do and he'll be in later,' Bobby answered mysteriously.

The carts rolled out one by one, leaving the Cavenors to watch over the sorters and grooms. Jared wondered what was so important that it would keep Toby McGuire from his work, but as he travelled the streets of Birmingham, his mind let it go. He knew he had to focus on his after-work meeting the following day with Tim Johnson and the information that needed to be gleaned. He might only have this one chance, and he didn't want to leave the meeting with any regrets.

* * *

Whilst Jared was thinking about his meeting, the tatter king was having breakfast with Alice. The previous evening, she had put him on the spot about that one question he'd wanted to ask for many years, but he'd managed to put her off by saying it was too soon after her losing Stanley. She should finish her mourning time first; he could wait.

Now, as he glanced up at the face he adored, he knew that waiting any longer would be impossible for him. He also knew that the gossipers would have a field day if he and Alice were to wed only weeks after Stanley was laid to rest. He didn't care about that for himself, but he hated the thought of Alice being the subject of people's callous words.

Hot tea burned his mouth and he began to cough and dab his lips with his napkin.

Alice shook her head, her eyes not leaving her plate. 'Whatever it is, you'd best say it before you choke to death.'

'Tea – hot...'

'Yes, because it's made with boiling water,' Alice quipped.

'Smartarse,' Toby muttered under his breath.

Alice grinned. 'Ain't you going to work today? 'Cos if you are, you're late.'

'I'll go this afternoon. I have something to do first.'

'And what would that be then?'

'Bejasus, woman, can a man have nothing to himself?'

'Ooh, don't get your drawers in a tangle, I was only asking,' Alice said, not at all put out by his answer. To rub salt in the wound, Alice blew noisily on her cup of tea.

McGuire's face split into a wide grin as he heard the soft whoosh. Once he'd finished his breakfast, he got up and said, 'Right then, I'm off. I'll see you later.'

Alice wiggled her fingers in a wave as she slurped her tea. She wondered what he was up to but decided not to dwell on it as she would find out eventually anyway.

Toby yelled for a cab and asked to be taken to the vicarage. He had a favour to ask of the vicar and he suspected that a large donation to the church fund would be sure to help. His business with the vicar was finished within an hour, and the waiting cab took him home.

'What are you doing back? I thought you were going to the yard,' Alice called out from the kitchen.

McGuire ignored her and skipped up the stairs to his bedroom. Pulling open the drawer in the bedside cabinet, he retrieved the little box. Lifting the lid, he stared at the diamond ring nestled on a tiny cushion of red velvet. Snapping the lid shut, he clutched the box tightly in his hand. It was now or never. He couldn't wait another minute.

Running downstairs, he strode to the kitchen determinedly. Wrapping his arms around Alice from behind, he whispered in her ear, 'Come and sit for a minute.'

Taken by surprise, Alice gave a little yelp, but then allowed herself to be led to a chair.

Without any hesitation, Toby dropped to one knee, the box in his fingers. 'Alice, will you marry me?' And with that, he flipped open the lid to reveal the sparkling diamond.

Without missing a beat, Alice replied with the warmest of smiles, 'I will, Toby, despite it taking you so bloody long to ask!'

Placing the ring on her finger, Toby was relieved and delighted it fitted rather well.

'Is this a real...?' Alice began as she scrutinised the gem.

'Yes, *mavourneen*, it's a real diamond. You said you always wanted one.'

Alice threw her arms around his neck, tears of pure happiness coursing down her cheeks.

Wiping away her tears with his thumb, Toby leaned forward and placed his lips on hers. A thrill like hot fire flowed through his body – Alice was almost his at last.

49

When their lips parted, Toby said, 'Our wedding is next month – so you'd best get to finding a dress.'

'Oh, my... There's so much to do! Toby, what will the twins say?'

'They'll be pleased for you, *colleen*, and they'll be in attendance, don't you worry about that. Now, I'm away to the yard to share our good news.'

With another kiss, Toby left Alice wondering if her sons would indeed be pleased that she was getting married again so soon. But quickly she realised that this was her time now; her boys were grown up with lives of their own. She wanted them to be happy for her, naturally, but then how often had she seen them since the financial handouts had stopped?

Staring at her ring once more, Alice decided now was as good a time as any to go wedding dress shopping. She would let herself enjoy every minute of it.

* * *

McGuire virtually ran to the yard, so excited was he about Alice accepting his proposal of marriage. Bobby and Dicky shook hands vigorously with Toby when he told them that he was to be wed at last. The brothers were delighted to see their boss so happy. Once the excitement had died down, the Cavenors filled Toby in on what had been going on at the yard, including the news that Jared had arranged a meeting with Tim Johnson tomorrow afternoon.

'Thanks for telling me. Do me a favour, boys, and keep an eye on Jared, I don't want anything to happen to him.'

'We will, Boss,' Bobby said before they sauntered away to stand sentinel at the gates once more.

McGuire was bursting with his news so went straight down to the yard and told the sorters and grooms about his forthcoming wedding, explaining that the business would be closed for that day and he wanted them all to attend. A loud cheer went up and congratulations were called out as McGuire returned to his office. He could barely contain himself for the rest of the day, wanting only to be home with Alice in his arms.

As daylight began to slip away, and a wintery coldness settled on the city, the carts came home one by one, and once the mares were bedded down, McGuire called the boys to his office. 'I just want you to know, Alice and I are to be wed next month, and Jared, I'd like you to be my best man if you will.'

When the applause died down, Jared answered. 'I'd be honoured, Mr McGuire.'

'Good. I'm so glad that's settled. And boys, you're all invited to celebrate the big day with us. Now, Jared, I believe you have a meeting planned for tomorrow and I know you can handle yourself. All I will say is – be careful. Take your pals with you or stay close to the Cavenors.'

Jared nodded, knowing the brothers would have informed McGuire about his conversation with Tim Johnson that morning.

Jared and Seth left work and walked towards the market, where they strolled between the stalls. The place was still busy even at this time of day.

'What sort of flowers should I get?' Seth asked.

'I don't know, but if you tell the seller what you want them for, maybe they'll be able to help.'

Arriving at a flower stall, the boys eyed the beautiful blooms standing in buckets of water.

'Them's nice,' Seth said, pointing to the hydrangea.

'Heartlessness, that's what they symbolise,' the vendor said.

'Crikey, maybe not those then, Seth,' Jared said, pulling a face.

'I'm looking to say a big thank you to someone,' Seth explained.

'Well, yellow lilies represent friendship, warmth and hope. Campanula is for gratitude...'

'Those then, the campa-whatsits please,' Seth interrupted.

The woman wrapped a bunch of Seth's choice of flowers with a sprig of baby's breath and passed them over.

Seth paid the seller with his thanks and the boys walked on. Leaving the vibrant colours of the flowers behind them, an aroma of pies and bread tickled their taste buds, reminding them that they were hungry. Women's voices rose high as they argued or cackled at something said. Vendors called out their prices to prospective buyers, only to be told where they could shove them.

Leaving the market, the two boys walked swiftly on to Mrs Shipton's street, and arriving at the right house, Seth knocked on the door. When it opened, he thrust the flowers into the face of the woman standing there.

'Oh! How nice,' she said, a surprised look on her face.

'Hello, Mrs Shipton,' Jared said, digging Seth in the ribs for his uncouth way of presenting the gift, 'we came to say thank you.'

'Ah, I see, hello, Jared, hello, Seth,' the lady answered.

'Yes, sorry, I… thanks, Mrs Shipton, for letting me know where my mum was.'

'You're most welcome, Seth. Thank you for the flowers.'

'No trouble.' He tapped a finger on a bloom, saying, 'They stand for gratitude.'

Mrs Shipton nodded and smiled. 'Well, they're beautiful, thank you. And I'm so glad you and your mum have found each other again.'

Jared dragged Seth by his arm and, with a wave, the boys wandered away, happy with their good deed.

* * *

Early the following day delivered another surprise visitor to the yard when Bill Cank knocked on McGuire's door and stepped into the office.

'Bill! Well, this is a surprise. Nice to see you,' McGuire said, extending a hand.

'You an' all, Boss,' Bill replied, as the two men shook hands.

'They let you go then – the coppers, I mean?'

Bill nodded. 'The beak said he believed what happened to Ned was an accident, but I still feel bad about it. Ned was my pal for years.'

'Aye, well, it really was his own fault, so it was.'

Bill twisted his cap in his fingers and looked down at it. 'Anyway, I wanted to come to see you to say thanks for seeing the missus right with money, Mr McGuire. I appreciate it.'

McGuire nodded and puffed on his cigar, before asking, 'When are you coming back to work then?'

Bill sighed loudly with relief. 'I wasn't sure there'd be a job here for me after…'

'It's there if you want it, and we'll say no more about it,' McGuire assured him.

'Thanks, Boss, but what about Seth, how's he gonna take it – me coming back?'

'Well, why don't go and ask him yourself if you're worried?' McGuire said simply.

Bill nodded and descended the steps to the yard, just as Seth and Jared walked into the yard themselves. Seth immediately went over to Bill, with his hand outstretched for shaking, saying, 'I'm glad you're out, Bill, welcome back.'

'I'm sorry about your dad, Seth, it really was an accident.'

'I know, Bill, and as I said to Jared, it was bound to happen eventually. I'm just sad he picked you to fight with. I don't hold you responsible for what happened at all. And I'm just glad the law saw it the same way.'

'Thanks, lad, that means a lot to me. It'll be good to be back, working alongside you boys.'

McGuire watched from the office doorway as Seth and Bill shook hands before Bill took up his post as sorter once more.

That evening, as everyone left the yard, Tim was waiting outside the gate as planned, wrapped up against the chill of early evening. Tim glanced around, looking uncomfortable. 'It's good to see you, Jared. We can't talk here, is there somewhere we can go?'

'You'd best come to my house then,' Jared replied, striding out, his friends close behind him, determined to support him.

No one spoke as they traversed the heath to the home Jared shared with Seth. The boys sat around on the floor as they did when playing cards, and Tim was given a chair and Jared took the only other seat.

Seth set the kettle to boil and prepared the huge brown teapot and an assortment of chipped cups.

Jared could tell that Tim felt intimidated being surrounded by the boys, but he waited for Tim to speak first.

'I... I think we should talk in private,' Tim said at last.

'It's not gonna happen, so say what you have to, then be gone. If you have something to say to me, then you're going to have to say it to my friends too,' Jared answered sternly.

With a sigh and a nod, Tim began and, as he told his story, his audience listened intently between slurps of tea.

When he had finished, Jared was the first to talk. 'How do I know that's the truth?'

'Why would I lie? I came straight from Stafford Gaol to find you.'

'That means nothing, you could still be anybody. Give me some sort of proof.' Jared was close to tears, so desperately did he want this man to be his long-lost father, for all he had rejected the idea in the first instance. He still felt the loss of his mum and sister keenly and he wanted family around him again.

'You were five years old, I think, and you fell down in the street and grazed your knees. You were trying to play football as I recall, and your little foot flew into the air, missing the ball completely; it was then you lost your balance and pitched forward. You wore a white shirt and navy-blue shorts, which didn't help save your knees. You howled like a wolf and frightened the life out of me. I carried you indoors and sat you on the table to bathe your cuts.'

The memory shot into Jared's mind like it had happened yesterday, but he simply shrugged his shoulders. It was something any father might have done, but Jared needed irrefutable proof.

The silence in the room was palpable as everyone waited. Then Tim began to whistle a tune very softly. It was 'Brahms' Lullaby' and Tim used to whistle this beautiful music to his children every night at bedtime. Jared was undone as he was again transported back in time. Holding his hands over his face, he wept openly.

The boys looked at each other as they saw their strong friend crumble before them, and it was Seth who stood and placed an arm around Jared's shoulders in comfort.

The whistling ended and Tim let out a sob of his own. 'I've missed you so much, my son.'

Jared sniffed and looked up. 'I've missed you too, Dad.'

Wild cheering broke out as all the boys celebrated as they realised father and son were reunited at last, that small whistled tune the proof Jared had sought.

Tim stood and held open his arms and in a second they were wrapped around the boy he thought he'd lost. Jared held onto Tim with all his might, never wanting them to part again.

The clapping died down and the boys left the house quietly. Seth went to his room in order to give his friend some private time with his dad.

'Stay and eat with us,' Jared said when eventually they let go of each other.

'Thank you, I'd really like that,' Tim said with a nod.

Jared yelled for Seth to join them and the three of them prepared a meal, chatting excitedly together; Seth sharing his news about recently finding his mother again too and they marvelled at the wonder of it all.

It was late in the evening when Tim finally left, after promising to visit again the following evening. Seth and Jared sat with their knees covered by an old blanket in front of a roaring fire.

'Whoever would have thought it? You find your dad and I find my mum.'

'I would never have believed it, that's for sure,' Jared answered. 'It's like it was meant to be.'

'And what about McGuire getting married!' Seth gasped.

'I think that was always on the cards, the only question was when.'

'Ooh, just think, if your dad and my mum got...' Seth began.

'Don't you even think it!' Jared said with a laugh.

'I suppose your dad will want to come and live here with you now,' Seth said sadly.

'No, mate, I don't think that would be a good idea. I've been independent too long and I like it that way.'

Seth grinned. 'So we stay as we are?'

'We do indeed,' Jared said, snuggling down beneath the blanket and enjoying the flames dancing around the coal and logs.

50

The following weeks seemed to pass in a blur for everyone. The Cavenors were dispatched to inform Marcus and Luke Crawford that their mother was marrying Toby McGuire and they were expected to attend the service, with or without their wives.

Seth saw his mother Molly every Sunday and revelled in the love she showered upon him.

To everyone's surprise, Tim Johnson was taken on at the yard as a sorter and he was able to rent a room at a respectable boarding house. Neither he nor Jared had broached the subject of moving in together as they seemed to both instinctively know it would be a big mistake. As it was, they spent many hours together reminiscing and making new memories.

Alice's wedding gown was made especially to her own design and was hanging in the wardrobe. Each day, she took a peek, and was eagerly awaiting the day she could finally wear it. Her fingers stroked the cream silk with its lace covering, high neck and long sleeves with the hem just touching her dainty shoes. A veil would be held in place by a three-rose headband, the whole ensemble stunning.

Likewise, Toby had a new suit which was also waiting to be worn, and the tatters, sorters, grooms and assorted friends were busily cleaning and mending their Sunday best in readiness for the big day.

Seth had visited Toby and Alice one evening to give his congratulations to the lady who had cared so tenderly for him and, as they had tea together, Alice had said, 'Seth, I wonder if you might give me away.'

Taken aback, but only for a minute, Seth answered, 'It would be my pleasure, Alice.' Then, as an afterthought, he asked, 'But what about your sons, how will they feel about it?'

'To be honest, Seth, if I asked one then the other's nose would be put out of joint. Besides, I like to think you and I have grown quite close; it's like having another son.'

'Then yes, of course I'll give you away, with all my heart, Alice.'

On the morning of the wedding, the congregation gathered at St Gabriel's Church including Jared and McGuire, who were nervously stationed in front of the altar. Meanwhile, Seth was waiting in the living room of Toby's house for Alice. When she finally appeared, he gasped. 'Angel Alice!'

'You called me that once before,' she said with a smile.

''Cos it's true. You look beautiful – my second mum.' Seth grinned when he saw her bite her bottom lip. 'The cab is here if you're ready.'

Taking his arm, Alice left the house. The neighbours lined the street, calling out their best wishes, and Alice felt like a queen. With a wave, she climbed aboard the carriage, holding up her long dress. Seth sat opposite her, his face adorned with a huge, happy smile.

'I'm nervous,' Alice admitted as they set off.

'It will be fine,' Seth soothed, 'everybody is there at the church including your soon-to-be husband. He can't get away 'cos all the boys would be on him in a minute!'

Alice laughed as she felt the tension flow out of her and before long, the cab halted and they alighted at the church. Seth looked her over, adjusted her headband and veil, then hooked his arm through hers.

The organ struck up as they entered and the pair slowly walked down the aisle. Alice beamed at her sons, who sat smiling in the front pews, their wives nowhere to be seen. And as she reached Toby, their eyes met and everyone felt the love they shared.

'I love you,' Toby mouthed.

'I love you too,' Alice mouthed back.

Seth stepped back and the service began.

'Dearly beloved...' Whilst the vicar spoke, a strong ray of winter sunshine shone through the stained-glass window to fall on the happy couple in an array of striking rainbow colours at the words, 'I now pronounce you man and wife.'

Alice then said in a loud voice, 'And about bloody time too!'

Laughter and applause accompanied the happy couple as they and their guests spilled out of the church under a hail of rice thrown by onlookers, and then they all headed to the pub for a rollicking good knees-up.

Once everyone was settled with a drink, Toby called for order. 'First of all, I'd like to thank Alice for becoming my wife...' Applause rippled around the room. 'I'm sure you know that I have waited a very long time for this day and now I have every intention of making the most of it.' Ribald comments, catcalls and whistles rang out and Toby rolled his eyes. 'What I mean is that I have decided to step back from the business.'

Silence descended over the room at this revelation. What

would they all do without the tatter king? 'I want to spend as much time as I can with my wife,' Toby explained.

All eyes went to Alice. Glancing around, she said, 'Don't look at me, it's the first I've heard about it an' all!'

'Therefore,' Toby continued, 'I'm putting a manager in at the yard.'

Nervous looks were exchanged as the workers wondered who would be brought in as their new boss.

'I have every faith in the man chosen, so please raise your glasses to the new manager of McGuire's Yard – Jared Johnson!'

The sound of enthusiastic clapping, whistles and feet banging threatened to throw the roof off as a very surprised Jared got to his feet. From a scavenger on the street to a boss in the tatters' yard, he'd come a long way in a very short time in the great scheme of things. Jared silently sent up his thanks to his mum for teaching him how to persevere and stand his ground in the face of adversity.

Slowly the applause died down and Jared said, 'Thank you, Mr McGuire, I won't let you down.'

And with that, someone started to belt out a tune on a piano and the festivities really began.

The boys congregated around Jared, congratulating him on his promotion.

'How does it feel being a boss?' Dan asked.

'I'm just the manager, Dan, but one day...' Jared's eyes slid sideways towards Toby, who raised his glass in toast. 'I intend to be the owner of my own yard.' Then, as the words spoken to him by a woman in the street a long time ago came to mind, he added, 'One day, I'll be a tatter millionaire!'

51

It was just a few weeks later when, still in the throes of married bliss, there was a knock on their front door whilst Toby and Alice were enjoying a leisurely breakfast.

With a frown, Alice got to her feet.

'I'll go,' Toby said and with a nod, Alice retook her seat.

A couple of minutes later, Toby returned, looking pleased with himself.

'Who was it?' Alice called from the kitchen where she'd taken their empty plates.

'It's us, Mum,' Luke said.

Alice whirled around in surprise, which turned to shock when she saw Luke holding a little boy's hand.

'Riley, go and say hello to your grandma,' Luke coaxed gently.

The boy stepped forward and in a strong voice said, 'Hello, Grandma.'

'Hello to you, Riley, it's nice to meet you,' Alice said, tears glistening in her eyes.

Little Riley held out his arms and Alice scooped him up into a loving hug, relishing the feel of her grandson's arms around her neck. Tears rolled from her eyes as she threw Luke a look of gratitude and he smiled widely in return.

After a minute, Alice reluctantly placed the wriggling child back on his feet, saying, 'Would you like some milk and biscuits?'

'Yes, please,' came the reply.

However, as Alice turned towards the cupboard, her eyes were drawn to movement in the doorway.

Marcus entered, carrying his daughter in his arms. 'Mum, meet Jenny.'

Alice sobbed as she reached out her arms. Jenny's blonde curls bounced as she went to her grandmother, willingly planting a kiss on Alice's cheek.

'Jenny, you're so pretty, you look just like a princess,' Alice whispered.

'Like you, Grandma,' the little girl said with a giggle.

'It looks like it's milk and biscuits for two then,' Alice said with a laugh.

With Jenny passed back to her father's arms, Alice busied herself with the refreshments and a pot of tea, and it was only then that Alice realised Toby was nowhere to be seen.

The children sat at the table enjoying their treat and listening in to the conversation taking place amongst the adults.

'Thank you, boys, this means the world to me,' Alice said tilting her head towards her grandchildren.

'It's our way of saying we're sorry, Mum,' Luke answered.

'We should have done this years ago while Dad was still alive,' Marcus added.

'Well, you've done it now and I couldn't be happier,' Alice replied.

Once the biscuits were eaten and the milk had been drunk, Alice and the children chatted and laughed together as she told them funny tales about when their daddies were little and the trouble they got into; the twins watched on, glad they had made the journey and the effort.

Suddenly there was banging and a quiet curse coming from the living room. A moment later, Toby came into the kitchen covered in dust and cobwebs.

'What the...?' Alice began.

'I've been in the attic and brought down some of my old toys, but they need dusting off.'

Alice beamed as she found two dusters, giving one each to the children. 'Come on, let's see what there is to play with.'

Everyone bustled into the living room and crowded around the boxes. Opening one, Riley exclaimed, 'It's a fort!' Luke and his son pulled out the wooden pieces and began to assemble them.

Another box held tin soldiers, but Jenny's eyes were on the rocking horse.

'If we wipe it down, you can have a ride,' Alice said. She laughed when Jenny dragged her duster over the toy once before throwing it down and climbing into the saddle.

Balls and wooden carts and horses were drawn from another box along with farm animals and tabletop games like tiddlywinks and snakes and ladders.

The excited children, their fathers and grandparents sat on the carpet playing games for hours until it was time to part.

Alice hugged her sons tightly, whispering her thanks, then cradled Riley in one arm and Jenny in the other.

'Daddy, I want to stay here with Grandma,' Jenny pouted.

Alice's heart melted. 'Sweetheart, you have to go home now, but you can come back any time you want.'

Jenny clapped her hands.

With a kiss from each of the little ones, Alice saw them to the door, Toby beside her.

'We'll see you soon,' Marcus said.

'We will, Mum, I promise,' Luke added.

Alice nodded, wanting to believe it with all her heart. Waving them off, she turned to Toby. 'Well, how on earth did you manage that?'

'It had nothing to do with me, I swear on those kiddies' lives!' Toby answered, pleased that the twins had finally come to their senses of their own accord.

Alice frowned. 'I wonder why all of a sudden...'

'Ah, now don't be giving yourself a headache thinking about that, woman – just enjoy it,' Toby interrupted.

Alice laughed. 'You're right.' She then hummed a little tune as she busied herself tidying up the toys.

Strangely enough, across the heath, Jared was whistling the same tune – it was 'Brahms' Lullaby'. All was well at last in the McGuire empire. Seth had found his mum and was visiting regularly. Jared was installed as manager at the yard but still enjoyed the occasional jaunt out with Bess. Toby and Alice were wed at last after many years of wishing it to happen. Alice had met up with her grandchildren and knew she would spend many more hours with them in the days to come. Jared had a nice home now, shared with his friend Seth, and was reunited with his father. The future looked rosy for everyone.

As Jared continued to whistle, he wondered just what that future held for him. Would he ever get his own yard, or would he be forever manager at McGuire's? Either way, he was happy with his lot – for now.

MORE FROM LINDSEY HUTCHINSON

We hope you enjoyed reading ***The Ragged Orphan***. If you did, please leave a review.

If you'd like to gift a copy, this book is also available as an ebook, large print, hardback, digital audio download and audiobook CD.

Sign up to Lindsey Hutchinson's mailing list for news, competitions and updates on future books.

http://bit.ly/LindseyHutchinsonMailingList

Explore more page-turning sagas from **Lindsey Hutchinson**...

ABOUT THE AUTHOR

Lindsey Hutchinson is a bestselling saga author whose novels include *The Workhouse Children*. She was born and raised in Wednesbury, and was always destined to follow in the footsteps of her mother, the multi-million selling Meg Hutchinson.

Follow Lindsey on social media:

facebook.com/Lindsey-Hutchinson-1781901985422852

twitter.com/LHutchAuthor

bookbub.com/authors/lindsey-hutchinson